GHOST UPS HER GAME

Also by Carolyn Hart

Bailey Ruth Ghost mysteries

GHOST AT WORK
MERRY, MERRY GHOST
GHOST IN TROUBLE
GHOST GONE WILD
GHOST WANTED
GHOST TO THE RESCUE
GHOST TIMES TWO
GHOST ON THE CASE

Death on Demand series

LAUGHED 'TIL HE DIED
DEAD BY MIDNIGHT
DEATH COMES SILENTLY
DEAD, WHITE, AND BLUE
DEATH AT THE DOOR
DON'T GO HOME
WALKING ON MY GRAVE

Henrie O series

DEAD MAN'S ISLAND
SCANDAL IN FAIR HAVEN
DEATH IN LOVERS' LANE
DEATH IN PARADISE
DEATH ON THE RIVER WALK
RESORT TO MURDER
SET SAIL FOR MURDER

GHOST UPS HER GAME

Carolyn Hart

This first world edition published 2020
in Great Britain and the USA by
SEVERN HOUSE PUBLISHERS LTD of
Eardley House, 4 Uxbridge Street, London W8 7SY.
Trade paperback edition first published
in Great Britain and the USA 2021 by
SEVERN HOUSE PUBLISHERS LTD.

British Library Cataloguing in Publication Data
A CIP catalogue record for this title is available from the British Library.

ISBN-13: 978-0-7278-9047-4 (cased)
ISBN-13: 978-1-78029-707-1 (trade paper)
ISBN-13: 978-1-4483-0428-8 (e-book)

All Severn House titles are printed on acid-free paper.

Severn House Publishers support the Forest Stewardship Council™ [FSC™],
the leading international forest certification organisation.
All our titles that are printed on FSC certified paper carry the FSC logo.

Typeset by Palimpsest Book Production Ltd.,
Falkirk, Stirlingshire, Scotland.
Printed and bound in Great Britain by
TJ International, Padstow, Cornwall.

A toast to Rhys Bowen, Donis Casey, Hannah Dennison, and Earlene Fowler. Wonderful writers, cherished friends.

ONE

Heaven expects our best. Whether solving a mystery or digging up radishes or maneuvering a tugboat, do your job and don't give up. Never give up. If it takes shenanigans to foil a bad guy or a borrowed trowel or an extra hawser to pull a barge, do what you need to do and don't be too proud to ask for help.

Heaven eschews pride. That's a twenty-four-carat verb for don't-even-think-about-it. Pride prompts us to think we can do everything by ourselves. I will admit I always feel confident about my accomplishments and I always look forward to continued success at the Department of Good Intentions as either a dispatcher or as a celestial spirit on an earthly mission.

Dispatcher? Earthly mission? Department of Good Intentions? Heaven? Before you either guffaw or flee the room, let me introduce myself. I am Bailey Ruth Raeburn, late of Adelaide, Oklahoma. Late as in Deceased. Bobby Mac, my husband, wildcatted for oil all over Oklahoma and Texas. We raised two redheaded kids, Rob and Dil. I taught English until I called the principal an idiot when he made the football coach the geometry teacher. It was time for a new career. I trouble-shot for the Chamber of Commerce. That was quite a while ago in earthly time, but one of Heaven's charms is timelessness. We are the best we ever were or could be. Twenty-seven was a very good year for me and that is how I appear and feel whether in Heaven or on earth, all five feet five inches of me, red curls, narrow face, inquisitive green eyes.

It isn't my aim to take you on a tour of Heaven. That glory awaits you. Besides, the Precepts for Earthly Visitation discourage revelations about Heaven. The Precepts are required reading at the Department of Good Intentions, which sends emissaries to earth to help those in trouble.

My next visit to earth will be my ninth return as an emissary. I look back with pr— with pleasure on the assistance I've given to people in trouble, ranging from a rector's wife trying to move a murdered man off her back porch to a frantic sister desperate for ransom money.

Honesty compels me to reveal that Wiggins – that's Paul Wiggins, who runs the Department – often finds my efforts lacking. To be precise, I try to follow the Precepts, but things happen. Wiggins in his heart doesn't believe 'things happen' suffices as an explanation for transgressions of the Precepts. I will agree that the Precepts are clear.

Precepts for Earthly Visitation

1. Avoid public notice.
2. No consorting with other departed spirits.
3. Work behind the scenes without making your presence known.
4. Become visible only when absolutely essential.
5. Do not succumb to the temptation to confound those who appear to oppose you.
6. Make every effort not to alarm earthly creatures.
7. Information about Heaven is not yours to impart. Simply smile and say, 'Time will tell.'
8. Remember always that you are *on* the earth, not *of* the earth.

I loved helping people in trouble but I was honored when Wiggins invited me to assist him in dispatching emissaries. I did wonder a bit if he thought I'd get into less mischief at his side. Wiggins was a stationmaster on earth. He recreated his red-brick station to house the Department. The Rescue Express thunders on silver tracks, its deep-throated whistle and clacking wheels announcing arrivals and departures.

Wiggins insists we are emissaries when on a mission. To me, a visitor from Heaven who arrives unseen but can materialize at will is a ghost. Oh, I know, Precept Four (4. Become visible only when absolutely essential), and all that, but sometimes Appearing is essential. Besides, total honesty here (honesty is a Heavenly attribute), Appearing is fun. It's a matter of form. You will forgive me the pleasure I take in making that statement. To Appear begins with the decision to be present. Colors swirl, gorgeous swaths of lavender and silver, magenta and royal blue, gold and rose, and in a moment here I am.

On earth I wear attire suitable to the occasion. Wiggins fears that I am rather vain and give too much thought to my appearance. I confess I adore lovely clothes. A woman owes it to herself to choose clothes that lift the spirits of those around her. If they make her feel good as well, that's surely a plus.

When working at the Department, I choose a style that makes Wiggins comfortable. This morning I selected an aqua sweater decorated with an adorable beaded silver corsage, a sweeping navy skirt that made me want to twirl, and aqua leather slippers with silver buckles. Wiggins was impressive in his customary stiffly starched white shirt with black elastic garters between shoulders and elbows and heavy gray flannel trousers supported by both suspenders and a wide leather belt with a large silver buckle. His stiff train-master cap hung from a coat tree. His green eyeshade was slightly askew as he worked as fast as possible to ticket passengers.

Back to pride. I confess I was feeling a bit full of myself. I'd chosen a handsome young cowboy to aid a young school marm in Tombstone, a flint-eyed centurion to protect Cicero in 63 BC, an accomplished actor (David Niven is as clever as he is charming) to investigate accidents backstage at a current Broadway hit. Any old emissary wouldn't do.

Wiggins stood by a wooden case mounted on the wall next to the ticket window. Open slots held colored tickets, everything from Siamese gray to royal purple. I handed him the files, murmured modestly, 'I looked for the right person for the right job.'

Whoo whoo. Steel wheels clacked on silver rails. There was a general rush as emissaries emptied the waiting room, spilled on to the concrete platform.

After a quick glance, Wiggins tucked the files beneath his arm, reached for the proper tickets. 'Well done, Bailey Ruth. Sterling choices.'

No peacock ever spread gorgeous feathers with greater

pleasure than my delight in what I confidently accepted as my due. I'd done a helluva . . . I mean, I'd nailed this one.

As the platform filled – the Rescue Express was rumbling near – there was a sudden clatter of the telegraph key mounted on one side of Wiggins's desk as it tapped out a message in Morse Code, just as it did in his long-ago train station. I recognized the call letters. A message from Adelaide: Urgent. High Priority. 'Wiggins.' Perhaps I sounded a bit breathless. 'Adelaide. Trouble.' No fire horse ever heard a bell with greater anticipation.

He looked over his shoulder.

I gestured at the telegraph key. 'A message from Adelaide. Urgent.'

He handed me a sheaf of tickets and his stamp. 'The Express must depart on time. There's no time to deal with the matter now.' He hurried to his desk. He grabbed a sheet of paper, transcribed the message.

As the final passengers reached the window, I gave them their tickets, but my attention was on Wiggins. As soon as the last emissary turned toward the platform, I reached up to a familiar slot, grabbed a ticket to Adelaide, used Wiggins's stamp. After all, I excelled at choosing the right person for the right job, and no one was better qualified to help out in Adelaide than I. I flew across the office to his desk. 'There's just time.' I grabbed his scribbled notes. 'I'm on my way.'

A stentorian shout. 'All aboard. All aboard now.'

Wiggins called after me. 'Irregular. Problematic. Out of the ordinary.'

I regret to say my smile was patronizing. I was Bailey Ruth Raeburn, proven emissary and native of Adelaide. I knew the routine. What could go wrong? 'I'll take care of everything.' I leapt for the caboose as the Rescue Express whooed and chugged. Coal smoke stung my eyes. Cinders flared. The wheels began to move. We were on our way. I gave a backward glance.

Wiggins stood on the platform, clearly distressed. 'The Precepts,' he shouted.

Poor Wiggins. He need have no fear. I would be on my best behavior. This time I'd aim to complete a mission without

Appearing a single time. I felt noble. I lifted my hand in a jaunty wave.

The Express sped through the starry night, swathed in light from the Milky Way. I felt the same thrill I did as a child when listening to the radio and I heard the glad shout of the Lone Ranger. Since I was alone on the caboose, I let loose a lusty, 'Bailey Ruth returns.'

In the last car, I slipped into a plush red seat next to a voluptuous blonde in a spangled dress. She was absorbed in *Movie Mirror*, the August 1935 issue with a picture of redheaded Myrna Loy on the cover, an actress I adored. Definitely this was a positive beginning to my journey. I wondered if the emissary would hobnob with Claudette Colbert or Clark Gable. They were so splendid in *It Happened One Night*. I was tempted to ask but she was immersed in the text.

The Rescue Express makes its run in Heavenly time, so I would shortly arrive where something was underway. *Irregular. Problematic. Out of the ordinary.* I read Wiggins's hurried scrawl on the sheet he'd ripped from his notebook: Robert just passed the bar. Knows he's an officer of the court. Could be disbarred. Might set a record. Attorney-at-law for one week. Iris is a—

The conductor took my ticket. 'Next stop Adelaide.'

As the Rescue Express departed, I hovered above a large terrace near an open French door. I entered the room, surveyed it. Rather dull-looking volumes filled floor-to-ceiling mahogany bookcases. The furnishings, mostly brown leather sofas, several circular cherry-wood tables, and comfortable easy chairs in dull gray fabric, reminded me of a library reading room, but there were no magazines draped over an armrest. No reading glasses carelessly flung on a side table. No crumpled paper twists from discarded taffy wrappers.

A young man stared at a tall, slender older woman. She was elegant in a two-button lavender linen jacket. I admired three slash flap pockets. A cream polo matched cream slacks. Lavender rosettes studded her tall cream heels.

Inspired, I imagined a gauzy light blue tunic with adorable pin-tucks in front and a navy scalloped hem, slim white crepe slacks, and navy heels with silver bows. As soon as I choose an outfit, presto, I am wearing it. Not, of course, that I felt the tiniest bit competitive.

Everything was picture-perfect for a civilized evening, except for the black blob that dangled from the woman's slender hand and the body lying on the parquet floor and the look of shock on the face of the young man.

The woman gripped one end of a man's long black sock. The bulging foot portion hung down, apparently filled with a heavy substance. The upper portion was knotted at the ankle. Remote violet eyes gazed at the dead man sprawled at her feet. A woman of grace and charm. Something in her face and posture reminded me of Katharine Hepburn in *The Philadelphia Story*.

The dead man was probably in his late thirties, early forties. The fleshy face was little touched by lines. He was a big man, likely six feet tall. His head was at an odd angle and a dark purplish bruise marred the side of his neck. It wasn't hard to picture a swift strike with the homemade blackjack and a broken neck.

Her arched brows drew down in a frown. 'Too bad I can't rewind today. I'd make a few changes.' Her breath caught. 'I imagine he would, too.'

The young man clawed at his collar. 'What's that in your hand?' He stared at the object as if it were a squirming centipede edging up his shirtfront.

The violet eyes dropped. 'I'm not an authority on weapons, but it's heavy. I think someone swung the bulky end and struck him. I stumbled over it,' she made a vague gesture with her free hand, 'and picked it up. That's when I saw Matt.' Her face crinkled. 'I guess I should have checked for a pulse, but no one lives with their neck bent like that. I couldn't help him. No one could help him.'

'Iris.' Her companion sounded as if he was calling to her from the bottom of a deep dark well. 'Iris.' His voice was imploring.

'Don't repeat yourself, Robert. Calling my name in a frazzled manner is unhelpful.'

Robert. And Iris. I wasn't sure which one I was ticketed to

help. But I definitely was in the right place. I felt magnani-
mous. I'd help both of them.

  Robert clenched his fists. 'I know you never lose your cool,
but there he is,' he pointed at the body, 'and there you are
with that thing in your hand. It looks bad. I mean, it looks
like . . . I don't know what to say but the police are going to
think you hit him.' He was young, early twenties, still filling
out. As a mature man, he would be impressive. Tonight, sandy
hair disheveled, brown eyes shocked, he looked young and
vulnerable. The collar of his shirt was slightly frayed; his blue
blazer a little too tight across the shoulders and short at the
wrists. What had Wiggins written about Robert? Newly sworn
in to the bar. Likely an impecunious recent law-school graduate
with a mountain of debt. His bony face held a mixture of
emotions, disbelief, uncertainty, a touch of despair. As for Iris,
Wiggins was concerned about her as well. Time would tell.

  For an instant her composure cracked. 'I didn't break Matt's
neck.' She looked down at the weapon, shuddered. She took a
deep breath, then gave the young man a rueful look. 'But you're
right. Here I am with a weapon in my hand and the police will
want to know why I picked it up, why didn't I leave it on the
floor. I know it looks bad.' A considering pause. 'Trust Matt
to get himself killed at the worst possible moment. And place.
For me. But he did and I' – a quick look at Robert – 'we have
to deal with the situation. Clear your mind, Robert. You did
not come in here. I did not come in here. *Blessed are the
forgetful for they get the better even of their blunders.*'

  He blinked several times. 'I don't understand.'

  'Nietzsche. To paraphrase, dear Robert, what we don't
remember can't hurt us. To put it even more simply, follow
the lead of the political class when interviewed by the FBI.
Simply say, "I don't recall." A myriad of problems are solved
when you open your eyes wide and murmur, "I don't recall."'
She glanced at her watch. Her chiseled features were abruptly
utterly determined. She leaned down to the body, fumbled at
the jacket, pulled out a handkerchief. 'I don't know if cloth
holds fingerprints but I don't want to find out.' She rested the
weapon on the back of a leather chair, used the handkerchief
to firmly swipe at the portion she had touched, then wrapped

the heavy sock in the handkerchief, took two quick steps, thrust the bundle at him.

He stared down at the wrapped weapon cradled in his large hands.

She was authoritative. 'Get rid of it.'

'An accessory after the fact.' His voice wobbled.

'How did you pass criminal law? Didn't you ever watch the Perry Mason reruns? That charge requires cooperation in covering up the commission of a crime. I did not commit a crime. You, I assume, did not commit a crime. If you refer to removing evidence from the scene of a crime, no harm will occur. Removing my fingerprints will not impede a future investigation. Only an idiot grips a murder weapon and leaves behind crisp fingerprints for the police to pursue.' Another pause and her expressive Hepburn face was shadowed by uncertainty and sadness. 'In fact, we are assisting justice because my fingerprints would simply sow confusion. Toss the sock in the shrubs outside. The police will find it. Stuff the handkerchief under some trash in the men's washroom. I need to get upstairs. I'm due on the podium.' As she turned, her gaze swept the area near the French doors. She stopped. 'Do you always hover a few feet above ground?'

I was shocked. When I arrived, I'd remained in the air, absorbed in the tableau below. I looked down, didn't see my aqua blue flats. I was still invisible. Besides, when I Appear I am subject to the same gravity as earthly creatures. 'You can't see me.'

'Of course I can. How tiresome. Go back where you came from.'

I dropped to the floor, faced her, hands on my hips. 'I'm here to help you and Robert.'

'Thanks, but no thanks. Robert and I are not in need of assistance. We are dealing with a situation and we are rather busy at the moment.'

'It is your duty to call nine-one-one.' I spoke in my English-teacher voice to the class clown.

'That's impressive. A spirit knowledgeable about emergency calls.' Her gaze was appraising. 'Chic sweater. I didn't know spirits shopped.'

'I love fashion and—' This was not the moment to discuss how I chose my clothes. 'The police must be informed.'

Robert's head swiveled between her and the windows, following the sound of our voices. His expression bordered on panicked. 'Iris, you aren't well. Those voices. Yours is deep and crisp and the other one husky. Like a chanteuse.'

I smiled my approval. A cultivated young man. I sing rather well, a soprano that can handle everything from country ballads to jazz.

Iris was sardonic. 'Don't flatter yourself, redhead. The closest he's been to Paris is some of my daughter's perfume.' A pause. 'I've always loathed red hair. Unnatural.'

'It isn't unnatural.' I was huffy. 'My brothers and my sister have red hair, too.'

'Spare me further—'

'Iris, please don't talk in different voices.' He brightened. 'I understand. You're disoriented. Confused. The attack must have been an accident. That's what we'll tell the police.'

'No police, Robert. And please absorb the fact that I did not attack Matt Lambert. I found him lying here, just as I found that homemade weapon. And there aren't any men's socks at my house.' A slight pause. 'Not any more,' and there was sadness in her voice.

I moved to face Iris. 'The police must be summoned. I'm here to help. I have a good relationship with Sam Cobb, the police chief. I have assisted him in past cases. He is a fine man.'

'No police. Thanks for your offer. Not interested. For reasons I don't have time to pursue, I can't afford to be found next to Matt's body.' She started for the door, called over her shoulder to Robert. 'After you get rid of the weapon, come back to the ballroom. The program is about to begin.' She gave me a brusque wave. 'Go back where you came from. Nice of you to drop by, but we will take care of everything.' With that, she hurried across the room. At the door, she lifted the edge of her linen jacket and polished the brass knob before she turned it and stepped into the hall. The door closed. The knob turned again and I knew she was polishing the other side.

I glared at the closed door. 'Who do you think you are, lady? Mussolini?'

'Muss . . .' Robert said faintly. 'I couldn't have heard that. There's no one here but me. Just me. I don't know anybody named Mussolini.'

'World War Two,' I said impatiently. 'I can understand not knowing Nietzsche. But Mussolini?'

His eyes, huge and strained, stared in the direction of my voice. 'If there's a voice, I'm crazy, too. But crazy isn't contagious. Maybe I'm drunk. I can't be drunk on two glasses of champagne. Stupid skinny little glasses.'

'Flutes,' I supplied.

He took one step back, two, holding the handkerchief-wrapped sock as if it were radioactive. 'I don't know anything about flutes. Drums, yes. Not flutes.'

I began to understand Iris's exasperation. 'Don't babble.'

'Babble? Why should I babble? Nothing to babble about, is there? Only a voice from nowhere and a dead body and a homemade blackjack. The blackjack. I've got to get out of here before anyone comes.'

There was a knock at the door.

'Oh God.' Robert stared across the room, eyes wide with panic.

I was at the door in an instant. I flipped off the light switch.

The door opened. 'Oh.' A disappointed voice. The door shut.

I flipped the switch on.

Robert was backing toward the French doors. 'Light on. Light off. Light on. Hallucinations, too?' He rubbed his chin with the knuckles of his left hand. I wondered if it was a gesture used when he was under stress.

I said soothingly. 'Everything's all right.'

'Yeah,' he muttered, 'just dandy.' He fumbled with the wrapped blackjack, tucked it under one arm, grabbed the handle to the partially open French door.

'Robert, wait. I can explain—'

'Voices. I do not hear voices. I do not!' With that defiant yell, he pulled the door wide and plunged into darkness.

I was torn. Should I follow him? Likely he was now hidden in shadows dumping the heavy sock. Iris was smart to wipe the sock just in case. Since my recalcitrant charges hadn't summoned the police, I needed to keep them as safe as I could. Thinking of fingerprints, I hurried to the French door, Appeared long enough to use the hem of my tunic to polish the handle. I gave a final swipe, disappeared. Iris of the violet eyes that saw too much instructed Robert to return to the ballroom after discarding the weapon. I would find them there in a moment.

I hurried to the body. Likely the dead man had a cell phone in a pocket. I would alert the police. So far, my mission was unfortunately not proceeding in an orderly fashion. Oh, face it. So far, so bad. Wiggins would not be pleased.

I knelt beside him, gently reached inside the Madras sport coat. I felt leather in a pocket and in an instant held an expensive wallet. I pulled apart the leather sides. A driver's license tucked in a plastic holder read: Matthew J. Lambert. He was forty-six and lived at 601 Robin Ridge Road. I found a business card: Matthew J. Lambert, Vice President of Outreach, Goddard College, Administration Building, 101. Civic membership cards. Medical insurance. Three credit cards, likely one was issued by the college. All the cards were in the name of Matthew J. Lambert. Another card proclaimed him a member of the Association of College Fundraisers. I opened the bill side of the wallet and lifted out several banknotes. I have a tidy instinct. I don't cram things willy-nilly so I pulled the sides apart to return the bills and saw a folded square of paper. I plucked out the square. I unfolded it, read: The door opened and I saw—

The hall door opened.

Startled, I dropped the billfold. Credit and ID cards skittered on the parquet floor.

'Matt, where are you?' A youngish woman with curly brown hair stepped inside, closed the door behind her. 'Come give me a kiss.' Her tone was inviting. She came around the back of an oversize red leather sofa and jolted to a stop. 'Oh. Oh. Oh.' She rushed across the room, dropped to her knees beside the still figure.

TWO

Just as in Heaven, there is instant mobility to a desired location. I thought *ballroom* and there I was. Almost as quickly, I recognized the surroundings. I was on the third floor of Rose Bower, the elegant estate willed to Goddard College by Charles Marlow. I'd visited Rose Bower as an emissary several times. That accounted for the impersonal elegance of the room where Matt Lambert died. The room wasn't in daily use. Likely it was used as a reading room by visiting scholars. The ground floor of Rose Bower also contained offices and a huge kitchen where banquets were prepared. On the second floor, distinguished guests visiting the college were housed in elegant bedrooms.

Goddard College celebrates big events in the ballroom. As I flowed up near a chandelier for a better view, I realized I still clutched that folded square of paper. Fortunately the glow from the chandeliers wasn't bright enough for anyone below to notice a square of paper in the air above them.

I felt an urgency to do what I could while I could. I was sure the woman who knelt beside the body had hurried for help or called nine-one-one on her cell. Likely she was now gasping out her discovery to a calm-voiced responder. 'Speak slowly, ma'am. Take a deep breath. Give me your location. Rose Bower? Yes, ma'am. A body? Can you . . .'

Very likely wailing sirens would soon announce the arrival of the police. I scanned the ballroom. Iris stood at the foot of the steps to the dais. She looked slightly harried as she spoke with a rotund man who scarcely reached her shoulder. He was balding, wore a rumpled blue suit. He gestured emphatically with a pudgy hand. Her smile was reassuring.

I moved outside the ballroom to a broad hallway. I made a careful survey. I was alone. As I Appeared, I checked in a mirror, tidied my curls. I felt justified in Appearing since the Precept allows Appearances when absolutely necessary.

'Absolutely necessary,' I murmured aloud. I tucked the small strip of paper in a pocket. I opened a door and stepped into the ballroom. I'd attended many college functions here. This was a big event, the ballroom filled with circular tables seating eight. Most chairs were occupied. Voices rose in excited chatter. The guests were a mixture of Town and Gown.

For those who have not lived in a college town as residents, the terms might need explanation. Town included upright earnest citizens concerned about finance, business, banking, and commerce. Gown embraced all faculty members and most administrators. I can tell them apart in a heartbeat. Town appears stolid, perhaps a bit paunchy, and has an aura of Friday Night Lights. Town's eyes are alert, a trifle wary. Town's smiles are broad and inclusive. Bonhomie greases the wheels of commerce. Gown tends toward overlong hair, dreamy eyes, and auras of self-satisfaction. There is nothing like tenure to create a state of contented arrogance. Speech is over-erudite and – for Town – a shade patronizing.

A steady rumble of conversation almost drowned out a string quartet playing Mozart. A huge banner on the wall behind the dais proclaimed: Midsummer Merriment.

Every summer the college presented awards in appreciation of gifts or support from people, groups, faculty, and staff. It was the custom for the college mascot to stand next to the table holding the awards. The mascot back in the day was an ill-tempered goat who tried to devour any hand held out with a treat. I recalled the night my husband Bobby Mac received an adorable bronze trophy of a catfish in thanks for restocking Rose Bower Lake with channel, blue, and flathead, along with a standing invitation to use one of the college motorboats to fish there whenever we wished. The goat wore a red ribbon around her neck and a malevolent expression. I was relieved to see a new mascot was on display, a golden retriever who looked like she was smiling. A definite upgrade.

I walked swiftly toward the dais, alert for sirens. Iris stood with her back to me, thankfully. At a front table I headed for a pleasant-faced woman in her sixties. Perfectly coiffed white hair framed a plump face at ease with herself and the world. Pearl earrings and a string of pearls – both genuine – gleamed against a navy silk blouse. By the time I reached her, I held a pad in one hand, a pencil in the other. Heaven does provide. No doubt the Department could supply an up-to-date laptop but they knew who they were dealing with. I can manage this and that on computers, but I don't claim expertise.

My quarry was speaking in a light, high, cultured voice. '. . . important to be persuasive to achieve our goals.'

Before her seatmate responded, I bent forward. 'Pardon me, ma'am. I'm late arriving from The City.' To Oklahomans, a reference to The City is immediately understood to mean Oklahoma City, the state's largest metropolitan area. 'I'm a reporter for Associated Press. Can you give me the name of the woman standing by the dais?'

Her gaze swung to the platform. 'That's Professor Iris Gallagher. She's presenting faculty awards.' A manicured hand with pink-tipped nails picked up a program. 'Here, this will be helpful.'

'Thank you very much.' As I turned away, sirens caterwauled, louder, louder, nearer and nearer.

Iris Gallagher gave a final nod to the portly man, squared her slim shoulders and started up the steps. As she climbed, she looked out at the audience. She saw me.

Looks can indeed speak volumes. Her gaze was steely, challenging. If she'd flung a dagger at my feet, the shaft would quiver from the force of the impact.

I gave her a pleasant smile, fluttered the program at her. I felt sanguine. I would have no difficulty finding her and finding out about her.

The sirens shrilled to a peak, abruptly quit. Guests looked about, possibly concerned that someone had been taken ill, searching the room for signs of distress.

I moved fast now, eager to leave the ballroom. Iris was at the microphone. 'Good evening. Welcome to Goddard College's Midsummer Merriment—'

I opened the door, stepped into the expansive landing. Twin stairways descended on either side. A balustrade between the stairs provided, as I recalled, a view of the ground floor.

A couple stood at the top of one stairway. They weren't facing me so I disappeared.

The tiny woman spoke emphatically. '. . . go down right now and find out what's happening.'

A distinguished-looking man with silver hair and a beaked nose made no move. 'Francie, it isn't our concern.'

A young woman peered over the edge of the balustrade. 'I see flashing lights outside.'

Sounds rose of clattering footsteps and terse commands.

'Cops and paramedics just rushed across the lobby and went down a hall.' She gestured to right. 'Probably an accident of some sort. We'd better stay up here.' She sounded regretful.

I still held the program and the folded square from the dead man's wallet. When I disappeared, so did the notepad and pen supplied to the reporter from Oklahoma City. However, the program and paper from Lambert's wallet were visible. I put my hand down behind a potted palm. As long as I held physical items, I couldn't move instantly from one spot to another. I put the folded strip inside the program, folded it. That made the expanse of paper smaller, less noticeable. People rarely look up so I began to rise.

The folded program was yanked from my hand.

'Floating programs not permitted. Not proper. Not academic.'

A scrawny man with bushy brown hair brandished the folded program and its enclosure. He tried to focus his gaze on the program. 'What have we here? Flying paper is worthy of note. And note it I shall.' He paused between words, almost managing to speak clearly. 'Some might attribute elevated papers to consumption of gin. But,' his hand rose and he waggled the program, 'I see what I see. Gin be damned.' He stared at the program. 'We have a conum . . .' He cleared his throat, dropped syllables with care '. . . a conundrum. A floating program. Floating olives in martinis, yes. Floating programs in the air, no. Can't say I know what to do with a floating program.'

I no longer needed the program, but I had to have that square of paper from the dead man's wallet. I grabbed at the program.

He held on tight, his face folding into mulish resistance. 'Not going to be flummoxed by a piece of paper. I yield to my wife, She Who Must Be Obeyed. Rumpole and I are brothers in arms.' He gave an uneven laugh. 'Sometimes arms are warm, sometimes not. I suspect Rumpole's experience is the same. But that's another tale. I defer to the IRS, though offshore tax havens shouldn't be just for the rich. I gracefully agree with the department chair. Some day it will be my turn. But I will not be thwarted by a flying program.' He ripped the program apart, flung the pieces high.

The couple and the young woman reached him. The man's voice was pleasant, 'Always rip up annoyances, Reggie. Now,' a deft arm under one elbow, 'let's go back to the table.'

Reggie looked up at the distinguished man. 'Ashton, deal forcefully with flying paper. I shall add that dictum to the syllabus. Perhaps I should go to my office tonight.' He tried to turn, but was steered straight toward the ballroom.

Ashton was admiring. 'Good show, Reggie. We can discuss at length . . .' They reached the ballroom door, opened it, moved inside. The door closed.

I dropped to my hands and knees, scrabbling for the scraps. The lighting was poor. I gathered up bits and pieces until a door squeaked open behind me. I swept my hand in a final frantic effort, curled the pieces in a sweaty palm, and scooted to the ceiling. A security guard, cell phone to one ear, thudded toward the stairs.

I needed a safe place for the remnants. I zoomed down the steps to the second floor to seek sanctuary. Each bedroom is named. I'd last stayed (unbeknownst to the college) in Will's Room (Rogers, not Shakespeare). I reached Will's Room. The hallway was empty. I put my bits of paper on the floor, moved through the panel. In a quick glance, I saw no evidence of occupancy. I unlocked the door, picked up my rescued scraps, shut the door. Moving to a bedside table, I dropped the pieces into an old-fashioned porcelain pitcher which had surely been a prized possession in a long-ago frontier cabin.

I was pleased to see Sam Cobb, Adelaide's police chief, standing to one side of the crime scene with his second-in-command, Detective-Sergeant Hal Price. A scruffy young man in a tie-dye T-shirt over a damp swimsuit and rubber pool shoes knelt by the body. Jacob Brandt didn't look the least like a medical examiner, but was a very good one. I'd been helpful to Sam in past visits to Adelaide. Wiggins regretted that Sam was well aware I was sometimes visible and sometimes not. Tonight Sam wasn't in his usual rumpled brown suit. Since the call came after hours, he was casual in a Hawaiian shirt and worn khakis. Hal was trim in a blue polo and denim cutoffs.

I joined their circle. Brandt came to his feet and gestured at the body. 'Death instantaneous. Broken neck. Maybe a karate chop. That takes skill. Likely a weapon. Blackjack or sap. Big stick. Body's still warm so I estimate dead about half an hour, could be forty-five minutes.' He looked at his oversize wristwatch which likely could chart constellations or navigate Antarctica. 'Seven thirty-two. Right around seven. For the record, body of well-nourished adult male, no other signs of overt trauma.' He gave a wave with his hand. 'Set your hounds loose. I'm back to the pool.' He looked aggrieved. 'I was sharing an inner tube with a good-looking girl. Five guys were circling like sharks. What are the odds one of them took my place.' He turned and slapped across the floor.

Crime-scene technicians were already at work, starting at the perimeter of the room, drawing ever nearer the victim. A photographer completed a video sweep, switched to a Leica for still shots.

I looked around for the woman who opened the door and asked for a kiss, instead found death. She was no longer here.

Sam jerked a thumb toward the ceiling. 'Station officers at every exit of the ballroom. Get somebody upstairs who has a guest list. Find out if Lambert was seated by anyone. If there's anyone with a connection, take them to the main office. That's on this floor not far from the main entrance. Text me on arrival. After that person or persons leave the ballroom, announce that a homicide has occurred. Emphasize there is no danger to anyone present and a police investigation is ongoing. Anyone who came in contact with Matthew J. Lambert this evening or has information about him is asked to inform an officer. Guests exiting the ballroom will be required to show identification and sign their names to a register.'

Hal nodded and turned away. Sam scanned the room, making sure everything was being done properly. He gazed for a moment at the wallet lying on the floor and the scattered credit cards.

I knew Sam wondered if attempted theft was the reason for murder.

He looked for a long moment, then gave a short nod and moved purposefully to the door. I was right behind him. He crossed the hall, tapped on a door.

Detective Don Smith opened the door, stepped into the hall. '. . . jealous. She killed—' Smith shut the door, cutting off the shrill voice. Tall, lean, dark-haired Detective Don Smith was a whiz with computers. His demeanor was always a trifle sardonic. Tonight, his face was flushed. 'We got a wild woman on our hands. Clarisse Bennett. She found the body, called nine-one-one. Apparently she was Lambert's sweetie in the office. She wants to storm up and yank Lambert's wife out of the ballroom and throw her over the balustrade. Judy's playing Soothing Sue but the woman's hysterical.'

'The wife's here?' Sam tapped his phone. 'Victim's wife is in ballroom. Detail Officer Mackey to find her and escort her to the main office.' He slid the phone into his pocket. 'Can Judy calm the witness down?'

Judy was Detective Judy Weitz, who was always patient, careful, and smart in her investigations.

'No progress yet. Bennett alternates between sobs and yells; says she'll report us if we don't arrest the wife.' Don lifted his shoulders, let them fall. 'She may have a point.'

'Tell Ms Bennett the police chief has been apprised of her allegations and wants to assure her that the information will be investigated. Get permission to record your interview. I want details. Last time she saw him. Times. Dates.'

A ping. He pulled out his cell phone, glanced at the message. 'I have to meet the widow.' His heavy face was somber. 'Tell her she's a widow.'

I joined Detective Weitz in the small office. I approved her new tidy haircut, an improvement on her previous flyaway look, and I admired her aquamarine shift. Though very plain, the dress was stylishly cut and the color flattering to her fair complexion. A great improvement from my last visit. I recalled one outfit with a shudder, a loose-fitting dun-colored blouse and slacks reminiscent of a Brownie uniform. Clarisse Bennett, hunched on a stiff chair, was much more dramatic in a skintight flaming pink sheath. She was in her mid-thirties. Brown curls cupped a face with makeup smeared by tears. The sheath was low cut to emphasize what in my day was called a full figure, appealing to men enchanted by a Reubens nude.

Detective Smith opened the door and stepped inside. He wasn't enchanted, but he tried to look commiserating. 'Is there anyone we can call to come and help you?'

'I'm not leaving until you arrest her.' Clarisse's voice rose in anger. 'She thinks she's so important, sitting at a front table with him. Next year I would have been there as his wife. He was going to dump her and she knew it.'

Detective Weitz murmured, 'Police investigations require corroboration. You can be assured all allegations—'

Clarisse's face twisted. 'Listen to me. Joyce killed him. She resented his success. He was so important and she was just a little shopkeeper. And she's in debt and wanted him to take care of everything. He was tired of all her problems and that son of hers. He's artistic.' The adjective was an epithet. 'Matt was going to tell her they were through. We had everything planned. All Joyce cares about is money. He was going to give her enough to get the shop out of debt if she agreed to a divorce. We were going to Florida and have a wedding on the beach.' She pressed her fingers against her cheeks. Her shoulders jerked with sobs.

I reached the main office before Sam. Officer Mackey, trim in the Adelaide police French blue uniform, was sympathetic but firm. 'Ma'am, I am not authorized to speak. Chief Cobb is on his way.'

Joyce Lambert clutched at her throat. Her pale face sagged in fear. 'My son?' The words pushed out, high and stricken. Her large brown eyes glittered with panic.

Officer Mackey pressed her lips together, then blurted. 'Ma'am, this does not concern your son.'

I suspected she was a mother as well. I was sure Sam would understand.

Joyce Lambert's body eased from its rigid posture. She brushed back a strand of pale yellow hair that had escaped from coronet braids. Heartfelt relief was obvious, relief that so dominated her mind she made no effort to demand further information. Now she was a shaken middle-aged woman who looked out of place in the businesslike office in her festive rose silk blouse and four-tiered white chiffon skirt and white heels.

The door opened and Sam stepped inside. Sam is a big bear of a man. His dark hair is frosted by silver, his heavy face lined by years of experience. His observant brown eyes had seen much evil, but could still soften in empathy. His deep voice was gentle and he spoke fast, knowing that bad news is best delivered quickly. 'Ma'am, I'm Sam Cobb, chief of police. I regret to inform you that your husband Matthew Lambert was killed tonight. He suffered a broken neck.'

'Broken neck?' Her shock was evident. 'You can't be right. It must be someone else. Matt's talking to people. That's what he does at social events. He talks to people, makes supporters of the college feel welcome. We have to look for him. Matt can't be dead.'

'Ma'am, we have confirmed his identity. The victim is Matthew J. Lambert.'

'A broken neck?' She tried to make sense of the words. 'Did he fall?'

'Ma'am, I'm sorry to have to tell you that an assailant struck him on the side of his neck. He is a homicide victim.'

'Homicide?' Her voice was a whisper. She stared at Sam in disbelief. "Someone killed Matt? Here at Rose Bower?'

'Ms Bennett found his body in the Donald S. Malone Room on the first floor. Bruising on his throat indicates he was attacked with a weapon such as a blackjack. We do not have a witness to the attack. Ms Bennett says no one was in that room when she found Mr Lambert. The weapon was not in the room. Officers are presently searching both the mansion and the grounds. At this time, we have no information yet to lead us to a suspect. Do you know of anyone who threatened Mr Lambert?'

Joyce looked bewildered. 'No one threatened him. No one at all.'

'Mr Lambert was attending the banquet on the third floor. Can you tell us why he was downstairs?'

'No.' Her voice was faint. 'He left the table about a little before seven. At events he always took every opportunity to speak to important donors. And he loved talking to people.' She pressed her lips together in an effort to keep them from trembling. Her gaze was wide and staring.

Sam was kind. 'Can we call someone to come for you?'

'I don't know.' Her tone was numb.

Sam looked at Officer Mackey. 'Talk to somebody in charge upstairs. Get someone to help.' He glanced at Joyce Lambert. 'Check for her purse and bring it to her.'

Officer Mackey hurried from the room.

Sam moved to a wall, picked up a straight chair and brought it to Joyce. 'Would you like to sit down, ma'am?'

Joyce sank on to the seat, staring blankly ahead.

'May I ask some questions, ma'am? It could be helpful with our investigation.'

She clasped her hands together. She nodded, but her gaze was distant as she grappled with an unimaginable reality.

'Did your husband have any enemies?'

'Enemies?' A trembling hand brushed back a strand of hair. 'Matt didn't have enemies. It must have been a robbery. Something like that.'

'Are you aware of any disagreements? Quarrels? Estrangements?'

She shook her head at each question. 'Matt got along with everyone. People like – liked him. He raised money for the college. Lots of money. He was going to get an award tonight. Are you sure it was Matt?'

'We are sure. His body was discovered at shortly after seven in the Malone Room by a Ms Clarisse Bennet. She called nine-one-one.'

'Clarisse?' For an instant Joyce's face was flat, either with dislike or dismissal. Then she slumped back against the chair.

'Clarisse would know. So it was Matt. Oh my God.' Her face twisted in a spasm of sorrow, sorrow and something more – a flash of sheer panic.

Sam's expression didn't change, but his brown eyes were intent, calculating. 'What was your husband's relationship with Ms Bennett?'

'She was a member of his staff. But I might as well tell you,' Joyce's voice was harsh, 'he intended to fire her. It's one of those pathetic things. She's recently divorced and of course Matt was kind and encouraging, but she took advantage of his kindness. Called him at home. Wanted him to meet with her on the weekends. He tried to be patient, but it was very awkward. She convinced herself that Matt was in love with her. He was appalled. Totally appalled. You say she found him?' Joyce came to her feet, reached out, gripped Sam's arm. 'She must have killed him. Oh poor Matt. He was trying to help her. How dreadful. How absolutely hideous.'

The door opened and Officer Mackey held it wide for a woman with a greyhound face and a lean body. She strode forward, gave Sam a stern look. She carried two purses. 'I'll take you home. Joyce.'

THREE

The ballroom was the scene of an orderly evacuation. Guests were funneled through three open doorways staffed by police officers. The process was slow. Each person was requested to show identification and asked to sign a register and provide contact information, including address and cell phone number.

I was alert for any sign of Wiggins's presence. I was sure he was aware of my Appearance at the crime scene. I was eager to justify my actions. It wasn't my fault that Iris was one of those rare individuals with the ability to see the unseen. Her insistence that I go back where I came from compelled me to inform her I was there to assist her and Robert and I had every intention of fulfilling my task. Her lack of appreciation was rude.

There was no doubt that our back-and-forth conversation distressed Robert; put him, in fact, in a pitiable state. Absolutely he required reassurance. Perhaps Wiggins understood my dilemma. To my immense relief, there was no scent of coal smoke, no clack of iron wheels. The fact that Wiggins saw no need to scold gave me a boost. I would keep on keepin' on, as we say in Oklahoma, and discharge my duties. I would, I thought grimly, assist Iris and Robert no matter how uncooperative they might be.

To that end, I hovered near a chandelier, checked out the lines, and found Iris and Robert. Standing with them, a hand on Robert's arm, was a young woman with a marked resemblance to Iris; just as lovely, but with a sweeter cast to her face. Not that I disliked Iris, but her attitude this evening lacked charm.

I dropped to the floor, strolled to stand beside Iris.

She saw me, of course. Her eyes glinted. She held her program over her hand, shielding it from Robert and her daughter. She made a fist, poked out a thumb, jerked it toward the ceiling.

I gave her a sunny smile, came close, and whispered in her ear. 'You might as well be pleasant. We will be seeing a lot of each other.'

If looks could kill . . .

'Mom, who are you glaring at?'

'Not glaring. Simply thinking.' Her voice was brisk.

Her daughter gave a shaky sigh. 'Don't do too much of that. I guess the police will want to talk to everyone in Matt's office.'

Iris managed a smile. 'It will be fine, Gage. Simply tell them you've only interned there for a month and you don't know anything helpful and you didn't see much of Matt.'

'More than I wanted. And he was—'

Iris cut her off. 'Stay out of it, Gage. Don't offer any observations. If asked your opinion of Matt, look bland and say you were an intern and your focus was on how to approach wealthy individuals on behalf of a charitable institution and he was highly skilled at raising money.'

Gage nodded, but her face had a haunted quality and her fingers were laced tightly together. Her gaze slid toward Robert.

He blurted, 'The police will ask if you knew of anyone with a motive.' They exchanged a long look. 'I'd advise you to say your only contact with him was at the office and you don't have any information about his personal life.'

'Right.' Her answer came through stiff lips. Her gaze skittered from her mother to Robert and back again.

I wondered what prompted that searching look. It seemed likely the three of them had been seated together at the dinner. At some point Iris left the ballroom and so did Robert. They ended up in a room with a dead man, but obviously arrived separately because Robert was shocked to see the weapon in her hand, possibly feared she had attacked Matt. That suggested Iris and the dead man were at odds. Did Gage follow Iris or Robert downstairs? Or did she leave the table before them?

The three of them moved as the line inched toward a door. Iris gave me one more malevolent glance, then folded her arms, her expression somber. Her eyes held worry and determination.

Robert gnawed on one finger, likely considering the penalty for a member of the bar hiding knowledge of a murder victim. Gage hunched thin shoulders, clearly tense and anxious.

Tomorrow I would find out more, much more, about Iris, Gage, and Robert, about Matt Lambert, about his wife, about his possible lover. If need be. But possibly the answer to his murder was already within my grasp.

I arrived in Will's Room. Perhaps an emissary with nerves of steel would have handled the situation better, but I wasn't prepared for two immediate shocks: a portly man in baggy red-and-black plaid boxer shorts, one hand scratching his belly, the other reaching for the porcelain vase which contained the scraps of the square of paper I'd taken from Matt Lambert's billfold.

His hand and mine grabbed the vase handle at the same instant.

'So sorry.' I tried to sound reasonable and reassuring as I gripped the handle.

He stiffened, stared at the vase in disbelief. One hand clasped a roll of fat, the other fell to his side. He peered at the vase. 'What the hell?'

I picked up the vase. 'Hell isn't involved,' I said firmly. I hurried toward the door.

His stricken gaze followed the pitcher as it moved through the air. He backed to a chair draped with discarded clothing. He grabbed a pair of trousers.

'So sorry. Everything's all right. You can have a nice dinner. Relax. Watch the Cardinals. Sure to be a game on tonight.' I opened the door, placed the vase in the hall, closed the door. The guest was frantically pulling on trousers, his face working, his hands shaking so hard he bunched the trousers at one knee. I felt it essential to reassure him before I flowed through to the hall and that all-important vase. 'Don't be upset. I'm leaving now.'

He turned and hopped to the window, still struggling with that bunched pant leg. He shoved at the sash with one hand, yanked at his trousers with the other. Bless his heart, the window appeared to be stuck. Of course, possibly he was pushing at an angle. It really takes both hands to lift a window properly.

Truly I was sorry. 'I'm done now. I'm leaving.'

I moved through the door into the hall. I picked up the vase, retrieved the paper scraps. I was putting the vase down, honestly it was within a foot of the floor, when the door was flung open. He looked at the elevated vase, yelped. I can only describe the sound as a yelp. He slammed the door shut.

To compound my distress, the smell of coal smoke was overpowering and the clack of iron wheels shattering. The swirling smoke and rumbling wheels combined to pulverize my self-esteem but, like the boy at the dike or a cowboy holding a rattlesnake by the neck, I was solely focused on my goal. I rose to the ceiling. If anyone else entered the hall and saw speeding bits of paper aloft, that was beyond my control. I found a window, placed the precious scraps on the sill, used both hands and pushed up the sash. I grabbed the bits of paper, undid the screen, and fled outside.

The Rescue Express careened beside me. Cinders flew. Coal smoke obscured the horizon. I ignored the moonlight-silvered cars and swooped from Rose Bower to downtown Adelaide and a ledge of a second-story window at the police department. I landed on a particular window ledge, that of Police Chief Sam Cobb. I knew his office well. It was the work of only a moment to carefully tuck the pieces of paper on the corner of the ledge, move inside, open the window, undo the screen, grab the pieces. I closed the screen, whirled, skirted the old leather sofa that faced the windows. There was enough light from the street to reach Sam's desk and turn on the lamp. Coal smoke pulsed around me. The mournful cry of the whistle was deafening. I covered my ears as I moved wearily back toward the window and dropped in defeat on to the sofa. Coal smoke surrounded me like Poe's vortex. Wheels clacked.

I spoke in a breathless, hopeful voice. 'I can explain.'

Wiggins's deep voice was a mixture of despair and disbelief. 'Precept Three. Precept Six.'

Quick as a star pupil called to recite, I said respectfully, '"Work behind the scenes without making your presence known."' A quick breath necessitated by the pall of coal smoke and chagrin. '"Make every effort not to alarm earthly creatures." Wiggins, I was doing my best. It absolutely was never my intention—'

He cut me off. 'In all my experience, no emissary has ever fled the Rescue Express.' There was shocked emphasis on *ever*.

'Only in service of the mission. Here.' I held out my hand with the now rather limp pieces of paper curling on my hot sweaty palm. 'The contravention of the Precepts occurred only because I was carrying out my duties.' I knew I was babbling, which would evoke a sneer from Iris Gallagher. 'When I opened the victim's billfold in an effort to discover his identity, I found a folded square of paper that he kept with the bills. That suggested to me that the paper was important to him. I was holding the billfold when the hall door opened. A woman came in and when she saw him, she cried out and I dropped his billfold but I still held—'

'Bailey Ruth.'

I fell silent. I knew what awaited. A return to Heaven in disgrace. Perhaps I would never again be permitted to serve as an emissary. Like a drowning victim, faces and lives flashed before my eyes from my first effort that saved dear little redheaded Bayroo, my grandniece and namesake, to the recent rescue of a woman desperate to save her sister. I drooped. Hot tears slid down my cheeks.

A strange sound. Not a cougar's wail. Not the squeak of air from whirl-a-cars at the amusement park. Not the rump-a-dum-dum of the bass drum in a parade.

Rumble. Humph. Rumble.

I sagged in relief. Wiggins was struggling to suppress a booming guffaw.

'. . . have to say . . . poor fellow . . . pulling on trousers while he tried to push up the sash . . . all bunched up . . .'

I was wise enough to maintain a respectful silence.

Two deep breaths. Another. 'Ah. But,' Wiggins tried to sound stern, 'next time when in a difficult situation, remember, Silence is Golden. If you had managed to wrest the vase from him and the slips had fallen out, he might have thought he'd dropped the vase, but hopefully . . .' Wiggins broke off. 'Oh dear. A situation in Tumbulgum.'

The lovely little Australian town at the confluence of the Rous and Tweed Rivers, pop. 349, occasionally received Wiggins's attention. A situation could be anything from a lost sheepdog to a broken heart. I wished the sheepdog/young (or old) lover resolution but hopefully not soon.

'. . . Oh dear – Bailey Ruth,' his voice was fading. 'The Precepts. Iris and Robert need—'

The Rescue Express roared away. Coal smoke faded.

Helping Robert was a pleasure. In my view, Iris needed a personality makeover, but she was also my charge, so I must deal with her. As an emissary, I would fulfill my duty, though taking Iris down a peg or two would give me great pleasure.

Sam's quiet office offered respite. And perhaps the square of paper so carefully kept with the currency might point to a solution to the murder and I would be free of Iris. In my experience, a sheet of paper secreted in a billfold or purse meant a matter of importance was involved. I was eager to deal with the scraps of paper. But first I required some energy. I pushed up from the sofa, walked around to Sam's worn desk. I dropped the limp scraps on the desktop, pulled out the bottom left-hand drawer, and seized a bag of M&Ms. I poured a handful. Crunch. Munch. Another handful and I was in Sam's chair, looking down at my booty.

I never excelled at jigsaw puzzles but, aided by a third handful of crackly candies, I separated out the pieces of the note from the slicker paper of the program. I shifted these bits of paper and guessed and said a little prayer to St Anthony. He is a great help in finding something lost and I thought he could stretch a point and suggest missing words to me.

The folded-up message obviously was short. Here's what I had with the pieces I managed to save:

> . . . door . . . and I saw Ev . . . take . . . he . . . ay. I watc
> . . . the reflec . . . in the mirror. The . . . ss was full. She
> . . . ut . . . ray on the tab . . . She didn't add anyth . . . to
> the gla . . . and drank all of . . . This occur . . . Marc . . .
> . . . hew . . . ert

I tried a version on Sam's yellow legal pad:

> The door opened and I saw Ev— (Eva, Evangeline, Eve, Evelyn, Evita) take the tray. I watched the reflection in the mirror. The glass was full. She put the tray on the table. She didn't add anything to the glass and drank all of it. This occurred March . . .
>
> Matthew Lambert

The last was a scrawl, obviously part of a signature.

I felt prickly. You know what I mean. The sound of a door closing in an empty house. A vulture circling in the sky. The shifting of unsteady snow on a mountainside. The folded square might have been anything, but the last thing I expected was a note written by Lambert with a peculiar message.

He saw a door open. He watched in the mirror as a woman accepted a tray. He reported that she added nothing to a glass, drank all of the contents.

Matt Lambert recorded the event and kept that information with him. Why?

I put the legal pad with my transcription squarely in the center of Sam's desk. I pushed up from his chair, hurried to the old-fashioned blackboard on one wall. Sam disdained modern dry erase boards.

I picked up the chalk, wrote:

Matt Lambert carried a folded square of paper in his wallet. The existing remnants are on the desk along with a possible transcription. Lambert reports an apparently mundane scene he observed, but thought the information important enough to carry with him.

I paused, searching for the right words. Sam wouldn't be interested in a door closing in an empty house or a circling vulture or the expectation of an avalanche.

I wrote on the blackboard: *No one carries information – secretes information – unless the facts contained are critically important. Respectfully, Officer M. Loy*

I underscored the message on the blackboard.

P.S. The note was accidentally damaged and some pieces were lost, resulting in an incomplete record.

The signature would alert Sam to my involvement. M. Loy was my tribute to Myrna Loy, who starred as Nora Charles in *The Thin Man* films based on Dashiell Hammett's characters. In the past I'd Appeared in a French blue uniform as Officer M. Loy. Perhaps tomorrow. But there was much to do tonight.

The clock struck midnight as I arrived at the administration building on the campus of Goddard College. It was utterly silent inside the venerable building, which was erected in the early 1900s. I hovered just inside the door of Matt Lambert's first-floor office. I had no need to flick the light switch. The flashlight in Gage Gallagher's hand afforded good vision.

Gage was dressed in black from the silk scarf that hid her hair to a tight-fitting turtleneck to yoga pants. Even her sneakers were black. They looked like old, worn, high-school basketball shoes. She wore black leather gloves. She was perfectly dressed to slip unseen through the night.

I remembered her scarcely concealed impatience as the line progressed across the ballroom floor. Was a surreptitious visit to Lambert's office the reason she'd been so eager to be free of the room?

I remembered Robert's occasional worried glance at Gage despite his preoccupation with Iris and the murder he had not reported.

I'd taken it for granted that Robert and Gage were in love or about to be in love. Robert was concerned about Gage's mother. He might better be concerned about Gage. Slipping late at night into the office of a murder victim suggested Gage was not an innocent bystander, that there was some incriminating information in the office that would link her to the crime.

She stood by an opulent desk with a fancy tooled red leather desk pad to protect the rosewood surface from scratches. A picture of Joyce Lambert sat on one corner, a younger, happier Joyce, brown curls cut short, soft lips curved in a sweet smile.

Gage aimed the flashlight beam at the top right drawer. All

the drawers were pulled out. Folders littered the floor. She pulled out another folder, skimmed the contents, dropped it on a growing pile. Ten more minutes and all the drawers were empty.

Gage stepped to the desk chair, perched on the edge. She rested the flashlight on the desk and turned to the computer monitor. She apparently knew the password. Several clicks later, the cursor moved to a file midway down the screen. She lifted her index finger to click on the mouse, stopped.

I'd learned enough about computers in previous missions to understand her frustration. If she called up a file, the last time that file was seen would be recorded.

Her face squeezed in thought. She leaned forward, highlighted at least fifteen files, held down the delete and shift keys, clicked, and the screen was blank. She put the cursor on Close, hesitated, gently returned the mouse to the pad.

'Oh, good.' I clapped my hands in approval. I intended to do a search of his contacts, type in *Ev* in hopes of discovering the person who took the tray with the full glass.

Gage rocketed from the chair, knocking the flashlight to the floor. She stood like a creature at bay, head jerking from side to side, panicked gaze searching the room.

I realized I'd spoken aloud. I'm afraid my impulsive speech reflected a lifetime and beyond of acting first, thinking later. Bobby Mac once urged me, 'Honey, the next time the principal makes you mad, take a deep breath, maybe five deep breaths, pretend you are in a monastery in Tibet. The gong just sounded. It means: Shut up.'

Gage's breaths came in quick, short gasps. She backed away from the desk, wide eyes flitting in every direction.

'Don't be frightened.' I hesitated. I enjoy swirling colors and the effervescent experience of becoming visible, but my unexpected Appearance might utterly unnerve a young woman engaged in a highly questionable endeavor.

Gage took several backward steps, her eyes still seeking me.

Glass shattered. The unmistakable sound was followed by the tinkle of shards striking the floor.

Gage and I both whirled toward the bank of windows. The only light came from the flashlight that had rolled across the room and lodged against a sofa. The low beam illuminated drapes billowing inward. Pieces of glass glittered on the floor.

My nose wrinkled at the rank stench of gasoline.

A gloved hand gripped a portion of drape, yanked. A grill lighter flared, igniting cloth wadded at the end of a stick. The stick with its fireball end sailed through the broken window and landed on the desk. The near drape blazed. Fire erupted on the rug, a sofa, a chair. Black smoke eddied in a current of air from the smashed window. In an instant, suffocating smoke was too thick for vision. Or breath.

Smoke rises. I dropped to the floor. I crawled on my knees, one hand out in front, seeking, searching. Flames seemed everywhere. Smoke stung my eyes. Despite the crackle of the fire, I heard labored breathing quite near. My hand touched a sneaker. I gripped an ankle, shouted. 'Get down. Crawl. This way.' I tugged and she dropped to the floor.

I released her ankle, found an elbow. I took a firm grip as I tried to recall the layout of the office. The desk faced a wall of bookcases with windows to the left, the door to the right. The door was our goal. Beyond the door was air and life.

I struggled to breathe. Gage coughed and coughed and coughed again. I pulled her elbow and steered us away from the windows. A foot. Another. Another. My right hand kept sweeping ahead of us and then I touched the wall. 'We're almost there.' I was gasping. I didn't know if she heard. 'Keep moving.'

It seemed forever in the foul smoke and growing heat from the flames until I touched the surface of the door to the outer office. I struggled to my feet, pulling Gage up. My shaking hand closed on a knob. I turned the knob, pulled. The door swung in. Blessed air soothed my nose and throat. Gage shook free of my grip, hurried forward. I heard her stumbling steps ahead of me. She was on her way to the outer door that opened into the hall.

Sirens shrilled. A whoosh. Pellets of cold water doused me as water spewed from automatic sprinklers. More cool air as Gage opened the hall door. In the light from the flames, I saw her slight figure in the open doorway. She half turned, called out in a shaky voice, 'Whoever you are, are you all right? Where are you?'

'I'm fine. Thank you.' I admired her willingness to brave the flames if necessary, to help her rescuer.

'I don't see you.' There were tears in her voice. Was her rescuer in that blazing room?

I spoke firmly. 'Leave now. No one will know you were here.'

With that, she took a last searching look at the empty anteroom and the fiery flames in Matt's office, then turned and plunged into the central hall.

I reached the hall and heard running steps. Gage would escape before the fire engines arrived. Now that she was safe, I willed myself outside the building to the windows of Matt Lambert's office. I wasn't surprised that I saw no one. I was too late to catch the arsonist. I rose in the air, looking for headlights, saw several. But there was no guarantee the arsonist had arrived or departed by car. I tried to estimate how long Gage and I struggled to escape. At least three or four minutes. A car would be long gone. I circled back to the nearest exit to look for Gage. There was no trace of her.

I sought refuge in a room at Rose Bower. This time I made sure there was no occupant. The nameplate on the door attracted me: *Repose.* The serene room was sparsely furnished. A contemplative Buddha occupied a wall niche. I took a leisurely shower, blew dry my red curls, chose a simple cotton nightie. The air conditioning was quite cool so I slipped on a scarlet silk robe embroidered with a golden dragon.

I settled on a rather austere sofa. I was discouraged. I couldn't pretend the day had gone smoothly. I reviewed my lack of rapport with Robert and Iris, my worry about Gage's suspicious actions, the damage to the square of paper from Matt's billfold, Wiggins's shock at an emissary fleeing the Rescue Express, the escape of the arsonist. To lift my morale, I thought how nice it would be to have a glass of cream sherry.

I smiled as I picked up the glass, lifted it to see the ruby shimmer. I took a sip and admired quotes from Confucius in bamboo frames. I took one to heart.

Think of tomorrow, the past can't be mended.

FOUR

Summer sunlight gilded downtown Adelaide. The early morning air was already warm enough for new chicks. Mama Mississippi kites circled above the park across from City Hall, alert for any approach to a tree with a nest. I stood in the entrance to a dress shop not yet open. I admired beach pants with a wild pattern of orange and blue swirls and a matching sky-blue T-shirt flung over a slatted white wooden chair. Bright colors. Bright day. I checked for pedestrians and Appeared. Cheered by the summery display, I chose a sky-blue cotton blouse with a lace-edged hem, a slim white skirt, white sandals. Each sandal sported a shiny blue bow. Bright me.

Today was a new beginning. I would do my best for Iris, no matter how rude she might be. I took a deep breath of summer and hurried to Lulu's Café. Lulu's is an Adelaide institution, offering breakfast, lunch, and dinner. I stepped inside and loved the mingled scents of coffee, bacon, and cinnamon.

The tables in the center of the café were occupied, the four booths full but, how Heavenly, there was a spot at the counter. I knew it was meant for me. I slid on to the red leather stool and flashed a smile at Sam Cobb.

'Claire's out of town so I planned to eat here anyway.' His deep voice was pleasant. 'Figured you'd come. No uniform today.' That was his tactful way of telling me he'd found the information about the square of paper and knew Officer Loy was back in Adelaide.

The waitress held up a carafe. 'Coffee?' At our nod, she poured. 'What'll it be?'

Sam ordered an egg-white omelet and side of yogurt. With a sigh.

I gave him a commiserating glance, but my sympathy didn't stretch to imitation. I smiled at the waitress. 'Bacon, two sausage patties, omelet with mushrooms, onions, cheddar cheese, and pimiento, hash browns, Texas toast with cream gravy.'

Sam looked pained, then as the waitress turned away, he was businesslike. 'Who're you here for?' His brown eyes were intent.

'I'm not sure.' My smile was innocent. 'There was some confusion on my arrival. I'll try to find out today.' I didn't feel dishonest, though possibly a bit disingenuous. But Iris not only spurned help, I didn't see she needed assistance. On the other hand, Gage might well be in trouble and Robert was hanging out to dry if anyone saw him jettison the weapon. 'I haven't learned much about Matt Lambert.' I rapidly explained my unintentional grip on the folded square from Lambert's billfold and its later adventures, resulting in the pieces on his desk. I gave Sam my most beguiling smile. 'I'm here to learn.' I was confident that Iris and Robert were innocent so it wouldn't be helpful to place them at the crime scene. As for the fire at Lambert's office, I knew nothing about the identity of the arsonist.

Sam took a big slug of coffee. 'Disappointing, Officer Loy. I hoped you could point a finger.'

Our food arrived. Sam stared at my big platter, then his eyes fell to his plate with the anemic egg-white omelet.

I reached for his plate, briskly divided my order. I pushed the plate toward him. 'When manna falls from Heaven, simply count your blessings.'

Sam beamed.

As my mama always told us kids, 'When you make someone happy, you'll be happy, too.'

Sam speared a sausage patty. 'The case is screwy. For starters,' he licked ketchup from his thumb, 'Lambert is a big man around Adelaide. Knows all the rich folks. Charms them. Gets cash for Goddard. He dealt in big sums but all he got out of the gifts was prestige. His office never handled a penny, all the money went to the Goddard Foundation. He was the Golden Boy. Who kills the Golden Boy? Somebody jealous of his success? Goddard has an acting president who's hoping to get the nod from the Regents. But there's a rumor one of the regents is pushing Lambert to be president. Maybe the interim president decided to increase his odds. Then we got dames calling each other names. Wife says there's no love affair. Mistress claims divorce was on the calendar. Now you come up with a hidden message in the wallet. But maybe he absentmindedly folded that slip of paper and stuck it in there and forgot about it.'

I tried to be tactful. 'The paper is crisp and new, not creased or wrinkled. A wallet isn't a place you absentmindedly tuck something. I figure the information was important to him and the message was written recently.'

'Kind of intriguing, anyway.' Sam was in a good humor as he doused the hash browns with ketchup.

Sam might not be impressed with my reasoning, but he would try to figure out why Lambert carried that message. Sam would pursue all leads. As for me, I needed to know why Iris Gallagher came to the room where Lambert was killed and why she was holding the weapon, but I couldn't ask Sam for help to find the answers.

Sam looked at me sharply. 'Cat got your tongue?'

'I was thinking about the place where he was killed. Why was he there? The Malone Room is a long way from the ballroom.'

Diverted, as I'd intended, Sam nodded agreement. 'The setup's weird. Why was he in that study? The staff at Rose Bower says the room's almost never used, but it's kept dusted and spruce in case a visiting dignitary wants a place to spread out some papers. The best guess is that he went there to meet someone. Lambert was fourth on the program and he told the president he'd have a big announcement. BIG. His wife said he was excited, pumped up, but he wouldn't tell her what was coming. Maybe somebody in his office knows.' Those canny brown eyes studied me.

I took a bite of Texas toast and looked expectant. 'Are you going to his office when you leave Lulu's?'

There was a glimmer of disappointment in his gaze. He gave a noncommittal humph.

'Do you have any leads?' My voice was eager.

'A few.' He watched me closely. 'A waiter slipped out for a smoke and saw a guy near a clump of trees at the edge of the terrace. Something about his posture caught his attention and he moved that way. The guy – the waiter said he was young, tall, and thin – raised his arm and threw something that splashed in a pond. We judged where a throw from the terrace might land, used a rake, brought up a soggy sock stuffed with sand. Makes a dandy blackjack. The waiter got a good look at his face as he turned and hurried to a terrace door. Waiter said he looked guilty as hell. We've got him looking at pix of the dinner guests. We took a photo of each person as they exited the ballroom.'

Robert raising his arm, throwing the sock, now documented. I tried to appear admiring. 'How did you do that?'

He looked smug. 'Lapel cameras on the officers at the ballroom doors. Guest signed the register. Snap.'

My heart sank. 'How helpful.'

I made a quick stop at the student newspaper office, which is housed in an old building on a hillside. The editor's office at this early hour was empty. I knew a new student editor was in charge because the office was quite tidy and a vase on the desk held a spray of orchids. But some things remain the same. I found a faculty-student phone book in the top center drawer. I looked up Iris Gallagher.

Iris stood at her kitchen counter and sprinkled brown sugar on a bowl of steaming oatmeal. She wore a pale lilac blouse and orchid slacks and sandals. The kitchen was modest but cheerful, yellow curtains at the window over the sink, matching curtains at a window that overlooked a back yard that was a testament to a resident gardener. One corner was thick with wildflowers. Corn, tomatoes, cabbage, and carrots flourished in the other corner.

I pulled out a chair from a white wooden breakfast table.

She turned at the sound. Her fine brows drew down in a frown.

I smiled cheerily. 'I'd enjoy a cup of coffee.'

She ignored me, scooped up the bowl and a pitcher of cream, walked to the table, sat down.

'You may not feel in need of help, but Robert – because of

you – will soon be the subject of a police inquiry. Where does he live?'

She put the spoon down. 'Robert?'

'I want to talk to him before the police do. I may be able to save him from arrest.'

Alarm flared in those intelligent violet eyes. 'Why are they suspicious of Robert?'

'A waiter taking a break saw him throw the sock in the pond, described him accurately. The police are scanning photos they made as the banquet guests departed. The police have retrieved the sock. I imagine its contours will match that purple bruise on Lambert's throat.'

Iris pressed two fingers briefly to each temple. 'Robert Blair. Nineteen Fulton Street. Primrose Apartments. Number Twenty-Two.'

I shared the sky above Rose Bower with a wheeling Mississippi kite. The hawk and I could clearly see, if she cared, the swath of woods between the back of the mansion and the campus. The pond near the base of the terrace glittered in bright July sunshine. I traced Robert's path after he exited last night through the French door. He'd likely darted straight ahead to a clump of bois d'arc, the small hardy tree prized by early settlers for its amazing hard wood. When he reached the thicket, his way was barred because not even a bull is strong enough to crash through bois d'arc (pronounced bodark in Oklahoma). I imagined his panic, fearing discovery with the handkerchief-wrapped murder weapon in his hand, and all the while trying to avoid thinking of a dead man, and two women's voices but only one woman in the room, then my Appearance. Iris instructed him to throw the sock in the bushes. Perhaps the glimmer of the pond in the moonlight caught his eye. In any event, at some point he lifted his arm and threw.

I looked down at the grove of bois d'arc and smiled.

Robert's wrinkled T-shirt was stained near his right shoulder. A brownish stain, likely mustard. A hem was unraveling on his faded navy-blue boxer shorts. Barefoot, he poured a mug

of coffee and slapped to a kitchen table. Bleary eyed, hair
sprigging in all directions, unshaven, he plucked two packets
of sugar from a disorderly pile, ripped them open, dumped
sugar in the steaming coffee. He sat down, picked up a spoon
with one hand, a folded copy of the *Gazette* with the other.

'Time is of the essence.' I spoke with some urgency.

At the sound of my voice, Robert's shoulders hunched,
his body went rigid, the *Gazette* fell to the floor. The spoon
remained at an odd angle in the air.

I took a deep breath and Appeared. 'No choice.' I spoke
firmly in case Wiggins was near. I was honoring Precept Four
(Become visible only when absolutely essential). I'm sure
Wiggins understood as well that it wasn't my intent to distress
Robert (Precept Six: Make every effort not to alarm earthly
creatures.)

Robert bolted to his feet, the chair crashing to the floor
behind him. He backed away from the table, still clutching
the spoon, watching me with huge, staring eyes.

'Stay where you are.' I again used my teacher voice,
edged with steel. 'We don't have much time. The police will
be here shortly.'

His lips moved, but no sound came. His eyes darted wildly
around the room, then back to me. He saw me. He knew he
did. He saw me but I couldn't be there.

I started toward him. 'Don't move. Listen to me. You
don't need to worry. I really am here. But if I choose, I'm
not.' I disappeared.

The spoon bounced on the uncarpeted floor. He covered his
eyes with both hands, stood stock still.

I reached him, gently patted his shoulder.

He shuddered, spread his fingers wide enough to be sure
no one stood near.

I gave him an encouraging pat. 'We have very little time.
Here is what we need to do.'

At the end of my recital, he was leaning against the wall.
His face sagged. 'I don't get this hereafter stuff but you kind
of have to be on the level or how do you know so much?
And sometimes you're here and sometimes you aren't. I don't
want to think about that. But I guess I have to play your game.

Whatever it is. And now you tell me I'm fingered for tossing the murder weapon. They'll know it's the murder weapon by now. Iris was on to something when she told you to take a hike. Iris sees you?' His tone was pleading.

'Yes.' My tone was short. 'It's unfortunate but she does.'

'I hear you. I saw you a minute ago. You can come and go?'

I swirled present. I thought a dressier appearance might reassure him. The basket weave grassy green cotton cardigan certainly cheered me, with the neckline, hem, and pockets trimmed in ivory and pink, pink ankle-length linen slacks, and pink ballet flats.

He gave me a sickly smile. 'Damned if you can't.'

'Not damned. Actually . . .' But this was no time to discuss what he described as hereafter stuff. 'I'm here for now and we need to hurry. Get dressed. No time for coffee. No time for anything.'

'OK. Whatever you say.' He backed away, hand behind him for the knob of the bedroom door. He opened the door, started to close it behind him.

'Don't bother. I won't look. Fast, Robert, fast.'

He did as I asked, even picked up speed as he led me downstairs and out to the parking lot beside the apartment house. Robert's sleek black Toyota sedan smelled new and I wondered if he'd bought it on the prospect of a lawyer's income. Interesting that he chose a sedan and not a sports car. Was he thinking of Gage and the future and perhaps toddlers in car seats in the back? Or did he think a sports car too flashy for a new young lawyer? He didn't look lawyerly this morning, uncombed and unshaven, a tie-dye T-shirt, jeans with a hole at one knee, sloppy tennis shoes. No socks. But sartorial splendor wasn't important. Speed was.

He was certainly a slow driver. 'Go faster.'

'A motorcycle cop lurks at the bottom of the next hill. But I guess a speeding ticket won't matter if I'm in jail for murder.' He pressed on the accelerator.

His apartment house was on one side of the college. Our goal was the opposite side. We zoomed down a hill, zoomed up again, then turned into a wide boulevard bordered by woods. A half-mile later, he pulled into a parking lot, pointed.

'Rose Bower on the far side of the woods. Your party. You lead the way.'

When we were out of the car, I charged toward the path, looked back. 'Hurry.' A hundred yards later we curved around towering oaks on a path shaded by overhanging branches. I disappeared.

'I wish you'd stop doing that.' His tone was querulous.

'Two people are more noticeable than one. Go faster.' When the trees thinned and I glimpsed Rose Bower through the branches, I reached out and clutched his arm.

He jerked. 'Tell me when you're going to grab me. It scares the hell out of me when I feel a hand that isn't there. I mean, I can't see it there. I can feel it.' Another shudder.

'Go to the edge of the woods. Make sure no one is near. Run to the bois d'arc—'

He stared. 'The what?'

I was shocked. 'Aren't you from Oklahoma?'

'What difference does it make? Look, I haven't had my coffee and you're here and not here and I feel kind of sick to my stomach and you ask me if I'm from Oklahoma.'

'Osage orange?' Another name for bois d'arc, though not commonly used in Adelaide.

He was irritable. 'Will you please start making sense. What's osage orange?'

'Another name for bois d'arc. I thought surely you were familiar with one or the other.'

'Sounds like some nutsy crossword puzzle. I want coffee.'

I gripped his arm tightly. My nails are sharp.

'Ouch. OK. Whatever.'

'Anyone from Oklahoma . . .' I broke off. 'Never mind. Remember the name. Bois d'arc.' I pronounced bodark with vigor. 'It's going to be important to you.' Bois d'arc is loved by some, loathed by many. The small sturdy trees spread fast and are hard to remove. I pointed at the clump of trees. 'Those trees. That's bois d'arc. AKA osage orange.' I gave careful instructions.

He slid a glare toward where he thought I was.

I rose in the air above Rose Bower. A lawn service was busy – thankfully there are no leaf blowers in Heaven – in the extensive grounds in front, but the gardens by the terrace area were free of traffic. I perched unseen on the low wall that marked the base of the terrace and gave my best imitation of an owl. I know owls are nocturnal but this morning an owl – me – was singing near the bois d'arc.

Robert heard the signal, sprinted from the woods, running in a half-crouch. He reached the bois d'arc. He stood up. One long arm grabbed a green seed pod. The hard-pebbled green seed pod is baseball sized. He yanked a pocketknife from his pocket.

I was startled. This wasn't in our plan. I moved close enough to hover at his shoulder.

He flipped out the knife, held the pod in one hand, scratched an R, drew a heart, scratched a G.

I would have clapped in admiration, but this was not the moment to applaud. Robert might be unnerved and he was doing splendidly.

He turned, judged the distance to the pond, heaved. The seed pod splashed on the surface and sank. Robert turned and ran toward the woods, again in a crouch. The entire exercise took no more than fifteen seconds.

I joined him in the shadow of a huge magnolia. 'Good job. Love the R and G and the heart.' He scarcely gave me a nod. He was breathing fast, but his pace picked up and he plunged into the woods on to the path to the parking lot. Feet pounding, he reached the lot in record time. He yanked open the driver's door, threw himself behind the wheel. His face was flushed and his chest heaved.

I'd scarcely settled in the passenger seat when the car haroomed out of the lot. 'Do you need gas?'

His head swung toward the apparently empty passenger seat. 'I thought maybe you'd stay there. Look, it's been fun, but why don't you go wherever you need to go. I want my coffee.'

'You need to stop somewhere and buy something.'

'I don't need gas. I want my coffee.' He lifted a hand, scratched at one cheek. 'And a shave.'

I was emphatic 'Stop somewhere and buy something.'

'Will you please go away.' He shot another glance at the

seemingly empty passenger seat. 'Or,' his voice was resigned, 'be here. It's better to see you. It spooks me to know you are somewhere around and I can't see you.'

'The police know me.' I was calm. 'It's better if I remain unseen. But don't worry, I'll be with you all the way.'

'Yeah. Dandy. You hanging somewhere and the cops wanting to talk about murder. I never intended to have anything to do with criminal law. Life is too short for that.'

I was a little impatient. 'The seed pod will make all the difference. Trust me.' I looked up the street. 'Oh, good, I see a convenience store. Stop there.' I pointed, remembered he couldn't see me. 'The one on the corner. Buy something.'

He was equally emphatic. 'I don't need anything.'

I reached over, yanked at the steering wheel.

The car swerved. He avoided a curb and managed to steer into the lot.

'Go. Buy. Now. Or I will Appear sitting on your hood.' I wondered if Wiggins might eventually add a Precept prohibiting emissaries from making threats. Did I smell coal smoke?

Robert's vicious glare would have done justice to Richard Widmark in *Kiss of Death*, but he braked, slammed the door, stalked inside. He returned in a few minutes with a white sack with grease spots beginning to appear on its sides.

I smelled cake donuts. I deserved one.

Robert thumped into the driver's seat, drove the car into the street, and ignored me for the next few blocks.

I didn't ask. I picked up the sack, opened it, pulled out a sugar-crusted donut, took a bite.

He tried to sound conversational. 'Elevated half-eaten donuts are damn strange.'

I continued my feast.

'Weird.' His voice was a little high. A piece of donut hangs over there and then it disappears. Pouf. There and then it's gone.'

'Watch the street.' I licked my fingers. refolded the top of the sack, placed it on the floor. 'That brown sedan parked in front of the apartment house belongs to the police chief.'

The sedan slowed. 'Uh-oh.'

As Mama always told us kids, 'Be gracious when you prove someone wrong. No one likes to feel foolish.'

I tapped the sack of donuts. 'Be sure to offer to share them with the policemen.'

He pulled into his parking slot, grabbed the donut sack.

'And Robert,' I kept my voice cheerful, 'it's a beautiful morning.' And it was, cardinals trilling, the bright blue sky promising heat but no clouds. 'You strike me as being a jolly fellow. Take the stairs two at a time and whistle. Try to look as though you don't have a care in the world. Your only plan is to enjoy a donut and coffee.'

At the foot of the stairs, he took a deep breath, rearranged his face. The two steps at a time turned out to be problematic as he stumbled near the top, but he caught the railing, righted himself. He whistled offkey, not a melody I recognized, that sounded vaguely martial.

He was halfway down the hall, when his steps slowed.

Sam Cobb, big and bulky, and Detective-Sergeant Hal Price, lean and muscular, waited at the door to Apartment 22. They watched Robert approach with stolid faces, intent and thoughtful and observant. They had the aura of men with authority, men who brooked no nonsense, men who were alert for danger.

Robert, his expression a mixture of curiosity and puzzlement, reached them. 'You waiting for me?'

FIVE

Sam was brusque, his deep voice businesslike. 'Police Chief Sam Cobb.' He and Hal pulled out IDs. 'Detective-Sergeant Hal Price. Like to have a word with you, if we may.'

'With me?' Robert clutched his sack, appeared bewildered.

I silently applauded. Robert looked puzzled but not in the least uneasy.

Sam's dark eyes were appraising. 'Robert Blair.' He spoke with certainty. 'You were at the Goddard event at Rose Bower last night.' It wasn't a question.

'Yeah.' Robert looked mildly surprised. 'Me and a couple hundred other folks.'

'We have some questions.'

'About what?'

Sam jerked his head toward the apartment door. 'This may be a lengthy interview, Mr Blair. I suggest we step inside.'

Robert shrugged. 'OK. If you say so.' He turned up one hand in a whatever gesture. He was clearly in a whatever frame of mind. Robert unlocked the door, held it wide. 'Come on in.' He waggled the sack. 'Just been out to get some donuts. You guys like some coffee and donuts?'

Sam and Hal declined, but Sam was genial. 'We don't want to interfere with your breakfast.'

Robert waved them to a ratty-looking green sofa. Sitting side by side, they looked big and formidable. The other furnishings included a lopsided bean-bag chair patched with black duct tape, a beach chair, and an easy chair covered with an army blanket.

'Make yourself comfortable. I'll be right with you.' Robert took the sack to the kitchen counter, pulled out two donuts, put them on a paper plate, popped the plate in the microwave, tapped 60. At the ping, he removed the plate, grabbed the coffee mug from the table, put it in the microwave, tapped.

I never underestimate Sam. He watched Robert and I saw realization in his eyes that a mug filled with coffee that was now presumably cold was being heated.

Robert looked utterly unconcerned when he joined Sam and Hal in the small living room, mug in one hand, plate in the other. He settled in the blanket-covered easy chair. 'How can I help you?'

Sam's deep voice was casual. 'You poured the coffee before you left?'

Robert's eyes widened. 'Did I – oh yeah. I poured my coffee and then realized I didn't have anything good to go with it. That's when I dashed out.'

I gave an approving though unseen thumbs up.

Robert took a big bite of donut. Powdered sugar smeared his chin. 'Glad I did. Real good.'

Hal leaned forward, his blue eyes cold. 'What were you doing on the terrace at Rose Bower last night?'

Robert stopped in mid-chew. 'Gosh, is that where the murder happened?'

Hal ignored the question. 'You were observed on the terrace. What . . .'

Robert was nodding agreement.

Hal has a good poker face, but I saw a flicker of uncertainty in his eyes. Someone observed discarding a murder weapon is unlikely to cheerfully admit to the same.

'. . . did you throw in the pond?'

Robert ducked his head, looked young and slightly embarrassed. Driblets of sugar on his chin added to a vision of an untroubled witness. 'I know there's a bunch of rules at that place. Fancy and everything. But I didn't know it was against the law to toss a seed pod.' He devoured half a donut, took a gulp of coffee. 'Some kind of endangered something or other?' He sounded genuinely interested. 'Like the snail darter? Oh lord, did I whack some priceless fish in the pond?'

Sam was crisp. 'You claim you were throwing a seed pod?'

'I *did* throw a seed pod.' Nothing sounds more truthful than the truth.

Robert used the back of his hand to smooth away crumbs, added to the sprinkles of sugar on his unshaven chin. 'Am

I in big trouble? Are seed pods on some kind of don't-touch list?'

'No rules against seed pods. Mr Blair, when did you—' Sam broke off, started again. 'Why did you throw a seed pod?'

Robert leaned back, at ease, drank coffee, shrugged, looked embarrassed. 'Yeah, well, I was down on the terrace, just standing there. I saw one and grabbed it.' He wriggled uncomfortably. 'See, I was thinking about a friend, and anyway I got the seed pod and I got out my jackknife and I carved some stuff on it and then I reared back and threw it.' A pause. 'I played right field for the Cougars.' The cougar is the Goddard mascot. The tawny wildcat is smart, fast, and elusive. Robert's face crinkled in puzzlement. 'Why do you care about the seed pod?'

Sam studied him for a moment, pulled out his cell, tapped. 'Weitz, get a net and go to the pond at Rose Bower. You're looking for a bois d'arc seed pod.' He clicked off.

Cops pride themselves on never being surprised, but I guessed Judy Weitz's expression at the moment was strange. However, I'm sure she said, 'Yes, sir.'

'A lot of odd questions are asked during an investigation,' Sam said smoothly. 'Now back to the terrace. What time did you come out on the terrace?'

Robert's sandy brows drew down. 'Around seven.'

'Why did you come out on the terrace?' Sam might have been a large cat crouched at a mouse hole. An unwinking gaze looking for the slightest hint of confusion or fear. Or knowledge.

I tensed.

Robert finished his coffee. 'No good reason. His tone was casual, good-humored. 'I get tired of banquets. The waiters were bringing desserts. The program was going to start around seven and I thought I had time to go downstairs and walk around for a few minutes.' He shrugged again. 'No big reason to be out on the terrace. I just turned that way when I came down the stairs. So I walked outside and there I was. I strolled over to the trees and reached up and grabbed a seed pod.'

There was silence as Sam and Hal stared at him.

Robert was the picture of youthful ease slouched in the

big easy chair. He looked back at them with a pleasant expression.

Hal snapped, 'What time did you see Matthew Lambert?'

Robert blinked. 'Matt . . . You mean the guy who got killed?'

Hal's gaze never left Robert's face. 'The guy who got killed.'

'I only kind of knew who he was. I think I saw him near one of the ballroom doors, but I'm not positive. Then I looked in another direction.'

'When?'

Robert looked vague. 'A little before seven, I guess.'

Sam placed his big hands fingertip to fingertip. 'Someone told us you were seen following him from the ballroom.'

'Somebody told you wrong.' Robert didn't sound worried. 'I didn't see him at the dinner so I for sure couldn't have followed him. Where did he go?' Robert jerked a thumb toward the table. 'I haven't had a chance to look at the *Gazette*. All I know is what was announced at the ballroom.'

Hal leaned forward. 'What were your relations with Mr Lambert?'

Robert was unruffled. 'Like zip. Zero. I never had any personal contact with him. I'm not rich so he never knocked on my door. I've never spoken to him. Sure, I've heard about him, but that's all. Yeah, I was on the terrace last night, getting a breath of fresh air. And yeah I tossed a seed pod. If that's a crime, you got me. But I don't know anything about what happened to him.'

Sam slowly nodded. 'That seems clear enough, Mr Blair. We'll be back in touch if we have any more questions.' He stood. Hal rose, too.

Robert came to his feet, opened the door for them. As the door closed behind them, Robert shoved a hand through his hair. 'I wonder if I left any fingerprints in that damn room.'

I didn't have to ask him what room. 'Did you touch anything beside the handle to the French door?'

'The French door . . .' His expression was sickly.

'Don't worry. I polished the handle after you left.'

He stumbled to the easy chair, flung himself down, buried his face in his hands. A mumble. 'I am not suited for a life of crime.'

'Did you touch anything else?'

His hands dropped. His face squeezed in thought. Slowly he shook his head. 'Nope, only the handle to the French door.' He stared in my direction, or where he thought I'd be from the sound of my voice. Instead I was at the coffee carafe. I opened a cabinet, found a mug emblazoned with a cougar – oh happy Goddard days – and poured myself a cup. I needed a boost. For good measure, I reached for the donut sack.

'Yeah. You get mixed up in murder and pretty soon you hear voices and things move through the air. I think I'll call my mother and ask her if I can come home and get my teddy bear. She insisted on saving Woolly Boy. I didn't think I'd ever need him. I was wrong.'

I laughed and Appeared. The green sofa was comfortable, reminding me that looks aren't as important as function. I took a bite of donut and a swallow of coffee. Excellent brew. I held up the mug. 'French roast?'

He managed a strained smile. 'Chin up and all that. Just saw a war movie. *Keep calm and carry on*. I don't know what kind of roast. It was on sale. You remind me of a humming-bird. Dart here. Dart there. Please hover for a minute.' He took a deep breath. 'I really don't get this heaven stuff, but you saved my as— saved me from going to jail. Do you think he bought it?'

I knew Robert meant Sam. 'I think he's neutralized for a while because Detective Weitz will find a seed pod. But,' I finished the donut, 'it's time to talk turkey.' Now my gaze was direct and demanding. 'Start with why you were at the banquet.'

'A girl. Most of the trouble I've ever gotten into started with a girl. But this girl,' his tone said it all, 'she's worth anything. Everything.'

'Gage Gallagher?'

'Yeah. Gage, well, she'll probably turn into her mom when she's fifty, but I want to be there.' He rumpled his tousled hair, tried to look casual, but his eyes held tenderness and longing and a hope for a joint future.

I slid pieces of the puzzle together. He said he'd never spoken to Matt Lambert. 'What's the connection between Matt Lambert and Gage?'

He sat up straight. 'Look, Gage is all hiss and no bite. I mean, she's like one of those wild kittens, dancing this way and that, ready to pounce, maybe making a run at a big dog because she never backs down, but she wouldn't ever hurt anyone.'

'The connection?' Should I tell Robert she'd been in Lambert's office last night? No. There was no telling what he might do if he thought Gage was threatened.

Reluctantly, 'She's interning this summer in the Outreach office.'

He was careful to use the formal name, not speak in terms of Matthew Lambert's office.

'What happened?' There was no doubt in my mind something had happened.

He clawed at his uncombed hair. 'Nothing big.' He wanted to believe what he said, wanted me to believe him. 'I'm sure it wasn't anything big. Just an idea she got.'

I was patient. 'What kind of idea?'

'I don't exactly know. Something she thought wasn't right about some donation. But I don't see that it matters now.' His face was bland, but his eyes were uneasy.

'So why were you in the first-floor room with Iris holding a weighted man's sock and Lambert dead on the floor?'

'Well, it was kind of funny. I mean, kind of accidental. We were at our table, me, Gage, and Iris. Just talking, waiting for the program to start. I was thinking maybe Gage and I could slip out pretty soon. Then, all of sudden, Iris looked across the room. She saw somebody and made a comment—'

'Robert.' My teacher voice.

'She looked across the ballroom and said, "He's a snake."'

'She saw Matt Lambert?'

Reluctantly, he nodded. 'Yeah. Then Gage said, "He sure is." Iris had her thoroughbred-horse look, you know, nervy and quick. She was still watching the exit, though Lambert was out of sight. Suddenly Iris stood up. She didn't say a word, just headed across the ballroom. Gage sat there for a few minutes, I don't know, maybe five. All of a sudden she tossed her head. She does that. A real quick motion and her hair ripples and . . .' He brought himself to heel. 'Anyway,

Gage got up, said something about checking and she headed for an exit. She didn't ask me to go with her. So I kind of sat. You know how things feel sometimes?' He looked at me earnestly. 'Like when there's thunder and the air's heavy? Anyway I didn't like the way I felt. I thought I better go see so I headed downstairs. I got to the first floor and Gage was standing by the stairs. She said she hadn't found her mom and would I take a look down the hall while she went out on the terrace. She said she'd meet me in the ballroom. If I found Iris I was to tell her she better hurry back upstairs, it was almost time for the program. I went to that hall and I got a glimpse of Iris going in that door. I kind of stood there for a minute. I mean, I didn't know how she'd feel if I came barging in on something, but Gage told me to find her so finally I went there and that's how I walked in on Iris holding the weapon.'

Iris Gallagher's austere office was sparely decorated. No drapes. A plain metal desk, likely garden variety issue from the college. The surface was bare except for several sheets of paper. An old, massive dictionary stood on a stand a few feet from the desk. A single print, *Nighthawks* by Edward Hopper, hung on a beige plastered wall. The emptiness of the other walls made even starker the sense of loneliness evoked by the print, a grill late at night, one couple at the counter but no sense of intimacy, a man alone a few stools away oblivious to them, the counterman, each immersed in solitary thought.

I looked at the slender woman seated at the desk. Summer sunlight flooding through an east window emphasized the glossiness of her raven-dark hair. Reading glasses perched at the end of her nose gave her a scholarly aura. I recalled my first view of her, an elegant and beautiful woman holding a weapon with a dead man at her feet.

A dowdy middle-aged woman sat in the chair facing the desk, hands clasped tightly together. Straggling gray hair framed a tired face, but the blue eyes were hopeful.

Iris looked up from a printed page. She was utterly still for an instant, her eyes meeting mine. She gave a slight headshake.

I understood. *Later. This moment doesn't belong to me. I am working.* I nodded in return.

She focused on the waiting woman, waiting anxiously. 'An excellent beginning, Gladys. I admire your effort to integrate Blake's personal experiences—'

I know teacher-speak. *Beginning . . . admire . . . effort . . .* Gladys had several drafts to go. I also recognized a kind and gentle approach where a student would never feel diminished.

Later . . .

The driveway at Matt Lambert's home was filled with cars. Cars lined the street in front of the house. There was no police cruiser, nor did I spot Sam's old sedan. Likely he and Hal had already spoken with the widow. She would be among the most important sources to interview. Did your husband have an enemy? Was your husband in debt? What were his relations with other family members? Did you have any sense he was in danger? What time did he leave the table at the banquet?

Inside the house, I looked into the living room, glimpsed perhaps a half-dozen women and a weary and pale Joyce Lambert seated in a rose-colored chair. Soft voices rose and fell.

The front door opened, making a distinctive creaking sound. A skinny six-foot teenager with curly shoulder-length brown hair, hands shoved deep in his jeans pockets, let the door slam behind him. Head down, he hurried for the stairs, shoes thudding on the tiled floor.

Joyce Lambert pushed up from her chair, came with quick steps to the archway. Her face was drawn, her eyes empty. Blonde hair loose on her shoulders, she looked older than the night before, much older. 'Jack.'

The boy was at the stairs. He turned. 'I don't want to go in there.'

She rushed to him, gripped his arm. 'We have to talk.' She tugged on his arm. He resisted for a moment, then, face rigid, walked stiffly across the foyer. She yanked open a door, held it for him.

Breathing fast, he looked up the stairs. He wanted to run.

She pulled again and they were in the small room, a den-cum-library, the door closed behind them.

Her voice shook. 'Where were you last night?' Her face held fear and despair.

He didn't meet her gaze. He stared at the floor, shrugged. 'I was around.'

'You didn't come home until two in the morning.' The words were uneven, shaky.

'Yeah. Well, I was driving around.' He stared at the floor.

'Why wouldn't you open your door?' Her voice cracked.

'Mom. Leave me alone. I don't want to talk about him.'

She scarcely managed to push out the words. 'Where were you last night?'

His face twisted. 'I drove around. Any law against that?'

'Were you near Rose Bower?'

His eyes flared wide. His eyes were a curious yellow green with thick, drooping lids. 'I was just driving. That's all. Just driving.' He turned and rushed across the room, was out the door into the entry hall. He pounded up the stairs.

Joyce stood in the hallway, hands limp at her side.

A kindly faced woman bustled from the living room. 'The poor boy's all upset. Better let him have a moment alone. You know how boys hate for anyone to see them cry.' The woman reached out, took Joyce's arm. 'Honey, let me get you some tea.'

If the shades of hell confronted Joyce, she would not have looked more desperate. It wasn't her son's tears that she feared.

SIX

The Administration building smelled heavily of smoke despite large fans in the lobby blowing at full capacity. Hot July air poured through open windows. Offices would be sweltering without air conditioning.

In the President's Office, heavy red velvet drapes were pulled back. All eight windows, four on each corner wall, were wide open. There was a hint of smoke, but nothing that wouldn't air out soon. Mahogany bookshelves filled two walls. Leather furniture emphasized comfort. A room of power and might. Had this been Matt Lambert's dream job? The mahogany desk was huge. An ornate bronze nameplate sat on one corner: President Everett Howard Morgan.

In the main lobby, a hastily scrawled poster on an easel announced that all offices were closed for the day but skeleton staffs were available for consultation in various rooms at Rose Bower. I noted two locations, the President's Office in the Marlow Suite and the Office of Outreach in the Gusher Room.

At Rose Bower, I wasn't surprised to see two police cars and a van parked in the front drive. The final scouring of the crime scene for evidence was likely nearing conclusion. Officers and technicians would be on the ground floor in the left wing. My goal was the second floor.

In the Marlow Suite, a secretary worked at a laptop on a card table. Sitting on Lorraine Marlow's upholstered love seat was the small man who'd spoken to Iris last night in the ball-room. He was possibly four inches over five feet, built like a dumpling. Light reflected both from rimless glasses perched atop his forehead and his shiny bald head. There was no police presence in the room.

I found an unoccupied guest room and Appeared as Officer Loy. A black stripe down each trouser leg added style to the French blue uniform. I stared at the mirror, chose a dim pink lip gloss and fluffed my curls.

At the Marlow Suite, I knocked briskly. A harried-looking woman opened the door. I flashed a smile. 'If President Morgan has a moment, there are a few points that need clarification.' I doubted either the president or his assistant were familiar enough with police protocol to question the appearance of a single officer rather than a duo.

'Come in, come in,' Morgan boomed. His voice was much bigger than he. He bustled toward me, plump hand outstretched.

I shook a soft, moist hand.

'Shocking. Just shocking.' He nodded toward a straight chair near an armchair with embroidered cushions. I sat primly on the edge of the seat.

He was avuncular. 'Tremendous loss to the college. Able man. Very able. I told the police this was an affront to all of us and a huge shock to have such a dreadful crime occur at Rose Bower. I've constituted a committee. We must determine if our security was lacking, though I have to believe this was an anomaly. Perhaps a hold-up. Someone followed a car to Rose Bower, attempted to enter through a terrace room and Matt confronted him. It must be something of the sort. I told the police they should be looking for a vagrant.' He nodded several times.

I wondered if he felt murder should be relegated to bars, but I gave him a pleasant look, noting the flush on his round cheeks, a trace of sweat on his shiny forehead. The temperature in the room was perhaps on the chilly side. After all, the suite was never used to house guests, but was a memorial to the late owners of Rose Bower.

I pulled a small notebook and a pen from a pocket. 'I understand Mr Lambert was superbly successful as a fundraiser for Goddard.'

His face remained cherubic, but there was a cold glint in his blue eyes. 'We have very generous patrons, both here in Adelaide and throughout Oklahoma. You might say Matt was more in a custodial role. The great bulk of the university's endowment was gathered in by his predecessor.' The unmistakable diminishment was delivered in such a civilized tone.

I lifted my eyebrows in questioning surprise. 'Oh, I see. But wasn't Mr Lambert to make a big announcement last night? What donor would that be?'

A pudgy hand waved a dismissal. 'Matt delighted in raising expectations. But I looked over the guest list. The major donors in attendance have a long history with Goddard. There was nothing new.'

Sam Cobb once told me he always looked for a trigger. Why did a murder occur when it did? The question seemed deceptively simple. Why was Matt Lambert's neck broken the night of the Midsummer Merriment banquet? Why that particular night? A wife who would rather see him dead than agree to a divorce? A staff member who was either a lover or deluded? Someone as yet unknown with a secret or a grudge? Or to prevent him from making his appearance on the dais? Lambert himself made a mystery of an announcement he intended to make. Was it possible a gift to the college was linked to his murder?

But as Mama told us kids, 'It's better to ask too many questions than not enough.'

'Mr Lambert said he intended to make a big announcement. That must mean a major gift. Who were the big donors attending the dinner?'

'The kind of people who give to Goddard aren't accustomed to inquisitions by the police.' He looked worried, obviously opposed to the prodding of any golden calves.

I gave him a reassuring nod. 'Benefactors are always substantial members of the community. I'm sure they will be eager to assist the investigation. Of course they will be treated with great respect.'

He cleared his throat. 'Three major donors were in attendance. The Kirk family, the Prichards, and the Mayers. As is customary, each donor hosted a table.' He looked across the room. 'Rachel, provide the officer with information about the donors.'

I looked at his assistant. 'Contact information will be very helpful.' I was pleased that a Prichard was a donor. That was a distinguished Adelaide family. I was familiar with the family mausoleum in the cemetery. I turned to Morgan. 'Were all three to be recognized last night?'

Morgan tapped the fingers of his right hand on the armrest. 'Matt was making such a production of his presentation. We always send invitations to those families because they are loyal to the college. I don't know who he intended to honor.' Morgan frowned. 'Such a fuss. Matt often failed to be collegial. And as president of Goddard—'

I glanced at my notes, interrupted in the tone of a junior officer focused on accuracy. 'Let me see, acting president, I believe.'

He pursed little pig lips. 'I am called President Morgan during this interim period.'

As if diverted, I looked eager. 'Will you become the real president soon?'

Stiffly, 'The regents will consider personnel matters in an upcoming meeting.'

Again I glanced at my notes. 'Let's see,' an innocent recollection of information received, 'I understand there was some thought that the regents were going to consider Mr Lambert for the presidency because of his success in fundraising.'

Morgan's blue eyes were guileless. 'Oh, that was highly unlikely. He had no academic achievements. But that question is now moot.'

I nodded. A dead man is scarcely ever elevated to high office.

I tapped my notebook. 'Are you aware of anyone with reason to want Mr Lambert dead?'

He turned those plump hands palms up. 'I am baffled.'

A wrought-iron sculpture was mounted on the door of the guest room at Rose Bower. Oil cascaded in perpetuity from an old-fashioned rig. The letters beneath the artwork – *The Gusher* – were wrought iron also.

I lifted my hand to knock, then decided to take a peek. I disappeared.

Inside the room, the early oil days motif continued with black-and-white photographs of wooden derricks in the Fitz Field. The sole occupant was an attractive young woman stretched comfortably on a blue denim-covered sofa, legs crossed. She held a cell phone in one hand, toyed with a long strand of bright blonde hair with the other. Her face held a mixture of boredom and complacency. '. . . Glad I caught you.

I don't have a thing to do and I didn't bring my books with
me and I am sooo bored. I have to stay another twenty minutes.
Listen, will you find out the name of that cute guy on your
floor, the one with that itty-bitty mustache?' Her tone was
wheedling. 'Now you promised—'

In the hall, after a quick check to be sure no one was near,
I Appeared and knocked three sharp raps.

The blonde opened the door. She saw the uniform and her
blue eyes widened. 'There's nobody here but me. I mean,
Mrs Caldwell talked to the two detectives and after they
left she told us to take turns because we can't do any work
because we can't access our computers and I can give you her
number and—'

I nodded and moved forward. 'Appreciate your cooperation.'

She backed into the room, looked at me rather helplessly.

I pulled out my ID. 'Officer Loy. I have a few questions.'
I gestured toward an armchair and the sofa.

She returned to the sofa, sat up straight, said uneasily. 'I'm
not official. I mean, I'm just a student. You need to talk to
Mrs Caldwell.'

I gave her a reassuring smile. 'I know you can help me. I'm
double-checking to be sure we have correct titles for staff
members. Please list them again for me.'

She wasn't bothered that this information had already been
obtained. Hers not to question why, hers to do whatever the
moment required. She counted on her fingers. 'Amy Caldwell,
chief assistant. Clarisse Bennett, executive secretary. Edith
Martinez, financial officer. Gage Gallagher, summer intern.
Ms Bennett didn't come in today. She called, said she wasn't
feeling well.' Knowledge flickered in her eyes. 'Everyone else
came in. Except Mr Lambert, of course. Gee, I still can't
believe what happened. Why, I saw him yesterday.' She took
a breath. 'Oh, and I'm Deanne Davis. I'm a junior majoring
in advertising. I work at the Office of Outreach all day on
Fridays. But not all day today because Gage is coming back
in a while to be here for an hour.'

I was matter of fact. 'We've gathered quite a bit of information about office relationships. It's necessary to confirm the
information. Please give me your observations.'

She looked uncomfortable. 'Well, they talked to each of us separately. I was last so I don't know what anyone else said. And this real handsome detective was real nice to me and we got to talking and I didn't want to tell them but they just kept after me and now I feel terrible. Mrs Gallagher's just the nicest person. I had her for English Lit and I don't know how they knew about yesterday but somebody must have told them and they asked me if I heard anything Mrs Gallagher said when she slammed out of Mr Lambert's office earlier that day. I didn't want to say anything but somehow they made me talk and I had to admit I heard her tell him he was a sorry excuse for a human being and he ought to stick his head in a pigsty because that's where he belonged. I feel terrible about quoting her because they didn't give me a chance to say how nice she is. I'll just die if I got Gage's mom in trouble.'

Iris put down a printed page. Her hand, holding a red pencil, hovered above the sheet. She sighed, put the pencil down. Sunlight slanting through the window behind the desk cast a golden glow over her, almost like a nimbus. Not in this lifetime, I thought tartly. But I sympathized. 'It might be easier to teach cats how to play croquet.'

She looked up and saw me. The fact that she saw me even though I wasn't visible always came as a shock. What gave her that ability? I pushed away the thought that she might be incredibly empathetic. If so, she didn't waste a second imagining how I felt. She definitely had a Katharine Hepburn look, the same high cheekbones, the same confident, dismissive gaze. In person, Kate has an enchanting smile and everyone adores her. Oh, that's not for me to share. Precept Seven.

'Much easier.' Her tone was wry. 'Someone has an ear for language. Or not.'

I settled in a director's chair a little to the left of her desk. It looked much more comfortable than the plain wooden chair recently occupied by the earnest student. I met her gaze and said conversationally. 'The police know about your shouting match with Matt Lambert yesterday.'

A shrug of those slender shoulders. Utter dismissal.

'You know,' I kept my tone conversational, 'the Department of Good Intentions sends help to someone in trouble, but that person is always innocent. If I didn't know better, I'd think you were guilty as h— as can be.'

'The Department of Good Intentions.' Her tone was almost wistful, then she said firmly, 'Neither that department's policy nor your thoughts are of any interest to me.'

'Excuse me.' Emphasis on second syllable. Great emphasis on pronoun. 'Are you rude for personal pleasure? Are you making some kind of political statement: laws don't apply to you and it's fine to help a killer escape, you didn't like the guy anyway?'

That struck home. Her wide violet eyes were suddenly stricken. 'That's not—'

Her office door opened. No knock. Sam Cobb loomed in the doorway, big, sturdy, impressive. His brown eyes gazed around the room, no doubt seeking the audience for her words. Hal Price was looking, too.

There was an instant of silence.

'Mrs Gallagher.' Sam's voice was gruff. Again, he didn't ask. He knew her identity.

'Yes.' Her tone was formal. She looked with a remote gaze at the two men, who exuded the threat of authority.

'Sam Cobb, chief of police. Detective-Sergeant Hal Price. May we have a word with you?' He was already moving forward.

She gave me a quick glance as she gestured at the chairs.

I eased out of the director's chair, floated up to sit on the top of a medium-sized bookcase.

Sam pulled out a notebook, but he didn't consult it. 'You are Iris Gallagher, assistant professor of English.'

'Yes.' Iris appeared completely at ease.

'Please describe your actions at Rose Bower last evening. Start with your arrival.'

Iris was perhaps a little sardonic, meticulously describing where she parked, her arrival in the ballroom at shortly before six, her purchase of a glass of Chardonnay and subsequent encounters with various faculty members, her arrival at Table Nine around six p.m. to join her daughter, Gage, with her escort, Robert Blair. They were seated with a Spanish professor,

the chair of the business department and her husband, and
Acting President Everett Morgan and his wife. She concluded,
'It was the usual banquet evening. Chicken with an orange
sauce. Asparagus. Rice. Faculty gossip, a great play last night
by Jose Altuve, and a devout hope the dessert would be
edible. I remained at the table until a few minutes before seven
when I left to visit the ladies' room.'

'You saw Matthew Lambert.' A statement, not a question.

'A glimpse.' Her tone was agreeable.

A glance at his notes. 'Professor Mullins recalls you and
your daughter speaking critically of Mr Lambert.'

I tensed. Sam and Hal had done their homework. I gave Iris
a warning look.

She looked amused. 'That would be correct.'

'Please explain why you and your daughter disliked Mr
Lambert.'

'No.' She spoke with finality.

Sam's face looked heavier. 'How long have you known
Matthew Lambert?'

'I knew him as I know other administration officials. It's
a small college. I'm familiar with almost everyone here. I
rarely saw him.'

'You saw him at his office yesterday.' Hal's voice was
deceptively pleasant. 'You were observed entering his office.
A quarrel ensued. You were overheard describing him in
pejorative terms.'

She made no reply. Her expression gave no indication
of stress. In fact, she appeared uninterested.

'You said he was a sorry excuse for a human being.' Sam's
stare was combative.

She remained silent, continued to look as though she were
listening to a boring presentation that had no interest for her.

Sam planted his big hands on his knees, leaned forward.
'Mrs Gallagher, what was the cause of your argument with
Mr Lambert?'

Silence. She was quite lovely, her elegant features aristo-
cratic, her violet eyes reminiscent of the flower that bore her
name, quite lovely and quite unaffected by the tense atmosphere
in the small office.

Hal was forceful. 'Had he made improper advances toward your daughter?'

Surprise lifted her eyebrows. Iris shook her head. 'My dispute with Matt had nothing to do with my daughter. Believe me, she knows how to handle that kind of trouble. And, to be fair to Matt, there's no suggestion that he ever crossed that particular line.'

Sam said smoothly, 'What line did he cross, Mrs Gallagher?'

She pressed her lips together, said nothing. She met Sam's stare with equanimity, displaying neither concern nor uneasiness.

Sam folded his arms. His dark brown eyes were somber. 'You were observed downstairs last night.'

Iris smiled and shook her head. 'I visited the ladies' room on the third floor. Your informant apparently mistook someone else for me.'

'Do you deny going down to the first floor?' Hal's tone implied she was going to be caught out in a lie.

'I had no reason to be on the first floor. I can assure you that I absolutely did not speak to or with Matt Lambert last night. I had no interaction with him.' She pushed back her chair, rose. 'I do not know who killed Matt Lambert. Should I obtain any information that would be helpful to your investigation, I will contact you immediately. And now, I have an appointment I have to keep.'

The men stood. Sam gave her a searching look. 'We'll be in touch, Mrs Gallagher. I will request that you not leave town.'

When the door shut behind them, she breathed out a sigh and sagged into her chair. She clasped her hands tightly together and gazed blankly at the wall.

I doubted her thoughts were reassuring. Iris Gallagher was in deep trouble and she knew it.

I returned to the director's chair. 'To continue our conversation—'

'Go away.' Her voice was abstracted.

'I am here. Here I stay. I understand now that you will need assistance from the department. Sam Cobb has you in his sights. I've seen that stare before. A lion looking at a gazelle.

Hands down the lion prevails. The next interview will be at the police station.'

'I won't answer questions.' Her violet eyes were determined.

'Sam can hold you as a material witness. Look, Iris, you can't win this battle.' I studied her, spoke without rancor. 'You understand a man was murdered. It is the duty of all citizens to assist in a homicide investigation. Why are you resisting? It's obvious you are shielding the person behind your quarrel with Matt Lambert. Who is it?'

'Not a murderer. But . . .' She broke off, shook her head.

'I suppose after all you are shielding Gage.' I liked Gage. I liked Robert. I wanted him to be there with Gage at fifty when she turned into her mother. I didn't want her to be in trouble. But Gage crept into Lambert's office at midnight, searched frantically, was almost a victim of the smoke. It was a toss-up in my mind. Did Gage hurry to the office because she killed Matt Lambert or because she had something to hide? Gage was not the only person with something to hide. Arson occurred to destroy contents in the office. Was the arsonist afraid Matt Lambert kept some kind of record or file or note that might lead to exposure?

Whichever might be true, Gage was afraid of something.

Iris was abrupt. 'Gage was an intern in his office this summer. Period. End of story. My argument with Matt had nothing to do with Gage.'

Truth always sounds true. So I spoke gently. 'Then why was Gage in Lambert's office at midnight?'

SEVEN

I watched Iris open the door to The Gusher guest room at Rose Bower, the temporary quarters for the Office of Outreach.

Gage looked up at the sound, popped to her feet when she saw her mother. Gage was slim and appealing in a pale coral-and-white-striped shirtdress. Deep smudges beneath her brown eyes and a generally wan appearance hinted at her late night.

Iris closed the door behind her, stood with her back to the panel. 'What were you doing in Matt's office last night?'

Gage lifted a hand. Her fingers clutched at the scoop neck of her dress. 'How did you know?'

Iris's deep violet eyes held fear. 'Answer me, Gage.'

Gage flung her hands wide. 'Because I was stupid. Because I didn't think anyone would believe me. Because he threatened me.' She had the look of a cornered cat, fierce and determined, at bay as dogs yapped.

Iris pushed from the door, hurried to her daughter, slid an arm around stiff shoulders, gave her a reassuring hug. 'We'll work everything out. But I have to know what happened.' She took her daughter's hand, tugged. They sat down side by side on a wicker sofa, a cheerful western piece of furniture unsuited for grand drama.

'Mom,' Gage's thin face was earnest, 'you always told me to do the right thing. You told me not to look the other way. If I saw somebody doing something bad, I couldn't think, oh well, that's their problem. If I knew, it was my problem. So when I thought Matt was extorting money from somebody, I knew I had to find out what was going on. I couldn't accuse him of anything, like go to the president, without some kind of proof. And the way I found out was one of those funny things, like serendipity, but in a bad way. I was on the terrace behind the Student Union . . .'

A two-story limestone building in the heart of the campus houses the food court on the ground floor and reading carrels, the alumni office, and faculty club on the second floor. The terrace has various levels and a series of blossom-covered arbors that provide little enclaves of privacy.

'. . . and I was having a latte.'

I smiled, remembering my college days and the unremarkable cafeteria and tepid, weak coffee out of big urns in white pottery cups.

'I picked a spot on the lower terrace near an arbor covered with honeysuckle. I heard footsteps. I didn't want to talk to anybody, I was texting Robert, so I slid inside the arbor. I was as far down on the lower terrace as you can go. Very private. The footsteps stopped a few feet from me. I recognized Matt's voice. He sounded slick, oily. It wasn't the words themselves. It was the way he said them. I'll never smell honeysuckle again without thinking of that creepy conversation.' She tossed her head, her silky dark hair rippling. I saw what Robert meant. The gesture was as wild and free as a mare galloping across a pasture at dawn, the wind stirring her mane.

Gage reached out, gripped her mother's arm. 'Matt said,' her face scrunched in concentration, '"You'll make it happen. One way or another. How about five million? It will be the largest gift ever announced at Midsummer Merriment. I'll give a huge shout-out at the banquet." He stopped talking. I guess the other person said something. In a minute, Matt laughed, a nasty laugh, an I've-got-you-where-I-want-you laugh, and said, "I wrote down what happened that day. The door opening. You handing her the tray. We can trade. You give me a piece of paper with the amount of the gift, signed by you. I'll give you the piece of paper with what I saw, signed by me. A win-win for both of us. Especially you."'

Gage gulped air as if she'd burst from deep water. 'That was all he said. I think he clicked off his cell. I heard him walk away. And then I guess I was stupid. I wanted to get out of there. I hurried out of the arbor and started up toward the Union but then I stopped and looked back. He was at the sidewalk to the Administration building but he was looking toward the Union. I think he saw me. I just hurried faster and got inside. My heart was thudding. I was scared. Something bad was happening. I sat at a table and thought about what I'd heard, but without his slimy voice, the words could be any conversation with a donor. I needed proof Matt was doing something wrong before I told anyone.'

She pushed up from the sofa, folded her arms tight across the front of the shirtdress, and looked down at her mother. 'I checked the list of people coming to the banquet. There were three donor families.'

I nodded in agreement. The Kirks, the Prichards, and the Mayers.

'I overheard the call Wednesday afternoon. I thought and thought and I couldn't figure out what to do. Thursday I decided to find out more about the families.' Gage swallowed hard. 'One conference room in the Outreach office has about twelve – I don't know what to call them – niches, maybe? Anyway, kind of like in a church where you put the saints but these hold pictures of donors and red leather books with a tribute and a history of donations and what they'd meant to the college. I went there yesterday afternoon. I started with the Mayer family. I was reading about their last donation – a new chemistry lab – when Matt came in. He gave me a funny look, asked what I was doing. I was all smiles, said I'd checked out which donors were coming to the banquet and thought I'd do a little research. He didn't believe me. He said, "Interns are expected to do work assigned to them. Major donors are not your concern. I suggest you go back to your cubicle." I started for the door. He said, "If there are any further un-authorized explorations or any discussion of donations," he stopped there and I knew he knew that I heard his call. He stared at me, his eyes like knives, "I'll describe your perform-ance this summer as unsatisfactory. Highly unsatisfactory. Unworthy of scholarships or internships."'

'He threatened you?' Iris's voice was tight with anger. 'Why didn't you tell me?'

'Oh Mom, I couldn't.' Gage looked thoroughly miserable as she sat down and turned to face her mother. 'You came in earlier and everybody knew you were mad at him. I didn't

want you to come back. It would only have made things worse
for me.'

Iris looked grim. 'Is that why you went to his office last
night?'

'I wanted to see if he'd written anything down about me.
I was afraid if it came out that he'd put something bad in a
file, I might lose my scholarship. And I thought maybe I
might find out which donor he called, asked for the big gift.
I checked his computer. There was a file with my name. I
didn't open it. I deleted a bunch of files including that one.
In the call he said he wrote down what happened that day,
like there was some special day that meant a lot. I didn't
think that would be in a computer file. You don't talk about
writing something down if you are putting it in a computer.
So I pulled open drawers, hunted for anything that looked
kind of secret or special. I didn't find anything. I was about
to quit when somebody outside smashed a window and threw
a fiery stick inside. It was awful, the glass cracking and a
gloved hand tossing a stick with burning stuff on one end.
The stick landed on the desk and all of a sudden there was
fire everywhere.' Gage's eyes were huge. 'I couldn't see. I
lost my flashlight and the smoke was so thick I couldn't
breathe and, Mom, you're going to think I'm nuts, but just
before the window broke, I heard a woman's voice, even
though there wasn't anybody in the office but me. But when
the smoke was so thick and I knew I was going to die, a
woman took hold of me and pulled and showed me the way
to the door. We got to the anteroom and I opened the hall
door and I called out for her and she said she was fine but,
Mom, there wasn't anybody there. Mom, she saved my life.
Do you think maybe she was a guardian angel? People talk
about that kind of thing and I know she wasn't there, but she
was and that's why I'm alive. When she said she was fine, I
heard a voice and that's all, just a voice, but she said she was
OK, so I got into the hall and ran to the door and outside
and then I went as fast as I could. I got away. But Mom, the
woman, I don't know where she went or who she was.'

Iris's violet eyes turned to me.

I nodded.

Iris sent me a look of gratitude and apology and heartfelt thankfulness. There was a depth of awareness in her eyes at how nearly Gage might not have survived. 'I think,' Iris's voice was uneven, 'we can thank your guardian angel. We will always thank her.'

I wondered if I would ever have a moment to explain to Gage that angels are a higher order of being and I would never ever claim to be one. But perhaps it didn't matter.

Gage looked solemn, slowly nodded.

I wished I could reach out and hug her, but instead her mom's arms went around her and held her tight for a moment. When Iris sat back, she lifted a hand to lightly touch Gage's cheek for an instant.

Gage looked at Iris. 'I woke up thinking about her this morning. That was a happy thought. And then I thought maybe I should tell the police about what I heard Matt say on the terrace. But I don't know if they would believe me.'

I lifted both thumbs up, nodded yes energetically.

Iris hesitated, but she was a woman who would always try to pay her debts. 'Whether they believe you or not, you need to tell them.'

Folders were spread across the top of Sam Cobb's desk. A plastic recorder sat within easy reach. As the recorder ran, it emitted a slight whirring noise, underscoring the reality of answering questions in the office of the police chief.

Oddly, to me, Sam evinced no surprise when Gage took a deep breath and said in a rush that she'd gone to the Outreach Office last night because she hoped to find proof that Matt Lambert was in fact extorting rather than cajoling a huge gift for the college.

Sam made notes, listened intently, his heavy face impassive. Gage described overhearing Lambert's phone call. She didn't mention her belief that he knew she overheard the call or his threat to give her a poor recommendation.

When she finished, Sam studied Gage for a long moment. 'About this phone call when you were on the terrace Wednesday. What time was it?'

Gage pulled her cell phone from a pocket. 'I can tell you.'

She scrolled. 'Here it is. I was texting Robert. It was nine minutes after three.'

Sam reached for a folder, opened it, riffled through some sheets. He stopped, made a note on his pad, closed the folder, looked again at Gage. 'What time did you arrive at the Administration building last night?'

'The clock in the tower was tolling midnight.' She gave a little shiver. When on a secretive mission, darkness and shadows are intimidating.

'How long had you been inside when the window was smashed?' Sam's gaze at Gage never wavered.

She squeezed her face in thought. 'Ten minutes. Maybe a little less.'

'What did you do when you heard the glass break?' His stare was intent, measuring.

'I looked that way.' Her voice shook and I knew she was remembering the rush of air and the smell of gasoline and red velvet drapes quivering.

'What did you see?' His face remained stolid, but his eyes were cold and suspicious. Did Sam believe Gage searched the office then hurried outside and ran around the corner of the building, used a flashlight to smash the window, lobbed material she had brought with her to create the blaze?

'The drape billowed toward me. A hand pulled the drape to one side and—'

Sam demanded, 'Big hand? Small? Man? Woman?'

'Could be either. A black leather glove. The glove looked big. But everything happened fast. The crash. The drape. The glove. Then fire. A ball of flame came through the air and landed on the desk. Fires burst out all around me.' A trace of the panic she'd felt made her voice shaky.

Sam's gaze was cool and impersonal. 'You used your entry code on the keypad to enter the building last night.'

Gage looked startled.

'There is a record of entries using the keypad. Were you aware each entry is recorded?'

'I never thought about that.' She sounded scared.

'Perhaps the fact occurred to you later.' He was sardonic. She shook her head.

'Perhaps you remembered and knew you'd be questioned so you decided to come see us, appear as if you are cooperating.' His voice was matter of fact.

'I'm trying to help.' She might be cornered, but she was going to keep on fighting. 'You have to find out who Matt talked to, who he was threatening.'

Sam asked in the same even tone, 'What caused the quarrel between your mother and Mr Lambert?'

The disconnected question, the danger-fraught question, jolted Gage. She looked smaller in the chair. 'My mother?' Her lips trembled.

'You were in the office when she was overheard berating Lambert. What did she say?'

Gage was mute, her eyes huge.

I clenched my hands into tight fists. The interview was harder, more challenging than I'd expected. His question revealed Sam was focused on Iris and Matt Lambert, despite Gage's midnight trip to Matt's office. He'd obviously already interviewed other staff members.

Iris intervened. 'Gage heard what everyone heard. I told Matt in rather colorful terms that he was despicable. My opinion has not changed. Gage has no knowledge as to why I hold that opinion.' Iris's smile was cool and composed.

'Really.' Sam did not believe Iris. He did not believe Gage.

He pushed the pad away, rose, making it clear the interview was at an end. 'The investigation is continuing.' He gave Iris a hard stare. 'We will be in touch.' The final words were a threat.

Mother and daughter stood, Iris as self-possessed as always, Gage half mad, half scared. As they walked toward the hall door, Gage looked back at Sam. 'I'm not making this up. Matt was forcing someone to give money.'

Sam merely nodded, his heavy face unmoved, his gaze skeptical.

When the door closed behind them, I attacked. 'Sam, you need to listen. Here's a gold-plated motive. Lambert wanted a big gift in exchange for keeping his mouth shut about what he saw.' I almost repeated 'gold-plated' for emphasis, but surely Sam agreed. 'Lambert had the goods on somebody with deep pockets and he wanted to make a big splash at the banquet, announce a major gift.' I pulled a straight chair a little closer to his desk.

Sam watched the chair move. 'Why am I not surprised?'

I rushed ahead. 'Guests seated at the donor tables will know who left the ballroom and when. All you have to do is find out which donor left the ballroom around seven and you will have your murderer.' This might be one of my quickest missions. Perhaps I would receive a special commendation for efficiency. A gold star on my file at the department? Not gold-plated. Genuine gold. Diverted for an instant, I wondered if Wiggins was still occupied in Tumbulgum.

Sam leaned back in his chair, managed a sort of smile. 'You have a nice voice, but I kind of like to see people I talk to.'

I Appeared in a pansy purple linen blouse with pearl buttons down one arm, silvery slacks, and silver sandals. I hoped my makeup was fresh. I like to look my best when enjoying success.

'That's better. I should have known you were here.' He punched the intercom. 'I'm in conference. No visitors.' He gave me a quizzical look. 'Haven't seen much of you,' he said conversationally.

'I'm here and there.' I waved a hand gracefully and admired the matching purple polish on my nails.

'I should have known you're working for the professor.' He shook his head. 'She's watched too many crime shows on TV, thinks she can blow off the police. She'll find out we don't give up and if she can't answer questions, she's signing a ticket to jail.' He raised a bristly eyebrow. 'Has it occurred to you that this time you're backing the wrong horse? Maybe you're supposed to be looking out for her daughter. The kid's a lot more likable. Anyway, the professor is on my radar. Big time. And it isn't just my antipathy for supercilious women.'

'Sam, believe me, Iris isn't supercilious.' I pushed away my previous appraisal of her. 'And Gage isn't making up the story about the phone call.'

'Were you there?' He was definitely eager.

'Of course not. I didn't arrive until last night. But clearly Matt Lambert threatened someone. He demanded a major gift to keep quiet about something he saw. And,' I was triumphant, 'we know he carried in his wallet a square of paper that described something he saw.' I almost tossed off *Duh,* but as Mama always told us kids, 'Pat a horse and you can ride far. Kick and watch his dust after he bucks you off.'

Sam eased back in his chair, clearly disappointed.

I was insistent. 'Obviously there's a connection between his threat and his murder.'

Sam shook his head. 'Ease up, Bailey Ruth. You mean well, but you are obsessed with that scrap of paper. I get it that you found the paper in his wallet. I understand how you struggled to find all the pieces after your tussle with the man who had a dislike for floating paper. Can't say I blame him. But even you have to admit there's no suggestion of wrongdoing or crime in the words we have or the message you guessed at. As for Gage Gallagher's eavesdropping, sure, maybe she heard something like related. But the sinister interpretation is all her own. The kid's hiding something and it doesn't have to do with gifts to the college.'

I hesitated, then took the plunge and described Lambert's threat when he found Gage checking out the donors.

Sam looked satisfied. 'I knew there had to be something else behind her visit to his office.'

'Her concern about losing a scholarship or internship isn't the point.' I was frustrated and sorry I'd told him. 'What matters is that Lambert was upset to see her in the donor room.'

'We don't know his warning about her file was linked to her visit to the donor room. That's her story. Maybe she was doing a lousy job. Maybe he came on to her and she blew him off. I agree, Lambert was a jerk. But that's no excuse for murder.' Sam pulled out the lower left drawer, grabbed the sack of M&Ms, plumped it on the desk. He pulled a folder near, flipped it open. 'I have the scraps of paper here along with your proposed draft.'

I didn't need to reread what I'd crafted. I remembered quite well:

The door opened and I saw Ev— (Eva, Evangeline, Eve, Evelyn, Evita) take the tray. I watched the reflection in the mirror. The glass was full. She put the tray on the

table. She didn't add anything to the glass and drank all
of it. This occurred March . . .

                                        Matthew Lambert

Sam poured himself a handful of M&Ms, pushed the sack
across the desk.

Automatically I tilted the sack, welcomed the candies in
my hand.

Sam was almost cheerful. 'In regard to the daughter and the
phone call, the whole thing's a smokescreen to protect Mama.
And maybe herself. Maybe he was after the intern for sex and
you can imagine how Mama would react to that.'

I clutched my handful of M&Ms, too shocked to eat them.

'Sam,' the M&Ms felt moist in my sweaty hand, 'I heard
Gage tell her mother about the phone call.'

'Yeah. But the funny thing is,' he tapped a folder on the
desk, 'I have a list of Lambert's cell phone calls for the week.
There wasn't a call at nine minutes after three on Tuesday.'

For an instant, I had that upside-down feeling you get in a
hammerhead ride at the carnival, then I clapped my hands
together. 'That's more proof he was up to no good.'

Sam looked at me as though I had suddenly broken into
song or spoken Portuguese.

I tried not to sound chiding. 'Lambert was using a burner
phone.' That's how the cognoscenti describe cheap throw-
away phones, picked up at what I used to call a five-and-dime
and paid for in cash, no records kept.

His big face squeezed in thought. 'I don't say that's not a
possibility. Maybe he was leaning on somebody and being
mighty careful, just in case there was a complaint about
his attitude. We'll hunt for a prepaid phone. I'll look at the
donors even though I don't think that's a real possibility.
No donor quarreled with him yesterday.'

'Someone set fire to his office. I was there. The arsonist wasn't
Gage.' This had to be the clincher that Gage was innocent.

'I got the call as soon as the flames were spotted. Nice to
know you were there.' Sam crunched another mouthful of
M&Ms. 'So she didn't set the fire. Maybe, just maybe, her
report on the sinister phone call is accurate. Maybe somebody

had a good reason to want his records to go up in smoke. But maybe the quarrel between Iris and Lambert was about something she didn't want the world to know. Maybe Mama was telling him to stay away from her daughter. Maybe Mama was afraid he'd screw up Gage's scholarship. There's not a lot of money floating around the Gallagher house.'

'Sam,' I came back to what seemed to me to be a clincher. 'He was killed with a homemade blackjack. You keep talking about Iris quarreling with him and getting mad when she sees him in the banquet hall. This wasn't a last-minute fight with Matt Lambert. His killer came planning to break his neck.'

'Yeah, the killer was prepared.' Sam was in agreement. 'That's why I think there's more to learn about Iris Gallagher and Matt Lambert and I intend to find it. Maybe it's about her daughter. Maybe it's something else entirely, but I'm going to find out.'

I wished I could alibi Iris for the fire.

It was as if he read my mind. 'Maybe Iris Gallagher smashed the window and tossed in a fireball. Be pretty ironic if she torched the office and didn't know her daughter was in there.'

'Iris didn't set the fire.'

He pounced. 'Were you with her?'

'No.' Regretfully. 'Even I can't be in two places at once.'

'If you could be in two places at once, that would bother me even more than your appearing and disappearing. I'm almost used to you coming and going, even if I sometimes wonder whether I made you up.' He shook his head. 'I don't have that kind of imagination. I'm stuck with you as a ghost, nutty as that is.' Abruptly he was serious. 'Back to Iris, how do you know she didn't set the fire?'

'I think the murderer set the fire and I'm sure Iris didn't kill Lambert.'

'You *think*. That's not proof. I want proof. The investigation has covered a lot of ground. Things are clearer. For example, the widow is alibied by four people at her table. She never left the ballroom after she arrived until an officer brought her downstairs.' He rubbed a cheekbone with knuckles. 'She looks terrified every time I see her. The police affect some people like that.'

I could have told him that Joyce Lambert was terrified for her teenage son. I didn't. I wanted to talk to Jack first.

Sam reached for a file. 'As for the office amour, Lambert may have convinced his wife he was being pursued, but we have some statements that suggest he was having an affair with Clarisse Bennett. I intend to nose around a bit more about her – was she stable, was she jealous, was she desperate? We're still asking a lot of questions. So far, we haven't found any leads. And sure, I'll check and see if any donors left their tables last night at the critical time, even if the conversation by the arbor doesn't impress me. I'll tell you how I see it. He was killed at Rose Bower. The odds are a hundred to one someone attending the dinner is the killer. The odds are maybe a thousand to one something immediate triggered the homicide. Like a confrontation in his office that afternoon. That brings us to Iris Gallagher.'

I was impatient. 'Sam, think about the murder weapon, a sock filled with sand. I suppose that's what you think every well-dressed woman carries in her purse when attending a banquet.'

He wasn't amused, said flatly, 'If she has an appointment with a man she intends to kill, yes. Pretty clever, actually. Easy to make. I've figured from the start he was meeting someone. Why else would he be down there? Sure, I can see the professor with a dandy weapon. Your client, I guess that's what you'd call her, gave me a my-good-man stare, claimed she knew nothing about what happened to Matt Lambert and declined to discuss the matter further. I could have brought her in for questioning. I decided to see what we could dig up. The digging is going well. I have witnesses that she left the ballroom shortly after Lambert, that she was seen going downstairs. The next time I talk to her she'll get the Miranda warning. We'll see how supercilious she is then.' He gave me a demanding look. 'When did you first connect with Iris Gallagher?'

I never lie to Sam, but all he needed for his case against Iris was my report that she was not only downstairs, she was in the Malone Room standing over Lambert's body with the weapon in her hand when I arrived. 'A little before seven last night.' I like to think redheads are special. There are so many who deserve acclaim: Myrna Loy, Agatha Christie, Agnes Moorehead, Greer Garson, Elizabeth I, Florence Nightingale, Lucille Ball. I once played Lucille Ball in a faculty skit. I can look as innocent as Lucy reassuring Ricky that of course she wasn't the one who did whatever. I widened my eyes. 'Oh my. A sudden call. Time to go.' Colors swirled. I went.

EIGHT

'd scarcely disappeared when I smelled coal smoke and heard the roar of the Rescue Express.

'Roof.' Wiggins's tone was genial.

I settled on a parapet overlooking Main Street. As Mama always told us kids, start off on a positive note. 'I trust Tumbulgum was a pleasant interlude.' I fervently hoped a follow-up might be required.

'A satisfactory conclusion. A shop girl wrongly accused of pilfering. The owner and family live upstairs and the culprit turned out to be a pet monkey. Clever fellow. He stashed the trinkets in a hollow tree. No more monkey business there.' A robust laugh. 'But here,' a sigh, 'first you rush away from the Rescue Express,' his deep voice still held shock, 'and now you are failing to provide the proper authority with material information. A usual emissary,' there was definite longing in his voice, 'would not Appear and converse with the police. Since you do, you surely owe the police chief an honest recital of facts. Such as the presence of Lambert's stepson near Rose Bower. Further, the minute he asked about Iris Gallagher, you disappeared. It seems obvious you do not want to tell him she was present at the crime scene. She likely can assist his investigation.'

I was grave. 'If I tell Sam, he will arrest Iris.'

'Oh dear.' Wiggins is not only kind, he has an appreciation for beautiful women, especially beautiful women in distress. Moreover, Wiggins knew Iris was innocent since she was chosen to receive assistance from the Department. 'That would be a shame.'

I was quick to emphasize further dire consequences. 'If Iris is arrested, the police will end the search for the murderer. All effort will be focused on building a case against Iris for the district attorney. Moreover, placing Iris at the crime scene puts Robert at risk. Involvement in a murder case as a co-conspirator could cost him his law license.'

Wiggins murmured something about slippery slopes as he gave an exasperated whuff. 'A difficult situation. I'm afraid the only solution is for you to find the murderer. As soon as possible.'

'I'm doing my best.' I gave my own exasperated whuff. 'Iris isn't making my efforts any easier. I need to know why she was in the room with the victim.' After an angry exchange with Lambert earlier in the day, Iris surely didn't seek him out. But she left the ballroom soon after his exit. Maybe she wasn't following Lambert. Maybe she followed someone else. Perhaps she saw that person leave the room where he was killed and something about that departure prompted Iris to go into the room. Iris insisted she wasn't trying to protect a murderer. She must feel confident the person she saw had nothing to do with his death. 'The situation is complicated. I'll keep trying.' Possibly I sounded grim.

'It's unfortunate you find Iris difficult to deal with. No doubt she is distracted by all that has occurred.'

As I said, Wiggins appreciates beauty. Her lack of charm apparently escaped his notice.

'It is very telling that she sees you.' There was a hint of reverence in his voice.

'That's part of the problem. I could get so much more done if she didn't see me. Is there anything you can do about that?'

'Heavens no.' Reproof was clear. 'She sees you because she is unusually empathetic. Life is hard for those with that quality. They often appear sardonic and flippant. That careless attitude serves as a shield against the pain that presses against them when they encounter unhappy souls.'

Oh. And oh. As Mama always told us kids, 'Walk a mile in her (or his) moccasins before you scold.'

Wiggins was firm. 'It is unacceptable for emissaries to obstruct the authorities. That course can't be tolerated. You must both protect Iris and do your duty as a good citizen. Today.' His voice was fading. 'The Department rarely

changes emissaries mid-mission but that . . .' His voice faded
away.

I was on notice. Work a miracle or climb aboard the caboose
for an ignominious return. Today.

I felt the wind was at my back, always a good thing in
Oklahoma, when I found Sam's office dim. True to his usual
disdain for the city rule that employees change their computer
passwords weekly and commit them only to memory, I found
his list of passwords in his center desk drawer. Apparently he
was feeling alliterative when he drew up this month's list:
wallaby, wombat, warbler, and woofer. The first was drawn
through. I typed in wombat.

It took only a moment to find the file I was seeking. Joyce
Lambert's son Jack Wells was nineteen and this fall would
be a sophomore at Goddard majoring in art. When questioned,
Jack said he was 'just fooling around' from six thirty to
eight p.m. Thursday, last saw his stepfather when he and
Jack's mom were leaving the house for the banquet, had no
idea why anyone would kill him. Judy Weitz's appraisal:
Seems like a nice enough kid. B average in high school and
at Goddard. Summer job at the city pool in the concession
stand.

A machine whirred and ice spun into a cone. A squirt and
the ice mound turned orange. Jack's hair was pulled back
behind a red bandana. He looked skinnier than ever in
a saggy blue polo, denim shorts, and flip-flops. Another
teenager was stacking cellophane-wrapped sandwiches in a
cooler.

The pool was thronged with big kids, little kids, and moms.
I found a spot between a weeping willow and the trash bin
and Appeared as Officer Loy. By the time I reached the
concession stand, my hair lay limp and damp against my
neck. It might not have been the right protocol for an investigating officer, but I pointed at the snow-cone machine when
I reached the counter. 'Strawberry, please.'

Jack saw my uniform, of course. He nodded, flicked the
switch. When he handed me a snow cone, I took a huge bite.

I wriggled my nose at the shock of cold, murmured, 'Officer Loy.' I retrieved a dollar from a pocket – Heaven provides – and put it on the counter. 'I have a few questions about your stepfather.' Perhaps it was the nose wriggle or a smear of strawberry on my chin or a question that didn't sound threatening, but Jack said, 'Sure.' He turned, 'Mickey, take over for me for a few.' Jack lifted a portion of the counter, joined me. We moved into the shade of an elm.

He squinted at me. 'Have you found out who killed Matt?'

'Not yet. We—'

He leaned forward. His eyes blinked rapidly. 'Listen, my mom is knocked for a loop. She thought he was wonderful. She didn't—'

I was quick to reassure him. 'Your mother never left the ballroom after she arrived. Lots of witnesses. She is not a suspect.'

Tension drained from his face. 'Mom's OK.' He tried to keep his lips steady.

I couldn't claim Iris-level empathy, but Jack's evident relief meant there might have been quarrels at the Lambert house, that all might not have been sunny between Joyce and Matt. His relief also suggested to me he hadn't been quite certain his mom was innocent, which meant he was innocent as well. I chose my words carefully. 'At present we are pursuing leads that suggest Mr Lambert threatened someone or was involved in a dispute. We are attempting to put together a complete profile of the victim. We know he was outgoing, enjoyed parties and pageantry, admired successful people. We need to know more about the private man. As someone who observed him close hand, can you suggest any character traits that might have led to a quarrel between Mr Lambert and those around him.'

Jack's mouth curled in disdain. 'Oh yeah. That I can do. He was mean. He liked insulting people. People like me or a waitress at a restaurant or somebody behind a counter. You know, people who don't count. People who aren't rich. Like Thursday night. Just before they left for the banquet. He came in my room. Didn't knock. Just came in. I was working on a charcoal sketch. He said, "Looks like chicken scratches in the dirt." Then he gave that big laugh. See, he always laughed when he gigged somebody so then you look like you're surly if you got mad. Everything was funny, but it wasn't really. He gave that laugh and said, "When I was your age, I was in the line at Goddard. Oh well, there are chicken scratchers and football players, right, Jack?"'

'Is that why you drove to Rose Bower last night?'

He tugged on the ring in his left ear. 'Did Mom tell you I was over there? Anyway, I got close – there's a girl I know who waits tables at banquets – but when I was almost there I changed my mind. It would be just my luck to run into him. So I turned off, drove through the park to the other side of campus. You know the Strip?'

I nodded. A street adjacent to the campus has two cafés, a tearoom, three bars, and an ice-cream shop.

'I hadn't had dinner. I had a banana split, three scoops, one dip each vanilla, butter brickle, and pistachio, caramel on the vanilla, chocolate fudge on the rest.'

Iris checked the rearview mirror. Clearly she saw me in the back seat of her Malibu sedan. She looked conflicted, as in yes, she could never repay Gage's rescue and no, she didn't want an unseen buddy.

Since Gage was in the front passenger seat, it wouldn't do to speak aloud. I pointed at myself, then at Iris, drew an imaginary heart in the air.

The car slowed as she darted a puzzled glance at the mirror.

I pointed at her, then at myself, tapped my fingers against my thumb, mouthed, 'Let's talk.'

Iris gave an infinitesimal nod. Her face was a study in uncertainty, determination, resignation.

'Mom, are we going to roll there?' Gage shifted impatiently in the seat.

'Sorry.' The car picked up speed. Iris made a left turn, pulled into a drive fronting several dormitories. 'Will you and Robert be over for dinner?'

Gage brushed back a tangle of dark hair. 'Mom, don't talk about dinner. That big man thinks you killed Matt.'

Iris said quietly, 'He's wrong. Not to worry, honey. Everything's under control.'

Gage took a quick breath. 'Mom, who's Nicole?' Her eyes were wide with concern.

Iris didn't change expression, but her hands tightened on the steering wheel. 'I'll fix lasagna. Would Robert like a green salad or Caesar?'

Gage's eyes shone with sudden tears. 'Mom, it's not a game. The police are asking people and they know everything that happened yesterday afternoon and you can't pretend like everything's all right.'

Iris reached out, gently touched her daughter's cheek. 'Everything will be all right. I promise. I know what to do. I didn't kill Matt. Now you get back to your life.'

'The police are after you. And I want to help but there isn't anything I can do.' The tears in her eyes brimmed, trickled down her cheeks.

Iris gave her a loving look. 'Just being Gage is all you need to do. I'll take care of the rest. I have some special assistance,' she glanced at me in the rearview mirror, 'that will see me through. So, no more worries.' She made a gentle shooing gesture with one hand.

Gage slowly nodded. She opened the door, swung out, poked her head back inside. 'Mom, call me if you need . . . anything.'

'Of course.' Iris watched as Gage walked quickly up the sidewalk, pushed open the door to enter. When the door closed, Iris pressed the accelerator, started up the drive. 'What do you want to talk to me about?'

'If you weren't in danger of arrest on a murder charge, we could talk about e. e. cummings or what it's like to see a cheetah run or your lasagna recipe. We don't have that luxury.'

She turned the car into the street, drove a couple of blocks in silence, pulled into a parking space at a park. 'Arrest?'

'If Sam Cobb knew you stood over Lambert's body last night with a homemade blackjack in your hand, you'd already be in a cell.'

'Who's going to tell him?' She arched a questioning eyebrow, fully aware I could easily expose her secret.

'I hope,' I said slowly, 'you will tell him. Something – or someone – drew you into that room. I don't think you wanted to talk to Matt Lambert. The police need to know what you saw, what happened.'

'I can't.' She spoke with finality.

'Why not? You didn't kill Lambert.'

A wry smile. 'Thank you. Even Robert wondered. But you know as well as I do that if I tell the police I picked up the weapon, I'll be in jail.'

'Why did you?'

She brushed back a strand of dark hair. 'I opened the door and stepped inside. I walked toward the French doors. I saw one was ajar. I wasn't looking down. My shoe hit something. That's when I saw a sock with one end tied and that fat bottom portion. I thought that was odd. I picked it up, thinking it was some kind of weird trash and I'd put it in a bin. Maybe the result of being a military wife for so many years. Everything is tidy on a post. I stopped for a minute, still holding it. I almost turned to go out but there was something about the room, I didn't like the way I felt . . .'

That empathy again. Could a place hold a sense of evil?

'. . . so I kept walking. I saw Matt.' The sentence reflected shock and dismay. She didn't like Matt Lambert. She abhorred the ending of life.

In the park, a woman walked a Dalmatian that looked alert and ready to bolt if unleashed. Two shirtless young men in gym shorts stood thirty yards apart on a soccer field. One lifted his arm and spiraled a football to his friend. It was an ordinary summer day except for Iris's bleak face. Iris's cheekbones jutted, her firm chin was elevated. This was likely the posture that elicited Sam's comment about supercilious women.

I reached out, gently touched a rigid arm. 'Why didn't you call the police?'

'Equal parts foolishness and fear.' There was a touch of defiance. 'I remembered the door to Matt's office was ajar yesterday afternoon when I told him cruelty to the defenseless was indefensible. And much more along those lines. Loudly and clearly. I looked down at his body and thought the police might well disbelieve the reason I picked up the sock. The very heavy sock. I knew that's what killed him.' A breath. 'We're supposed to speak up and shame the devil. Now the shame's on me. I argued with him that very day. I thought – and maybe it was stupid – that I didn't know anything about who killed him. I'd just been unlucky enough to walk in on the murder of a man I despised. I thought I didn't have anything useful to tell the police. And I didn't want to explain why I opened that door.'

I was surprised. 'You planned to see him?'

'Lord, no.' The disclaimer was quick and firm.

I persisted. 'Why did you open the door?' There had to be a reason why she came to the first floor and went to that particular room.

She was silent, her chin tilted at that stubborn angle.

I knew the reason. 'You saw someone follow Matt Lambert from the ballroom. You hurried, but a conversation delayed you. You went downstairs and saw that person leave the room. Perhaps the person looked upset or frightened. You went inside the room.' I took a deep breath. 'By this evening, you must go to the police and tell them what you know.' Before she could object, I rushed on, 'You told me you aren't protecting a murderer. Your silence may be doing just that. The person you saw might know something that will lead the police to the murderer.'

Finally she gave me a quirky half-smile. 'You have almost everything right, but not quite. I didn't see anyone leave the room. I did see someone I know start up the stairs and there was an odd look . . . I thought maybe Matt had been mean again . . . I guess I don't have to tell you I'm impulsive.'

I didn't fault her. I'd been known to speak first and think second more than a few times.

'Anyway, I got mad all over again. I charged up the hall, tried all the doors. That room was the only one with the light on. So I went in. That's why I was standing there, that sock in my hand, when Robert arrived. I thought Gage would be furious with me if I involved him in a mess. So lots of reasons jumbled in my mind to get us out of there. I was due to make a presentation in the ballroom, so that's why I asked Robert to get rid of the sock. I was due upstairs in only a few minutes. Like I said, I can't be proud of that performance. I thought about everything that happened last night and knew I couldn't leave it that way. I was afraid the person I saw might have been near the room, might actually be able to help the police. If that turns out to be true, I will go to the police, tell them everything. I'll know soon. If there's anything the police should know, I'll make sure they find out. But I can't go to the police and put someone in jeopardy just because they were downstairs.' Her chin still had that decided jut. She was determined to do what she felt she needed to do.

'Is the person you're seeking someone you know well?'

She looked a little surprised, slowly shook her head. 'Not in a personal sense. I know there's a fine mind. I know there's no family and a background of poverty, a student working two jobs to pay tuition, able to take only a few hours a semester. That came up once during an office visit. That's why I suggested the Outreach Office when I heard there was an opening. It would pay better and look better on a résumé someday. When I found out how that interview went, really demeaning, making poverty a barrier, I was furious.'

A student then. A student whose work she admired. A student without the means to dress up for an interview. It would be very like Iris to focus on intelligence and eagerness to learn and want to help.

She met my gaze directly. 'Now I know exactly how difficult it is to defend against suspicion. I can't put anyone in that situation simply on the basis of a facial expression.'

I understood. I reached out, again clasped her arm, this time an encouraging squeeze.

She smiled her thanks. 'I'll let you out here. Don't follow me.' A quick smile. 'I'll see you. I promise to let you know what I find out. But,' that uplifted chin, 'I will not tell you or the police about this person if I'm positive there's no useful information to be had.'

On the sidewalk, I watched the red Malibu drive away. Iris made it clear I wasn't welcome when she spoke to her quarry. But perhaps I could find my way by myself.

I scarcely recognized the woman slumped in an easy chair in the living room of a small apartment. Likely it was a furnished apartment. The furniture was shabby, undistinguished, tired, used by transients, not cherished and cared for.

Yesterday evening, when she had opened the door to the Malone Room, Clarisse Bennett was buoyant in a bright pink dress, her curly brown hair glistening, her makeup carefully applied. She was eager and happy until she walked around the sofa and saw the body of the man she loved.

I didn't doubt as I observed the shrunken figure in the overstuffed chair, hair uncombed, no makeup, still in a nightgown, dressing gown, and house slippers, that she grieved. Lambert's widow dismissed Clarisse's claim of a love affair as wishful thinking, a recent divorcée's infatuation. Whatever, whichever, the passion had been real on Clarisse's part.

Did that assure her innocence? She might have killed out of jealousy or despair and yet be heartbroken, her grief intensified by guilt. Of course if she were a murderer, she would already have been playing a part when she opened that door, known a body lay there, arriving to find Lambert and emphasize her innocence by her shock and sorrow.

In the apartment house hallway, making sure no one was near, I Appeared as Officer Loy. I knocked firmly on the thin wooden door.

It seemed to take a long time before the door slowly opened. She stared at me dully.

'Officer, M. Loy. Clarisse Bennett?'

She nodded, gazing with a numb, hopeless stare.

'Ms Bennett, it's urgent that I speak with you regarding an episode in the Outreach Office yesterday that may relate to the murder of Mr Lambert.'

When she said nothing, I took a step forward. 'I have a few questions.'

She held the door for me, gestured at a sofa in a frayed orange slipcover. By the time I was seated, she seemed to

come to life. She stood over me, her arms folded, the volu-
minous sleeves of the dressing gown bunched against her.
'When are you going to arrest Joyce?' Her voice held venom.

I spoke firmly, definitively. 'Mrs Lambert is not a suspect.'

'She killed him. I know she did.' Tears rolled down her
sunken cheeks. 'Don't be fooled by her lies. She was furious
with him. They'd been arguing and arguing.'

I spoke with emphasis. 'Mrs Lambert never left the ballroom.
Those at her table have given statements. She did not leave
the ballroom after her arrival with Mr Lambert at shortly after
six p.m.'

'She must have. Someone's lying.'

I was gentle. 'I understand your feelings, but there's no
question of her involvement. Mr Lambert was observed
leaving the ballroom a little before seven. You discovered
his body shortly after seven p.m. We have six witnesses who
will testify that Mrs Lambert arrived at the table at approxi-
mately six minutes after six p.m. and remained seated until
an officer asked her to come downstairs at twelve minutes
after seven p.m.'

Her face slack, Clarisse walked unsteadily to the chair, sank
into it. 'Not Joyce.'

'The identity of the murderer is unknown. That's why I am
here. You knew Mr Lambert well. You were also an integral
member of his office staff. You may have information that can
assist in the investigation. Can you tell me why he was in the
Malone Room last night?'

Her face folded in thought. 'Probably to meet someone.'

Was this to disarm a police officer, suggest Lambert had
an appointment? Or did she have an appointment with him?
Was she angry with him, had he told her that Florida was a
fantasy? I watched her carefully. 'How did you know he was
there?'

'I went out in the foyer after he left his table. I ran into a
friend and visited a minute. Matt went downstairs. When
he didn't come back up, I checked my cell and he was on the
first floor.'

I felt claustrophobic for an instant, glad I'd lived and loved
in a day without electronic tethers enveloping me.

Clarisse's voice trembled. 'I went down. I thought we could visit for a minute. He was going to Austin next weekend to visit a donor and I could meet him there.' Again tears flooded down her face. 'I tried the door earlier but the room was dark. Then I was sure he had to be there and I came back. This time the light was on and I went inside.' She dissolved again in tears.

She was telling the truth. I knew because I was there when someone knocked at the door and I just managed to switch off the light to protect Robert. I heard the disappointment in that soft 'oh' when she looked inside.

Knowledge of her innocence softened my approach. 'I know this is very difficult for you, but you truly may be able to help us in the investigation. We've been told that Mr Lambert quarreled with Iris Gallagher Thursday afternoon. Is that correct?'

She sat straighter, shook her head. 'That's all wrong. Matt didn't quarrel. He was perfectly pleasant the whole time. He hadn't done anything wrong. Iris Gallagher was acting like an idiot. He laughed about it later.'

See, he always laughed when he gigged somebody . . .

Her face flattened in dislike. 'She thinks she's better than everybody. She's academic, not staff. But who's she to tell everyone how to act? She's just an assistant professor living in a little frame house. She was lucky the college took her on after her husband was killed in Afghanistan. A major. She thinks she's special because she was an officer's wife and is a professor. Matt knew all the people in the big houses, people who matter. It was just like Iris to make a fuss about a girl like that, a nobody.'

I remembered Gage's unanswered question to her mother. 'Nicole?'

Clarisse sniffed in disdain. 'Iris sent this girl over to see about a job. I suppose Gage told her mother we have an opening for a clerk. Matt was absolutely right to send her away. If she felt insulted, why maybe she learned something. You can't come to an important office to apply for a job dressed like wait staff. She looked real tacky in that white shirt and black pants and clunky black shoes. She should have gone home and put on a nice dress if she wanted to work in our office.' Clarisse tossed her head and the uncombed curls quivered. 'Matt told Iris that rich people expect things to be nice. He said when he took them to dinner, he ordered the finest wine, lobster and filets, crème brûlée. He wouldn't dream of showing up in a shirt with a stain of something or other and shoes that were run down at the heel. He didn't want anyone in his office who didn't know how to dress. He said it didn't matter if she knew Chaucer, she had to know what mattered.'

I maintained a pleasant expression, but I understood Iris's fury. She'd heard of a job opening, one that was a step up from waiting tables, and she'd told a student.

'You are very helpful and we need to interview the student.'

Clarisse was happy to provide a name, address, and phone number.

NINE

I peered around the corner of a crepe myrtle shrub at a shabby three-story wooden apartment building that needed a coat of paint and repair to sagging gutters. A mother pushed a baby in a stroller not five feet from me. Of course, she didn't see me. But I knew to my chagrin that I was visible to Iris. My caution was repaid as I watched her departing Malibu sedan turn right at the end of the street.

A dog-eared 'Kitchenettes for Rent' sign was propped against a tricycle minus one wheel. A broken Coke bottle lay near the front step. Dandelions flourished in a yard that badly needed mowing. I suspected Kitchenette meant a microwave and a small fridge in a combo living/sleeping area. If Matt Lambert had seen where Nicole Potter lived, he certainly wouldn't have hired her.

A moment later, I was in a dingy second-floor hallway. My nose wrinkled at the smell of popcorn. It seemed incongruous in the dim and dusty corridor. I Appeared as Officer Loy and knocked. The flimsy door rattled in its frame.

The door swung in. The girl who stood in the doorway was so thin that the white shirt and black pants hung on her. Today the shirt, though wrinkled, was stain free. I was struck by the intensity of her gaze, brilliantly dark eyes in a skinny face bare of makeup, eyes that glittered with intelligence and with barely held-in-check anger.

'Nicole Potter.' I spoke as though confident of her identity.

She nodded, watched me with cool reserve.

'Officer M. Loy. I understand you were on the wait staff at Rose Bower last night.'

'Yeah.' Her thin face was devoid of expression.

'May I come in? I have some questions about the evening.'

She gave a slight shrug, held the door. The room contained a sofa, two metal folding chairs on either side of a card table, a bunk bed with a ladder missing a rung, a sink, small refrigerator, and microwave. No oven.

She waved at the sofa, walked to a folding chair, turned it to face me, sat down. 'Why do you want to talk to me?' There was an edge to her voice, a surprisingly deep voice for such a slightly built person, an edge of wariness, a hint of hostility.

'You interviewed for a job in the Outreach Office.'

She nodded. Her young face with its bitter cast remained impassive.

'Describe the interview.'

She flicked thin hands over as if waving away mosquitos. 'A flop. Wasted my time. I wasn't fancy enough to work for him.' The deep voice was even, but there was a hotness in her eyes. 'Win some. Lose some.'

'Why did you follow him downstairs last night?'

'Him? I could care less about him. Where he went. What he did. What happened to him, if you want to know the truth. I guess maybe he pissed off somebody *important*.' She put the word in italics. 'I didn't follow him.' The deep voice was assured. 'I went downstairs because I wanted to use the bathroom. Nobody much would be down there and I wouldn't have to wait in line. So,' she spoke with finality, 'I went down, went to the bathroom, came back up.' She stood.

So much for my uniform. Or me, for that matter. Nicole Potter wasn't impressed and, as far as she was concerned, we were done.

I tried to sound sharp. 'Did you see Lambert downstairs?'

The door swung in and a plump blonde stepped inside. She saw me and her eyes were huge. 'Oh. Hey Nicole, I came home for lunch.' She looked from Nicole to me and back again. 'Everything all right?'

Nicole's mouth might have curled in the smallest of smiles. 'Fine, Jolene. Just doing my civic duty. The police are talking to people who were at Rose Bower last night. You know,' she pointed at a laptop on an end table by the sofa, 'there was a murder.'

'Yeah. I heard about it at the Union. Scary.' She looked at me with big blue eyes. 'Do you know who did it?'

'We have some leads.' I stared at Nicole.

She met my gaze with a cool look which said not her murder, not her problem, she didn't care.

'I asked if you saw Lambert downstairs.'

'No.' Bored, totally bored. Not her problem.

'Did you see anyone in the hallway?'

'Nope. Like I said, I knew the ladies' room would be empty. Sorry I can't help.'

I liked Iris's house, an old-fashioned bungalow in a modest area adjacent to White Deer Park. Fancy homes on hillsides overlooked the park from the other side.

Iris's living room was small but charming, ivy twined wallpaper, a silver-and-rose Persian rug on the wood floor, several easy chairs, all with reading lamps, and, of course, filled bookcases. I noted some titles. *Green Mansions. The Good Earth. Vile Bodies.* Iris sat in a chair near a small piano. A half-dozen photographs sat atop the piano. Gage. Gage and Robert. An assured man with a warm smile in a major's uniform. The husband who didn't come home from Afghanistan. And now she had no men's socks in her house. She was reading and suddenly she laughed, a light gurgle of amusement.

I looked at the front cover. *The Passionate Witch* by Thorne Smith. 'A laugh a page.'

Her gaze lifted. For the first time in our short acquaintance, she smiled upon seeing me. She rested the book in her lap. 'He's famous for *Topper*, but he wrote several funny books. You aren't as entertaining as George and Marion Kerby.' The amusement slipped away. 'They didn't have to deal with murder.' She tapped the page. 'I needed some fun after yesterday and most of today. But, I have good news. The student I saw on the first-floor stairs at Rose Bower knows absolutely nothing about Matt's murder. When I asked about the look on her face, she told me she was afraid she'd be late getting back upstairs and the boss was a beast. She had no idea where Matt was. She said he was the last person she'd ever try to talk to. So,' Iris's violet eyes looked hopeful, 'don't you think it's OK to keep quiet about my sojourn downstairs? Nicole was the only person I saw. And there's the weapon and Robert. I don't see good things happening if I contact the police.'

'I agree.' I hoped Wiggins would approve.

'They're suspicious enough without admitting I was in that room.' Iris was no fool.

'That's true. I hope to divert Sam from you.'

'How can you do that?' She looked bewildered.

'Find out what really happened.'

She studied me for a minute. A smile flickered. 'Gumshoe Ghost?'

'Absolutely.' My tone was much more confident than I felt. So far I'd not discovered anything that convinced Sam of Iris's innocence. I had to know more to find out more. 'I need your help. Tell me what you did after Matt left the ballroom.' So far I only knew she followed someone downstairs and ended up standing over the body with the improvised blackjack.

'When Matt went out the door, I saw Nicole Potter and I thought she was watching him. Her face was . . . well, she was angry. I've sensed anger in her as a student. I think she's one of those people who have always had to fight for what they want. It looked like she saw him and started after him. I thought this wasn't going to end well. I started after her, but Ollie Baker stopped me. A Shakespeare scholar. He was livid, a new book about the Earl of Stratford.' A sigh. 'Honestly, after four hundred years, let it rest. He clamped his fingers on my arm and held tight. It took time to get free. When I finally reached the foyer, I didn't see either Matt or Nicole. I suppose I was only a few minutes behind them, but they were out of sight. I hurried downstairs. I'd just reached the ground floor when Nicole came from the hall and started up the opposite flight of stairs. She didn't see me. The look on her face bothered me. I wondered if she and Matt had spoken.

'I got mad all over again. Here he was, a star at the banquet with all the money he's raised and a girl who came up the hard way. I rushed on down. The ground floor was deserted. No lights in the offices. A student on duty at the welcome desk was working on a laptop. She never looked up. I turned right into that hallway. There are a half-dozen doors, two or three on each side. Several doors were locked. I opened three, the first two rooms were dark. The lights were on in the Malone Room. I stepped inside, saw the sock, picked it up. I'd just found Matt when Robert walked in.'

'Did you see anyone in the hallway?'

'No one.' Her eyes were dark. 'That's bad, isn't it? There was no one down there but me.'

I was working out times. Matt Lambert left the ballroom shortly before seven. Iris was delayed, likely didn't arrive downstairs for another five minutes. Within those five minutes, Matt Lambert was struck down and his murderer escaped.

Iris looked frightened. 'I didn't see anyone. I didn't hear anything. It seems unlikely Matt could meet someone in those few minutes and quarrel.'

My voice was quiet, but firm. 'There was no quarrel. The time for quarrels was past.'

She stared at me. 'I don't understand.'

'The decision to kill Lambert was already made. The murderer likely greeted him pleasantly, perhaps with a rueful comment about there being a lot of different reasons to contribute to the college. There would have been no hint of threat, more a sense of resignation. Lambert had only a few minutes to live. The killer likely said something about a noise outside. Lambert looked toward the French doors. The killer pulled out the sand-filled sock from a pocket or purse and swung. The weighted sock slammed Lambert's throat. He was dead within a minute or two of the time he walked into the room. The murderer left by a French door on to the terrace and returned to the ballroom by a back stairway.'

It took more than an hour for Officer Loy to track down the clerks who were behind the counter at the ice-cream shop last evening. My third attempt was successful. A redheaded girl – I liked her at once – stood at the side of the Olympic pool, swim cap and goggles in her hand.

I introduced myself. 'If I could speak with you for a moment.' I smiled reassuringly.

'Practice starts in just a couple of minutes.' She shot a glance at an angular man in his forties who stood at the deep end, looking down at a clipboard. Likely a coach who didn't tolerate late arrivals. 'What's wrong?'

'Simply a matter of information. Last night at the ice-cream shop, do you remember making a sundae with a dip each of vanilla, butter brickle, and pistachio, caramel sauce on the vanilla, chocolate fudge on the rest.'

'Yes, ma'am. He ate real fast. I think maybe he hadn't had any dinner.' A quick smile. 'He's real thin and tall like my brother. But my brother has short hair and this guy had kind of long brown hair.'

'Can you tell me about what time that was?'

She quickly nodded. 'Ten to seven. Just before I clocked out.'

I settled on the parapet and took several deep breaths. Heat radiated from the asphalt roof of City Hall. Whew. Double whew. Not a choice locale at noon in early July. I'd often conferred here with Wiggins. Usually he sought me out. I didn't know if I could summon him. I don't meditate. That requires sitting still for too long, but I concentrated hard: Wiggins, Wiggins, Bailey Ruth here. Wiggins—

Whooo. Coal smoke. The clack of wheels on silver rails. 'Wiggins!'

'Ah, Bailey Ruth.' His voice came from near a structure a few feet away that housed the trapdoor to the building. There was a small patch of shade there. I resisted envy.

'You have made great progress.' His voice was approving.

I basked in the geniality of his tone. If I were visible. I would have stood straight and saluted. I spoke in that sort of voice. 'Pleased to report that Lambert's stepson is alibied for the time of the death and that there's no need for Iris Gallagher to reveal her presence at the crime scene.'

'Well done, Bailey Ruth. Glad that young artist is all right. That sundae sounds rather good.'

On impulse, I urged, 'Come with me, Wiggins. I've not had lunch. It's a very nice ice-cream shop.'

There is Heaven and there is heaven. Wiggins looked quite sporting in a blue polo and khakis and loafers. Without his stiff blue station cap or green eyeshade, he looked much less formal. He took a spoonful of chocolate-fudge-topped butter brickle. 'Interesting tastes.' I doubt soda fountains in the 1910s had quite this array of flavors. In the spirit (couldn't resist) of summer and sodas, I wore a sleeveless white dress with bright yellow, lime, pink, red, blue, and gray stripes. Pink wedge sandals matched the pink stripe.

Our red leather booth at the front of the shop offered a view of the Fine Arts building across the street.

The pistachio flecked with fudge sauce was beyond delectable. 'Try the pistachio.'

Wiggins studied the boat-shaped bowl.

I pointed. 'Green.'

He took a bite, nodded approval. 'It's nice to conclude in this cheerful spot. Except for your evasion of the Express early on . . .'

Clearly my defection still rankled.

'. . . this has been a successful mission.' He put down his spoon and beamed at me. 'When you finish, let's hop aboard.'

Coal smoke. Clack of wheels.

'Not yet.' If a plea can be firm, my reply qualified.

His brows wrinkled in a frown. 'You arrived to safeguard Iris and Robert. You have done so. She need not reveal her presence at the crime scene since she has no critical evidence to impart to the police.'

Wiggins was right. My job appeared to be done.

As Mama always told us kids, 'If you suddenly feel frightened, pay attention. The angel at your shoulder is tapping.'

I leaned forward, reached across the table to touch his arm. 'I'm afraid for Iris.'

He looked into my eyes, made his harrumph noise. Men dismiss feminine intuition. Of course, if a man has a hunch, that's different. I added hurriedly, 'A hunch, Wiggins. There's trouble ahead for Iris.'

'Hmm. A hunch. Very well. See what you can do.'

In Sam's office, I relished the air conditioning, serious air conditioning as befitted a hot July afternoon in Adelaide. I plopped on to the brown leather sofa that faced the windows. Perhaps I gave a soft sigh of relief.

Sam's office chair squeaked.

I turned to look at the desk.

Sam held a half-eaten hamburger in one hand, a can of Mountain Dew in the other. 'Bailey Ruth?'

'It's hot outside.'

'July.' He took a bite. 'Anything else I can help you with?' He sounded like a blackjack player with a king in the hole and a bright diamond ace in his hand.

'How's everything going?'

He looked in the direction of my voice. 'Is that a tactful way of asking whether I've found a suspect other than Iris Gallagher? I'll bring you up to date on the investigation. The widow's in the clear. The lover had opportunity, but there's no evidence of a motive on her part and we've asked people who would know. A lot of people. And there was a little love note from him to her on her computer Thursday morning. The acting president never left his table. We haven't found any disgruntled former employees, estranged friendships, debts, or quarrels. He and the stepson didn't get along but no recent problems that we know about.'

'Officer Loy can report that Jack Wells was eating a sundae at the campus corner soda shop at seven o'clock.'

Sam made a note on his pad. 'Good to know.' He glanced again at his pad. 'When assured of confidentiality, some people were pretty frank. Lambert was something of a self-important ass, but that usually doesn't lead to murder. His humor was on the mean side, but it takes a pretty big insult to get you a broken neck. No serious debts so no money motive.'

That gave me the opening I wanted. I pushed up from the sofa, walked to the chair that faced his desk.

His eyes moved with me as he listened to my footsteps. 'Make yourself comfortable.' His voice held a hint of discombobulation.

I laughed, Appeared in a loose – so cool – white linen tunic, very short A-line skirt with bright scenes of Paris, and open sandals.

'Thanks.' He took a last bite of hamburger, followed by a gurgle of Mountain Dew.

I was direct. 'Let's talk money. How about a five million gift coerced to hide a donor's secret?'

'Dog with a bone,' but his voice was pleasant. Sam finished the soda, crushed the can, dropped it in the wastebasket.

I refrained from asking if the discard met the city standard for recyclable items. This was no time to aggravate him.

'But,' Sam was good-humored, 'it's cheerful to have you here. You are much better company than my most recent visitor. The mayor just left. On her way to a campaign picnic. She hates to be hot but she'd do a tap dance on a griddle if the donations were big enough. She's on a cut-the-budget binge, thinks it will help her re-election. She's threatening to make us keep the thermostat at seventy-two. I told her she didn't want riots in City Hall.' He gave me a wicked smile. 'I put the thermostat down another notch.'

Sam and Neva Lumpkin were not soul mates. The mayor longed to replace Sam and their relations were frosty.

'She arrived breathing fire. Homicide at Rose Bower apparently is far, far worse than homicide anywhere else in town. You'd think she might understand I don't pick the location for bodies. Or the time homicide occurs. Yeah, the nine-one-one came after hours. I had to call in some detectives who'd already put in a full day. She'd rather hug Dracula than pay overtime. She was practically in tears as she figured out how much it cost for the crew out at Rose Bower last night. But it soothed her down when I told her I have a suspect in sight and I'm looking for some physical evidence before I make the arrest.'

I didn't have to ask the suspect's name.

'Sam, it's ab—' I broke off. Men do not appreciate having their actions termed absurd. 'Absolutely unreasonable to think a woman like Iris Gallagher would haul a homemade weapon to a banquet and murder a man because she was upset about the way he treated a student who applied for a job.'

Sam's stare was level. 'How do we know their discussion had anything to do with that job interview?'

I tried not to preen. 'Officer Loy talked to Clarisse Bennett. Matt Lambert told her all about the interview, that's how we know.'

'Lambert told her?' He wasn't troubled.

'Yes.' I was emphatic.

'Clarisse Bennett said Lambert *told* her that was the reason Iris came to see him?'

I felt uneasy. 'Exactly.'

'Would he tell Bennett if there was a darker reason for that talk? Like maybe sexual advances? Bennett didn't actually hear Lambert and Gallagher, right?'

I was silent.

He nodded in satisfaction.

I began to sense I was on a raft tipping over in a stormy sea and I was almost in the water. I tried again. 'The call Gage overheard on the terrace is a much bigger deal than Iris quarreling with Lambert. Iris said what she had to say, went on from there. She isn't a neurotic woman nursing a huge grudge. But demanding a mega-million gift qualifies as a big-time motive.'

'Like I said, you're like a dog with a bone. What Gage claimed to overhear could be perfectly innocent. OK, let's agree Lambert said the donor had to show up last night and there would be a big celebration. Everything depends on Lambert's tone. Maybe it was a donor he knew well. Maybe he was having a little fun to encourage a reclusive donor to come. I talked to the donors who were there . . .'

The Mayers, the Kirks, and the Prichards.

'. . . and not one of them had spoken with him recently and all were attending the dinner because they always did, not because of any announcement to be made that night. Maybe he struck out and a reclusive donor stayed home. Your idea of a homicidal donor is a bust, Bailey Ruth. But you can't say the department doesn't follow up. Mrs Prichard, her son, Alexander, and daughter-in-law, Winifred, never left their table. August Mayer remained at the table. Jill Mayer went to the ladies' room about a quarter to seven. George Kirk, ditto. Melissa Kirk, ditto.'

'I even printed some photos from the *Gazette*. Just for you.' He rummaged and pushed a sheet across his desk.

Jill Mayer smiled in a studio portrait. I estimated her age at sixty-five to seventy. Silver-frosted brown hair was drawn back into a chignon. Her face was thin, sensitive, intelligent.

She was lovely in a cashmere sweater set and I thought the strand of pearls on her throat was real.

George Kirk was muscular in white tennis shirt and shorts, holding a racket, broad face red from sun. Curly brown hair. Smiling. A man accustomed to having fun. Melissa Kirk stood in the shadow of a huge redwood, hands on her hips. Dark windblown hair. Her face was thin, intense, nervy.

I don't know why I expected older people. There are young rich, too.

Perhaps Sam understood my expression. 'A different world for some. But money doesn't make people the brightest bulbs in the marquee. George strikes me as a good-time Charlie and I bet someone else made the money. He went downstairs and stepped out on the terrace, said banquets bore him. Pleasant guy, though. Speaking of the terrace, we found the seed pod Robert Blair threw. R heart G. Plus, his fingerprints. So, that's that. As for Melissa,' there was a trace of distaste in his tone, 'she thought the whole exercise was funny, said, "I never thought I could add *Interrogated by police re homicide* to my bucket list. That's a hoot."'

'Three donors left the ballroom.' I said it with as much force as I could muster, but even I had to admit that no one in that small photo gallery looked a likely killer.

'During the critical period,' his tone was indulgent, 'several people were absent from the table hosted by George Kirk.' He rustled through a sheaf of papers, 'In addition to George Kirk and Melissa Kirk, Camille Dubois and Alice Harrison also left the ballroom. Those four were among the thirty-six people known to have left their tables. The point is, thirty-five of them had no quarrel with Matt Lambert. That brings us to Iris Gallagher.' He ticked off the charges, one by one. 'She quarreled with him Thursday afternoon. She refuses to admit she went downstairs. She refuses to discuss the quarrel. My guess is that Gallagher lit into him over the daughter, one way or another. Maybe not sex, but he was overseeing an internship, maybe he was treating the girl wrong. Gage Gallagher went to his office at midnight, which shows she was pretty desperate about something in there that could jeopardize her scholarship. Anyway, Iris Gallagher's seen too many cop shows

on TV. When we ask a question, she says, "I decline to answer."
Of course, she declines to answer. And that, Officer Loy, is
where the investigation is.'

'She's innocent.' But I knew Sam didn't agree.

'I recall that at one point you were unsure she needed
your assistance. I can assure you she does. Except I thought you
were sent to aid the innocent. Maybe you got it wrong and
Gage is the one to help. Looks like you have a screw-up in
your orders this time.'

I repeated my claim forcefully. 'Iris is innocent. Your
investigation is headed in the wrong direction.'

He frowned. 'Nobody can fault my investigation.'

That got my dander up. Mama always used to tell us kids,
'I know you're a passel of redheads, but think before you speak.
Words said in anger are harder to swallow than a mouthful of
marshmallows and not nearly as sweet.'

I stood. Remembering Mama's declaration, I was polite.
But firm. 'Except you won't consider a motive big enough to
buy up most of Adelaide. If you won't look at the Kirks or
the Mayers, I will.'

He stood, too. He was equally polite, equally firm. 'On your
own time, Bailey Ruth. I better not hear of any knocks on
their doors by Officer M. Loy. The Adelaide police do not
harass outstanding citizens.'

Oh my, how thankful I was that I'd not boarded the Rescue
Express. I told Wiggins I had a hunch and now I knew how
right I was.

TEN

Oh for the long-ago days of phone books. This might well be a generation unfamiliar with the concept. Long ago, before devices reigned supreme, the telephone company produced a phone book, which contained the names and addresses of every phone subscriber. If I wanted to know where the Mayers and the Kirks lived, the listings would be in the phone book. Not now. Heaven does provide for emissaries, such as proper clothes, which in my case includes a purse. But a cell phone with access to Google? This was not the moment to try. I was in a hurry and wished to move from place to place merely by thinking of a location.

Sam's office – and his computer – would be off-limits to me until he left for the day. I would return later to keep on top of the investigation, but right now I wanted addresses for the Kirks and the Mayers. I went to the public library. I found an office with the computer on. However, a librarian occupied the swivel seat at the desk.

In the hallway, after making sure no one was near, I Appeared, choosing a shirtdress with a paisley patchwork design. Cheerful and light. White sandals. I knocked.

'Come in.' The tone was crisp.

I opened the door, smiled. 'The director would like a few minutes of your time.'

The librarian, short and plump with piled-high chestnut curls, looked surprised. 'I don't think I know you.' She studied me.

I hoped my smile wasn't too strained. 'I'm new.' A chirp. 'First day on the job.'

'I suggest you be sure of your information in the future. The director is on holiday. In Italy. You may close the door.'

Iris Gallagher looked up from *The Passionate Witch*. 'Please stand on the floor. It unnerves me when you hover.'

I settled in a rattan chair opposite her. 'It isn't easy being a spirit.' I tried not to whine. 'The simplest tasks are fraught with challenges. Can you get me the addresses of George and Melissa Kirk, and Jill Mayer.'

She put the book aside, picked up her cell phone, tapped. 'The Mayers live on King's Road. Three eleven.'

King's Road was Adelaide's old-money street on the crest of a hill.

'The Kirks live on Comanche. Nine fourteen.'

Comanche is a lovely road that winds around part of White Deer Park.

'Thank you.' I was grateful for her help.

'Any time.'

Her cell phone rang.

I gave her a farewell wave.

The Mayer house of gray stone was substantial, but it was old wealth, not new. There were no turrets, no copper spires, and no battlements. Inside, there was formality – French furniture, tapestries, cabinets with china, fine paintings – but there was also dog fur on a damask-covered sofa and a plump brown tabby atop a Sheraton table.

It was late Friday afternoon now. A golden retriever wandered into the main hallway, came near, pressed a moist pink nose in my hand. I patted her head.

I heard faint strains of Debussy.

Upstairs I found Jill Mayer. She rested on a chaise longue in a living area adjacent to a bedroom. She was frail, perhaps all of five feet two inches tall, weighing around ninety pounds. She looked to be in her seventies. Her thin face was kind. A cane leaned against the side of the chaise longue. She kept time to the music with a slight waving motion of her left hand. Her right hand was withered. Perhaps from a stroke.

She left the ballroom at Rose Bower. She did not crush Matt Lambert's neck with a homemade blackjack.

The Kirk house had an inviting air, windows framed by recently painted white shutters, flower beds bright with red and cream roses. Daisies lifted smiling faces in a huge blue porcelain pot on the front porch. Elm trees shaded a circular drive with an assortment of cars, a red Ferrari convertible, a cream Lexus sedan, a black Jeep, a tan Camry, and a blue Ford.

The number of cars surprised me. I'd assumed there would be two people in the house. George Kirk, an amiable young man. Melissa Kirk, an intense, possibly abrasive young woman. Opposites often do attract.

A siren shrilled in the summer air. The sound came from beyond the house. One siren. Another. I rose in the air, passed over the house, came down to the terrace to stand by a sparkling swimming pool with patio furniture and striped umbrellas that fluttered in the hot afternoon breeze. The pool was gorgeous with a waterfall at one end. I looked down the hillside at a lake rimmed by willows and a pier. I realized I was looking at the lake in White Deer Park.

I immediately felt at home. Bobby Mac and I often walked to the end of the pier. We gloried in swaths of Monarchs in the spring, watched mama ducks launch broods in early summer, felt the year ebb as geese flew south against gray skies in the fall, stood arm-in-arm on chilly winter days, bundled in down jackets.

Another siren shrilled. The alarming shriek was joined by another and another, shattering the late summer afternoon calm. Four police cars, a fire truck, and an ambulance squealed into the park, one by one. They jolted to a stop, forming an ominous line of vehicles next to the carousel.

White Deer Park was somnolent in the heat. Only a certified idiot would jog – oh, here came one, a sweatband on a red face, bronzed skin, brief sweat-drenched nylon shorts, expensive running shoes. He slowed for a moment to scan the official vehicles and the carousel next to a willow tree.

The carousel looked hot and cheerless. During the summer, the ride opened at seven in the evening for an hour and from six to eight on Saturday and Sunday evenings. The carousel was operated by a volunteer group, the Merry Merry-Go-Rounders. The old-fashioned wooden animals, everything from a unicorn to a tortoise, were kept in tip-top shape, freshly painted every spring. My favorites were a pair of flamingos and a buffalo. We called him Buffalo Bill, of course.

The only movement was the willow fronds blowing in a hot breeze and then a woman moved out from the willow. A woman . . . There was no mistaking Iris Gallagher, even from this distance. She held a cell phone to her face and walked toward the line of official vehicles.

The jogger veered to skirt the congestion, picked up speed. Fire, famine, or forensics, no matter, a runner runs.

I dropped down beside Iris.

She looked at me, her elegant features bleak, shock and horror in her eyes. She was speaking into the phone. '. . . I'm sure she's dead. Her neck is . . . bent. I won't leave.' A pause. 'Officers are walking this way.'

Another police car, a forensic van, and a low-slung MG pulled into the park. In a moment, Jacob Brandt, the ME, swung out of the sports car, walked fast, head down toward the carousel.

Sam Cobb's brown sedan squealed to a stop. Sam heaved out of the driver's seat, moved fast. Detective-Lieutenant Hal Price slammed shut the front-seat passenger door, hurried to catch up. Sam's black shoes sent up little plumes of dust from the heat-cracked ground. His heavy face was rock hard, eyes cold, jaw set. Hal looked grim as well.

I left Iris, went to the carousel. A young uniformed officer with a golden ponytail stood rigid next to the seats with swan sides. Sweat beaded her upper lip. She was trying hard to stop a quiver of her lips.

Nicole Potter looked even slighter in death than in life, white shirt sloping over her shoulders, black slacks obviously too large. She lay on one side. Blood welling beneath the skin turned her throat a dark purple and her neck, as Iris said, was bent. So young to die. Too young to die.

The ME knelt beside her. 'Just a kid.' His voice was brusque.

'Same MO. Lambert kill. Blunt-force trauma, broken neck, death instantaneous. Estimate death within the last hour. Could have been minutes ago.' He used his stethoscope. A formality. He curled the stethoscope in his hand, pushed it into the small back bag, came to his feet, looked at Sam. 'You got 'em dropping like flies, man. Who's the silent assassin who leaves no trace?'

Sam half turned, stared across the dusty ground at Iris. He gave the ME a brief nod, then started toward Iris and the weeping willow.

I got there first, whispered, 'Call Megan Wynn, Smith and Wynn, attorneys-at-law. Decline to answer any questions until your attorney is present.'

Iris heard me, but she made no reply. She watched Sam's determined approach, tried to calm her breathing. She struggled not only with the reality of Nicole's death, but the growing awareness that her presence here put her at risk of arrest.

I had time for a few words more. 'Tell Megan that Bailey Ruth gave you her name.' I'd been in this park with Megan Wynn when she was upset and when she was exhilarated. Megan had faced an accusation of murder and she understood how black facts can look for an innocent person.

Sam stopped a scant foot from us, recited the Miranda warning rapidly. He gazed at her with a hint of anger. He must have felt that Nicole would still be alive if he'd moved faster, taken Iris into custody. 'You came to the park to meet Nicole Potter.'

How did Sam know the identity of the dead girl in the carousel? Perhaps they'd already looked at her billfold, found her ID. She was in her uniform, but her name tag read N. Potter, not Nicole. Had Sam confirmed the reason for Iris's disgust with Matt Lambert? Very likely someone in the office knew about Nicole's job interview, that she had been recommended by Iris, that Iris confronted Lambert the day he died. Sam would also know that Nicole Potter had been a server at the banquet. Now Nicole Potter was dead, struck down just as Matt Lambert had been, and Iris Gallagher was on the scene.

That's all the information Sam needed to reach a deadly conclusion: Nicole Potter saw something to incriminate Iris in Lambert's murder, she contacted Iris, asked to meet with her at the carousel, and that call signed her death warrant.

Iris's mouth opened. I gripped her arm. She glanced at me. I put a finger to my lips.

She took a quick breath. 'I decline to answer.'

'You can,' his voice was cold, 'decline to answer at the station.'

He made an abrupt gesture at a group of officers near a car. Detective Judy Weitz hurried toward us, the hot humid wind ruffling her brown hair. Her magenta top, though short-sleeved, looked hot. A poor color choice for July. Her long skirt was gray with vertical magenta stripes. I longed to take her shopping.

Sam turned a thumb toward Iris who, as always, appeared elegant and contained. 'Take her into custody. Handcuffs. Material witness. Book her. One phone call. Put her in a cell.'

When Detective Weitz snapped handcuffs on Iris's slender wrists, I knew Sam had no doubt about Iris's guilt. There was no need for handcuffs. Sam was bringing pressure to bear. You are accused. You are a prisoner. The detective and Iris walked toward a police car.

I felt utterly alone and desperate.

Iris was the only occupant of the cellblock in the basement of City Hall. Bed, toilet, cement floor, bars. The air was cool but stale. No nice whoosh of air conditioning. The bed sheets looked grainy. I don't know if it would have been better or worse if other cells were occupied. Even untenanted, the cells held memories of despair and fear.

Iris stood in the center of her small square of space. I joined her. She looked at me with a sad, grave face. 'Poor Nicole.' Her eyes were bright with unshed tears. 'That's what breaks my heart with some students. When I know where they came from and the effort they've made to try and start up a steep ladder. Nicole was a cast-off. How would you like to be a cast-off? Father disappeared years ago. Mother on street drugs. Had an aunt but she was mad at everything, her sister, her long-gone husband, at life, at Nicole. She was homeless at fourteen. Somehow she made it through high school. Smart. Worked all kinds of jobs, plucked chickens, emptied trash, cleaned toilets, got a scholarship here. Scholarships don't cover everything. Now she's dead.'

'I'm sorry.' And I was. Sorry for Nicole. Sorry she'd made a wrong choice that cost her life. We all make bad choices. But she didn't get a second chance to be the person she could have been. 'I know you are upset, but right now we have to focus on what we can do to save you.'

Those violet eyes widened. 'What do you mean?'

I talked fast. 'We don't have much time. They'll come for you pretty soon, take you upstairs to an interrogation room. Don't say anything, demand your lawyer. You are in a tight spot because you were present at the scene of Nicole's murder. How did you end up at White Deer Park?'

'Remember the call I received just before you left? The call was from Nicole, so of course I answered.'

'How did you know the call came from Nicole?'

'She's in my contact list.' She saw my puzzlement. 'Her number was on my contact list on the phone so her name came up on the screen.'

I feel fairly *au courant* with communication devices I encounter, but I'm a little fuzzy on the fine points.

Iris's voice was thin. 'She was whispering. I could barely hear her. Just scraps of words. Fast. Something about seeing someone and she needed a witness and please could I come to the carousel at White Deer. And then she said, "I have to go. Please come. Hurry." The call ended.'

'Are you sure the caller was Nicole?'

Iris slowly shook her head. 'A voice whispered. The call could have been made by someone else. But the call was made on her phone.'

'Would you be in her contact list?' I could learn fast when I had to.

'That's possible. And my number would be in her list of "recent calls" because I called her earlier today to arrange to meet at her apartment.' She looked frightened. 'Do you think the murderer called me. Why me?'

'Maybe it's as simple as your number being the most recent one that rang Nicole. The murderer called back to ask whoever answered to come to the carousel. The murderer didn't care who came, but it would be someone who had been in contact with Nicole and possibly the police would be suspicious of whoever found her body. Or perhaps Nicole told the murderer she'd spoken with you, that you'd been downstairs Thursday night too and Nicole could ask you to

confirm she was downstairs if she ever decided to go to the
police.'

Iris thought about the call and how she might have spoken
with a murderer. 'If she mentioned me, it was easy for the
murderer to call me because my number was right there at
the top of her recent-call list.'

Cell phones contained more powers than I knew. I thought
about a whisper and how either a man or a woman could hide
behind breathy indistinct speech. 'I don't think Nicole called.
Nicole met someone at the carousel. Now she's dead, killed
the same way as Matt. After she was dead, the killer got her
cell out of her pocket, called you, put the cell back in the
pocket. Nicole may have seen someone enter the room
where he was killed. Maybe she saw Lambert open the
door, greet someone. Maybe she waited at the end of the hall
in the shadows. She was mad. Maybe she planned to knock
and tell him his car had been broken into or he was wanted
at the president's table, there was some kind of problem.
Something, anything to cause him some discomfort. She didn't
care if she interrupted a meeting. She probably thought he
had time for somebody rich, but not for her. So she opened
the door and went in and found him. Nicole should have
called for help. Instead, she hurried upstairs.'

Iris shivered. 'I saw her going up the stairs. No wonder her
face looked so strange.'

Nicole must have been shaken by what she had seen.
But she must already have been thinking, fast and hard. 'As
she served, she looked around, spotted the person she saw
with Lambert. Somehow she found out who the person was.
A rich person. She couldn't be sure that person was the
murderer, but there was one way to find out. She called,
probably using a landline in an office at the college. She said
something like, "I saw you go into the Malone Room last
night. Meet me at the carousel in White River Park at four
o'clock. Bring five thousand in cash." Then she hung up.'

Iris walked the few feet to the bed, sank down. 'I'm afraid
that's what happened.' She sounded tired, sad. 'I'm afraid Nicole
lied to me. I asked if she talked to Matt. She gave me a derisive
smile, said, "If I was starving and Lambert was the last person

on the planet and had a key to the pantry, I'd look him up. Otherwise, no way."' Iris was grim. 'The police will find out I went to Nicole's apartment today, talked to her. They'll either think she saw me go into the Malone Room and was worried about not telling the police or that she tried to black-mail me. Either way, they'll say I met her at the park. Killed her.'

I wished I could tell Iris she was wrong. I couldn't.

A door opened at the end of the corridor. A rush of air conditioning from the hallway beyond stirred the lifeless air.

Iris's head jerked toward the bars. 'They're coming for me.'

'Quick. Did you see anyone in the park?'

'I wasn't looking. Not really. I was hurrying.'

Footsteps on concrete. It took less than a minute. A jailer at the lock. The cell door opened. 'This way, ma'am.'

A screen separated Iris Gallagher and Megan Wynn.

Our bodies tell the story of our lives at a precise moment.

Iris Gallagher's air of elegance was undiminished, a lacy white top, slim turquoise slacks, white sandals. She was still classically lovely with her fine-boned intelligent face, but her eyes held fear and the destabilizing understanding that she was no longer free, that she would soon return to a cell, a prisoner.

Megan Wynn brought with her an aura of success and happiness. She was not only a partner in Smith and Wynn, her own encounter with fear far behind her, she was also Mrs Blaine Smith and that union would buoy her forever.

Megan said carefully, 'I understand an old friend recommended me. Bailey Ruth?'

I smiled. Iris was in good hands. Megan would represent her with skill and passion, but it was up to me to save her.

Sam stood in the broiling late afternoon sunshine, watching as a tech held up a cell phone with metal pincers. 'Victim's prints. Some smeared.' His young face was pink with heat, too. 'Most recent call at six minutes after four p.m. to Iris Gallagher. Duration of call one minute, forty-three seconds. Phone was found in back left pocket of uniform pants. Right front trouser pocket contained driver's license, a five and four ones. Left trouser pocket held a comb, lipstick, and two wrapped peppermint candies.' The tech blinked.

Was a peppermint candy Nicole's treat during a long afternoon or evening at work?

'Yo.' The sudden shout came from the bank of the lake.

Sam turned to look, shaded his eyes.

'Found it.' The shout was exultant. A cluster of officers stood on the bank. Several held long large rakes in their hands. The ground was littered with an assortment of debris from the lake bottom: pop bottles, a hubcap, sodden plastic bags, tangled weeds, a tire, a rusted trumpet, a half-dozen beer cans. The shouter clutched the lower portion of a rake handle, held it high in triumph.

Sam strode across the dusty ground.

The homemade blackjack was a replica of the weapon which killed Matt Lambert, a man's black sock with the weighted bottom, the upper portion twisted in a knot that left enough length to grip and swing.

Sam was brisk. 'Good work, Daniels.' He turned to gesture, but two crime techs were already on their way. When they arrived, Sam pointed. 'Compare the weapon to the first one. See if the analysis is back from the lab. See if this one contains the same kind of sand. Check to see if the sand matched the sand here in the park. Get a search warrant for the Gallagher house and grounds. Look for sand in Gallagher's yard. Look for men's socks in her house.' He turned to Judy Weitz. 'What do you have on Gallagher's personal life?'

Judy held a small iPad, tapped several times. 'Widow. Husband a major killed in Afghanistan. She came here to teach. Originally from Scottsdale, Arizona. BA in English, University of Arizona. MA University of Oregon. As an army wife she lived at various posts and overseas. Came to Adelaide in 2012 from Fort Sill.'

A ping. Sam pulled out his cell. His jaw jutted. 'Chief Cobb.' His hot face looked hotter. 'We have a person of interest, Neva.' Sam jerked a thumb at the cell phone as Detective-Sergeant Hal Price, his face flushed in the heat, joined him. Hal gave him a sympathetic glance.

I understood his brusque tone. Adelaide's mayor would replace Sam with her own handpicked favorite, Howie Harris, in a heartbeat, given the chance. Her Honor was a big woman with a politician's plastic face, wide eyes, smile on demand, and bleating tone that reached the back of any hall. 'We've taken the suspect into custody . . . Yeah, I'll keep overtime to a minimum. I'll get everything to the DA Monday morning. I'll give you a heads-up. You can have a news conference . . . City Hall steps? It should work out fine.' He clicked off.

Hal was sardonic. 'She wants to campaign on how she keeps the streets safe, but don't have any detectives on overtime.'

Sam shrugged. 'We've got lots of overtime on this one from last night. But announcing the arrest on City Hall steps will put her in a good humor.'

By this time Monday morning, Iris would be publicly identified as a murder suspect.

I stood at the end of the pier, my hands gripping the top railing. I was close to panic. All the facts supported Sam. By now the police likely had a witness who saw Iris on the ground floor. Sam would unearth Iris's visit today to Nicole's apartment. Iris would refuse to answer questions. Sam would conclude she'd gone to see Nicole about Thursday night and met her at the park either promising to go with Nicole to the police to explain what they did downstairs, or that Iris agreed to bring money to the carousel but instead killed Nicole.

Sam would build a strong, powerful, persuasive case. Her arrest, possibly as a material witness, possibly on a murder charge, would be broadcast to the world Monday.

I had one slender hope.

ELEVEN

In the hallway outside Nicole's kitchenette, I Appeared as Officer Loy. I knocked.

The door opened in an instant. Jolene's round face was slack with shock. Tears welled in her blue eyes. 'I'm getting ready to go to my mom's house in Rolf. I can't stay here now.'

'Of course. I'm so sorry, Jolene.'

'I told the other officers, they just left, that a redheaded policewoman was talking to Nicole when I got here for lunch. They said there wasn't a redheaded policewoman.'

'New hires,' I murmured. I tapped my name badge, gold letters on black, Officer M. Loy.

'Oh. Well. I guess it's like everything now. Here today, gone tomorrow.' A gulp. 'Gone . . .' That brought a fresh rush of tears.

I moved forward. 'I'll just take a moment. I know those officers asked about Mrs Gallagher's visit.'

That reassured her. She nodded and held the door open.

I led the way to the sofa. 'Of course you told them all about Mrs Gallagher.'

She nodded. 'They said Mrs Gallagher found Nicole. They said Nicole was hit on her neck and was lying in the swan seats at the carousel.' Her lips quivered.

I wished I could take her in my arms, make the world better, strip away horror and fear and the realization that her friend no longer moved fast, spat like a cat if provoked, was fun and clever when she felt safe. I hoped Jolene would some day feel safe again.

I spoke quietly. 'Finding Nicole's body was a great shock for Mrs Gallagher. Nicole called, asked her to come to the park. But she arrived too late to save Nicole.'

Jolene's face changed. 'I guess those officers didn't know that's what happened. They asked what Nicole said about Mrs Gallagher. Nicole didn't say much, just that Mrs Gallagher was really nice. They asked if Nicole acted scared of her. I said that was silly. Nobody would be scared of Mrs Gallagher.'

'Did Nicole say anything to you about what happened when she went downstairs last night at Rose Bower?' I kept my voice matter of fact, as if this were a question like any other, just a search for information, no big deal. Inside I hoped with all my heart for something, anything, a pointer, a hint, an arrow that turned away from Iris.

Jolene wiped her sleeve against her damp cheeks. 'She . . .' Jolene stopped. Her gaze slid way from me.

I was swift. 'Anything Nicole said about that night can help us find the person who killed her.'

Jolene clasped her hands together. They twisted and turned. 'The officers asked who to notify. I told them there wasn't anybody. Just me. We were friends. We went all that way through school. Nicole's dad left when she was real little. Her mom took some of those drugs and didn't wake up. She had an old aunt but the aunt didn't like Nicole, turned her out when she was in junior high. My folks let her stay with us. We were all she had. She got jobs, even as a kid, worked all the way through school, insisted my mom take that money to help with food and stuff. She almost never got to buy anything new. We came here to go to school and all the time she worked. My folks could help me some. Nicole had to do everything on her own. So she was . . . like mad if she thought somebody wasn't treating her right. Not that she expected to be treated right. That's why she loved my mom and dad so much. They were good to her. She told my mom she'd make her proud. Nicole never gave up. She was determined to go to school and get a good job and have the things other people have. Like nice clothes. And a car. And a nice place to live.'

I knew why Jolene told me. She wanted me to understand why Nicole did what she did. 'What did Nicole say about last night?'

Now those blue eyes looked haunted. 'After you left, I said it must be awful to be some place where somebody got killed. Nicole said it was kind of neat to know something people would like to know. I asked what she meant. She said, "Good thing I don't give up. I went downstairs to tell that jerk" – she meant Mr Lambert – "what I thought of him. He was walking into the room with somebody. And maybe the police would be real interested to know who it was. I heard him say, "Glad you could come." The door shut. I didn't have much time. I had to get back upstairs. I decided to barge in, tell him what I thought of him. When I opened the door, I took one look and beat it. I can tell the police. Or not." I told her she might get in trouble. She said she wasn't the person in trouble, and she didn't owe anything to Matt Lambert.'

I once again looked from the terrace of the Kirk house toward the lake in White Deer Park and the cordoned area of the carousel. Uniformed technicians continued their painstaking investigation of the ride and the area around it. Police cars and vans still glinted in the late afternoon sun, including Sam's old brown sedan. An ambulance was parked next to the carousel, ready to carry Nicole Potter to the morgue after the last photo was taken, the last measurement made.

If I could grip Sam's arm, turn him toward the hillside where I stood, I'd tell him he had the case wrong. Nicole didn't choose White Deer Park for her meeting with a murderer. The murderer suggested the park when Nicole called, made her demand. Nicole surely realized she was threatening a dangerous person, but what could seem safer than a park late on a summer afternoon? When the call came from Nicole, the murderer suggested the park and the carousel. 'The carousel is close to a nice parking lot.' Nicole's childhood might not have included visits here or a ride atop the zebra or buffalo or a chance to lunge for the gold ring, but certainly she would know the location.

As realtors say, 'Location, location, location.'

'Sam,' if only he were here to hear me, 'the Kirk house is right above the park. The Kirks are big donors. The Kirks were at the dinner last night. Both of them left the table. How easy was it to persuade Nicole to come to the park? Easy, right? Parks in daytime are busy, safe. There are people about. Somebody fishing on the pier. Joggers. Mothers with strollers. Safe, right? But the murderer slipped down the hillside, moved through the grove of trees, watched for Nicole's arrival, then strolled to the carousel.'

There was no reply. There would be no reply. If I spoke these words to Sam, he'd point out the Kirks were not the only banquet guests last night who lived near the park. Iris Gallagher's home was on the other side of the park and access equally easy for her. I could make the point that Iris's home was modest, but he would counter that – to Nicole – Iris must seem quite well-to-do. I might insist Nicole surely wouldn't try to blackmail Iris. Iris was her champion. Iris tried to help her. Sam would shrug. Maybe Nicole tried blackmail, maybe she told Iris she didn't feel good about not telling the police she saw Iris downstairs. Whatever, Iris couldn't afford to let Nicole tell what she'd seen. I would insist Iris cared about the girl, wanted to help her have a better life. Sam would shrug again. Sure, Iris championed Nicole, but now Nicole was a threat. Murderers don't ignore threats.

I was convinced that someone from the house behind me selected the park, arrived at the carousel, met Nicole. A casual wave to suggest they sit on the seat with the swan sides, the tall swan sides that provided privacy. An agreement was reached. So much money. The murderer rose, nodding, then reached into a purse or pocket and, quickly as a forehand smash, yanked out the bludgeon, swung and struck the still-seated Nicole. And she died.

The house behind me.

I stood in the foyer and felt a chill. Did silent death move freely about this place? I suppose I expected to feel a sense of evil, as if a snake coiled in one corner, a rack of poisons loomed on a wall, or a miasma of gloom tainted the air. Instead I found myself in joyful surroundings, a hand-painted azure ceiling with gold crescents that evoked an early morning sky and fading moon. Borders on the cream floor tiles matched the bronze hands of the antique tall clock. The clock hands glittered in sunlight streaming through a side window.

I looked through an archway at an inviting living area with custom wallpaper of bright daisies on three walls. On one wall was a hand-painted scene of an old-fashioned bandstand festooned with Fourth of July bunting.

I knew that bandstand in the park across the street from City

Hall. I'd listened to 'Stars and Stripes Forever', shepherded my
kids through the ice-cream line, Bobby Mac one of the servers,
grinning when he saw us. Memories tugged at my heart.

As if he understood, a black Lab, stretched out on a tan linen
sofa, lifted his head and looked at me with a smile. Yes, Labs
smile. A Siamese cat stretched on a window valance, blue
eyes watching me. I walked into the room with its contented
creatures and lovely furnishings. A paperback book lay on a
side table. The cover featured a pyramid against an orange
sky framed by blue above and below, the title *Cry in the Night*
in white letters.

The dining room was formal, Chippendale table and chairs.
Crimson velvet drapes framed tall windows. The hue was
repeated below the chair rail. Above was a hand-painted
desert scene, brilliant with sunlight. One cabinet held delicate
Limoges china, another crystal wine glasses. Everything about
this house spoke of good taste and comfort and welcome.

Hundreds of volumes filled pine bookcases in a small library.
I drifted by the shelves. Chaucer. Shakespeare. Blake and
Cowper. Rabelais and Sartre. Dumas and Dickens. Colonial
American writers, eighteenth- and nineteenth-century novelists.
Poetry. Biographies.

I looked at an oil painting above the fireplace. A slender
blonde in her forties held firmly to the tiller of a sailboat. A
gusty wind tugged at her white shirt and slacks, rippled the
water with foaming crests. She wasn't quite pretty, but she
would always get a second glance, a high forehead and thin
nose, deep-set brilliantly blue eyes, high cheekbones and a
square chin, perhaps a Scandinavian heritage. The artist
captured her delight in speed, her determination to prevail
against the wind. Her smile was triumphant. Her posture said:
My boat, my day, my life. The painting exuded vigor, excitement, enthusiasm. She was the kind of person picked as a jury
foreman or CEO or committee chair – smart, quick, impatient.
I wondered if I would soon see her.

I regained the hall, walked through an archway into a family
room. Large screen television, pool table, comfortable leather
chairs and sofas, Navajo rugs on a planked floor. The drapes
were drawn against the late afternoon sun.

Where was everyone? All those cars parked in the drive certainly suggested people were in residence.

At the back of the house, I poked into the kitchen. A tall, heavyset woman with broad shoulders and strong hands added sprigs of mint to three tall tumblers on a serving tray. She picked up the tray, turned toward a door. She wore a plain white blouse, dark skirt, and sturdy leather shoes. I noted a small tattoo of a lizard on her left arm. She was big enough that she could have been formidable, but her face in repose was pleasant and good humored.

The kitchen was large with three doors. She walked to a back door, opened it. She held the screen with an elbow as she carefully took the three steps to the terrace. She carried the tray around a row of potted ferns and turned toward the inviting pool with its cascade of water at the far end.

A man stood with his back to the terrace, vigorously toweling. He blocked my view of two people seated at a table with an umbrella. A one-story white stucco building, decorated with murals of Adelaide landmarks, was likely a facility for swimmers. Some twenty feet beyond at the end of a flagstone path was a fairly large structure with floor-to-roof windows.

Once again I looked down the hillside into White Deer Park. Three police cars and two vans remained near the carousel. The ambulance was gone, and with it the body of a girl who had made a fatal mistake.

By the time I reached the table, the housekeeper had served the drinks and was on her way back to the house.

I recognized George Kirk and Melissa Kirk.

George's curly hair was plastered to his head. He gave a final swipe with a towel then plopped into a webbed chair. His bare chest was muscular. Water dripped from his yellow-and-blue-stripe swim trunks.

Aviator sunglasses hid Melissa's eyes. The bones in her face looked sharp and she moved restively in her chair. I didn't know their companion, a young woman, likely mid-twenties, with an exotic heart-shaped face. Shining auburn hair was pulled back in a chignon with one tendril loose near her cheek. Spectacular thick dark lashes fringed almond-shaped brown eyes, accentuating their rich chocolate depth. A char-treuse blouse emphasized the glow of dusky skin and was a contrast to a pale watermelon bubble skirt, quite short. Her bare legs were crossed.

George wadded the towel, dropped it to the concrete. His gaze traveled from an ankle, up a shapely leg to the hem of the bubble skirt, and down. His interest was intense and obvious.

I glanced at Melissa. Her lips quirked in a sardonic smile. Neither George nor the woman with shapely legs noticed.

It was as disconcerting as confidently stepping off a curb and plunging into an abyss. Melissa could not be George's wife. There are many responses to a husband's intense physical interest in another woman. Amusement is not one of them.

Melissa pushed back her seat. The metal leg tips scraped against cement, a sharp screech, startling both George and the woman next to him. George looked up irritably. 'Lis, why can't you ever relax?'

'We all have different interests.' Her tone was suggestive, a quick side glance at the other woman, whose face was suddenly blank. 'I'm going out to dinner. With a friend.' Emphasis on the noun. 'See you later.' She whirled and moved fast across blue tiles.

There was silence at the table until a door slammed shut on the terrace. The young woman abruptly rose. 'I've a port-folio to examine.' Her voice was soft and she spoke in slightly accented English. A French accent.

George was on his feet, looming over her. 'Don't go, Camille. Please.'

'I am meeting a student in my office at six and I must prepare.'

'On Friday night?' He sounded bewildered.

'I must see students when the time works for them.' She shook her head. 'I must do the right thing. I feel a duty.' She shot a glance at the large two-story structure with its bank of windows. And she too moved fast across the tiles, sandals making a quick snap of sound.

Again a door into the house closed.

George scowled. 'Damn.' His voice was low and hard. He

turned and strode toward the pool, dived into the water, scarcely making a ripple.

I stood there at a loss. I'd come into the house, a beautiful house that would always make visitors welcome, in search of a murderer. The sun was hot. The splash as George's body arched in a butterfly stroke was such an ordinary midsummer sound.

George swimming to burn off anger, Melissa saying somewhat defiantly that she was going out to dinner with a friend. An exotic young woman with a French accent. There were odd currents swirling around the three of them. But I had no sense of the sinister. I looked toward the house. Somewhere in this house, I hoped to find answers.

On the second floor, I heard a squeak. I followed the sound down a long hall with an Oriental rug runner. At the far end, a door was open. I looked inside. A faded blonde in her fifties with a pale face dominated by a large nose sat in a desk chair, staring at a computer screen. Light blue eyes, cold eyes, read swiftly. Her lips pursed in a frown. She shook her head, swiveled, reached for a cell phone. She swiped, tapped, held the cell to listen. 'Hey Fran, Alice Harrison. So you're working late, too. I thought I might catch you. I'll be glad when we get this wrapped up. I need the papers you filed re the Cosgrove land. Can you send that to me? . . . Great. Thanks.' She ended the call.

I studied her for a moment. Alice Harrison. She had been at the Kirk table at the banquet and she left the ballroom.

She glanced at her watch, turned back to the computer, clicked several times. The screen went dark. Her work day was likely done.

In the hallway, I saw closed doors on either side. Bedrooms. I moved through the nearest door.

Such a tidy room. Not too large. A guest bedroom perhaps. A red-and-blue patchwork quilt covered the bed, a brass bed with shiny finials. An end bench was covered in a lovely fabric with a rose pattern. There was room for a bedside table and lamp. A single bookcase rose on one side of a window, an easy chair upholstered in a quilted material on the other. Near the door were a small desk and a table. Several penciled sketches lay neatly in the center of the table, a raccoon's face, a hawk against a morning sky, a skinny pigtailed girl in a T and shorts playing hopscotch. I moved to the desk.

It didn't take long to find what I wanted. A red passport with the emblem of France on its cover yielded the name of Camille Elise Dubois. I picked up a blue leather diary, opened it and saw elegant flowing script. In French. My French extends to *s'il vous plaît* and *merci*. I returned the diary. If it became necessary, a search warrant and a French speaker could investigate Camille's thoughts.

I didn't want to think about the low odds that the police would ever confiscate the diary and read the contents. Yet I believed the killer came from this house, the killer was at the banquet, and so was Camille Dubois.

I imagined Sam shaking his head. So she was at the banquet, so she left the table. So?

A shower hissed through an open bathroom door. I sniffed a carnation scent. Music blared from an iPad, loud thrumming drums and a high screech with indistinguishable words. Quite irritating. My preference? The songs of the forties and fifties. As in 1940, 1950. On my missions I hear the twang of steel guitars popular today. Trust me, earthly creatures, you don't know music until you hear Nat King Cole croon 'It's Only a Paper Moon' or Frank Sinatra plea for 'Luck Be a Lady Tonight' or Vera Lynn's heartbreaking wartime ballad 'We'll Meet Again'.

This room, to put it kindly, looked lived in. Clothes strewn on chairs, an overflowing basket of tissues next to a cosmetic-laden vanity, a bolster propped against an easy chair. A straw hat was perched atop one end of the bolster. A window seat served as a repository for one shoe, a sack of taffy, an iPad, a jangle of beaded bracelets, and an oversize cloth purse with wooden handles.

I opened the purse. The driver's license, though current, was from California. Melissa's hair was much longer in the photo and the name was Melissa Kirk Fulton. The street address was in San Diego.

*   *   *

I Appeared in a generic blue police uniform and knocked on the door of a stucco house.

A tall heavyset man opened the door. His Hawaiian shirt was wrinkled. Baggy Bermuda shorts hung near his knees. Shower shoes exposed hairy toes. He frowned. 'Yeah?'

'I'm looking for Melissa Fulton.'

'She doesn't live here anymore.' The door started to close.

'Sir, it's urgent that I contact her.'

He shrugged. 'Try her brother. George Kirk. Adelaide, Oklahoma.'

The door shut.

George's room was a thoroughly masculine enclave. It was much more than simply a room. There was a living area, large screen television, two red leather sofas, a wet bar. I lifted a cut-glass decanter, removed the stopper, sniffed. Gin. The next was rum. The third, Scotch. The refrigerator was stocked with lemons, bitters, sodas. The mini-freezer held two pints of Häagen-Dazs, vanilla and strawberry. The dark cherry bedroom furniture was massive, queen-size bed, dresser, chest. Unlike his sister's room, there was no disarray. A big closet held mostly sports clothes, only two suits, both dark. Shoes were arranged on shelves.

I opened the top dresser drawer, plenty of socks. I picked up a pair, neatly rolled, of black dress socks. Was one pair missing? There would be no way of knowing. The crime lab could determine if the socks filled with sand and made deadly were the same brand as these.

I came into the house looking for a murderer. I came, too, seeking a person Matt Lambert could pressure for a big sum of money. It was like watching the needle of a compass swing to true north. George Kirk was the one with money.

I shivered, the kind of shiver that shakes you when you are desperate and afraid. This lovely house with a handsome room for a handsome man offered nothing that linked him or any of the other occupants to the murders of Matt Lambert and Nicole Potter.

When in need, think of a saint. Saint Anthony helps find something lost. I remembered the childhood rhyme, *Tony, Tony, come around, Something's lost that must be found.* St Anthony, help me. I've lost my way. This request might be a stretch for him, though I remembered the time I despaired of finding my car keys and I had ten minutes to get to the train station to pick up a company president the Chamber wanted to wine and dine in hopes of landing a factory. I made my plea and the keys suddenly rolled off the mantel and landed on the tile hearth with a musical clink sweet as an orchestra's overture. I reached the station in time and the pottery factory came to town, bringing 112 new jobs.

I squeezed my eyes shut, turned in a circle just for good measure, opened them. Ahead, just to the left of the wet bar, was a door. It was as if an unseen hand gently propelled me to that door. I clutched the knob, turned. The door opened to a very fine room, a feminine room.

I was enchanted by the room, a woman's retreat just as the room behind me was a man's retreat. Pale lemon walls, lime drapes, white French provincial furniture, walls adorned with framed paintings. The paintings were splashes of color, stripes, whirls, blocks, vivid, arresting, vibrant. I suppose I am partial to specifics. I like precise speech, art-deco architecture, geometrical shapes, Edward Hopper paintings, but the brightly colored paintings evoked sun-spangled days, huge waves curling to break, glittering headlights in the rain.

I studied the paintings until the quietness of the room touched me, the sense of emptiness, a feeling that this door rarely opened, that footsteps rarely sounded on the wooden floor. The room should be a setting for an interesting woman, but heavy stillness indicated disuse. No book rested on the bedside table, no magazine lay open on a coffee table in front of the satin-upholstered love seat. The vanity surface was bare. There was no summer sweater carelessly flung on a chair.

Quite near was a white bookcase filled with photographs. I recognized the woman on the sailboat. So many pictures. Riding a chestnut mare. Playing tennis. In one photo, she arched in an overhead smash, features set in concentration. Several in evening dress, one on the arm of George, both looking at ease, she with a regal aura, he the handsome courtier. In a much younger photo, she cradled a baby with a pink bow in sparse hair. Standing at a dais. Hiking on a mountain trail.

I looked past the bookcase into the large room. Stillness, stillness.

I closed the connecting door to George's room behind me, moved slowly across the planked flooring. I walked to a closet. The rods held nothing. No hangers. No clothes. The shelving for shoes was bare.

I crossed to a lovely white desk. Ebony Nefertiti bookends braced a row of blue leather books, likely diaries. I opened a drawer. Stationery. I picked up a sheet . . .

The hall door opened.

I dropped the sheet of stationery into the drawer, eased it shut. The door panel screened the visitor from my view. And then I looked across the room at an ornate ormolu-framed wall mirror that reflected the image of Camille Dubois, auburn hair drawn back in a chignon, still that tendril across one cheek. She looked young and appealing in the chartreuse blouse and pale watermelon bubble skirt.

The image was for an instant only. She walked into the room leaving the door to the hall open. She carried a flattish rectangle bundled in thick butcher paper. She moved without hesitation to the wall of paintings. She pulled to loosen tape, carefully removed the protective wrapping. In a moment, the painting was hung in an empty space.

She smoothed and folded the wrapping, turned and, carrying the paper, crossed the room to the open door to the hall.

I looked again at the ormolu mirror and watched the door close behind her.

Like words flashing on a screen, I remembered the message I recreated from the scraps that remained from the square of paper in Lambert's billfold:

> The door opened and I saw Ev— (Eva, Evangeline, Eve, Evelyn, Evita) take the tray. I watched the reflection in the mirror. The glass was full. She put the tray on the table. She didn't add anything to the glass and drank all of it. This occurred March . . .
>
> Matthew Lambert

On a March day, Matt Lambert stood here and looked into
the ormolu mirror and watched the hall door open. He saw the
reflection of someone bringing a tray with a full glass to
the room's occupant.

I whirled and hurried to the white desk. I pulled out the
drawer, picked up a piece of stationery.

> Evelyn Murray Kirk
> 914 Comanche Avenue
> Adelaide, OK 74820

Someone brought Evelyn a glass, a full glass, a glass she drank
without adding anything to its contents. Why did Matt Lambert
carry a note with that information?

Who was Evelyn Murray Kirk?

I walked to the desk, reached for the last of the blue leather
books. Her initials were embossed in gold leaf on the cover.
I flipped to March.

The last entry was on Monday 19 March. Bold back-slanted
writing, overlarge; a pen with a thick nib. *Tahiti definite.*

It took only a few pages to realize this was not a personal
journal, that the woman who penned these words likely
dismissed as indulgent the practice of recording personal
emotions. These entries reflected a full life of sports, travel,
committees, finances, charitable giving. I soon figured out
titles in block letters referred to paintings followed by sums,
I assumed the amount for which they sold. The information
was factual. not personal. She played doubles every Wednesday.
She and her partner usually won, often 6–2, 6–0. On the rare
occasions of a loss, perhaps a comment: Told Lisbeth to get
her racket restrung. Or, Iola double-faulted four times.

I rather thought I was glad I wasn't Iola.

I took away from the jottings a sense of a businesslike
woman – an artist? – who was hugely generous to her community and enjoyed an active social life, dinners, luncheons, and
coffees were listed. I also had a sense of an imperious woman
who expected excellent effort from everyone around her. The
only personal comments were mentions of letters from her
daughter. *All going well for Madeleine and Jimmy. Madeleine*

and Jimmy in Paris this weekend. Madeleine will be home over the Fourth. And once, it tugged at my heart, *Looking forward to seeing Madeleine.* I replaced the appointment book. I wouldn't describe it as a journal.

The stillness of the room made me feel cold. This was Evelyn Kirk's room. Now the room was empty. The last entry in the blue leather book was 19 March. On a March day someone brought a tray with a full glass: 20 March.

TWELVE

I Appeared in the shadow of a magnolia outside the public library. I chose a simple wardrobe, white cotton blouse, peach slacks, plain flats. This was no time to think about style. I moved fast, hurrying up the steps. I scarcely wanted to take time to breathe, much less Appear, but it would be much more distracting if I settled at a library computer unseen and someone noticed a mouse moving on its own. I sat at a monitor on the end of a row.

I entered the website for the *Gazette*, typed Evelyn Kirk March, clicked. I stared at a three-column headline below the fold on Page One:

GODDARD BENEFACTOR EVELYN KIRK DIES AT HOME

There was a photograph: sleek blonde hair, an intelligent face, features not quite regular, eyes that looked, watched, observed. I recognized the woman in the painting above the fireplace in the Kirk house, the woman who steered a sailboat on a windy day taking pleasure in mastery, exhilarated by challenge.

The news story was a tribute to an accomplished life cut unexpectedly short by a heart attack.

Evelyn Murray Johnson Kirk, 47, died unexpectedly at her home Tuesday. A family spokesman said Kirk had been diagnosed with atrial fibrillation earlier this month and was on medication. She complained of fatigue early in the afternoon and retired for a nap. She was found unresponsive at shortly after four p.m. by the family housekeeper Bess Hampton.

A family spokesman reported that her physician, Dr Kenneth Thomas, said she suffered a myocardial infarction. Cardiopulmonary resuscitation was unsuccessful.

Evelyn Marie Murray was the only child of the late

Wilhelm Murray and Katherine James Murray. She was the great-granddaughter of early day Pontotoc County oil baron Gustav Murray.

Gustav Murray was a fabled name in Pontotoc County. Everything he touched turned to gold, black gushers in the Fitts Field, a ten-thousand-acre ranch famed for its Hereford cattle, a chain of whatever-you-need-we-have-it stores that were gobbled up by a national conglomerate in the 1980s.

Kirk attended the University of Oklahoma and received a BFA. She was a gifted artist and was often featured in galleries in Scottsdale and Los Angeles. She was active at St Mildred's Episcopal Church where she served on the vestry. Kirk was a generous donor to many Adelaide charities and to Goddard College. The softball field is named in Kirk's honor.

Kirk received her master's degree in fine art from Southern Methodist University. She spent several years at Marlboro Gallery in Pasadena. She was also a film enthusiast. Her former husband, director Holton Cramer, credited her as the inspiration for *Dare Me Now*, his Golden Globe-winning adventure film. They divorced in 2014.

Kirk returned to Adelaide and opened Blue Sky, a gallery which drew visitors from around the world with an eclectic collection of southwestern art, California impressionism, and New England realism. Kirk's paintings featured masses of bright color that one critic described as 'formless with form'.

Eugenia Pierson, director of the Adelaide Chamber of Commerce, described Kirk as brilliant, engaging, and inspiring. 'Her energy level was phenomenal. She moved fast, thought fast, expected everyone to do the same. She believed promises made should be kept.'

A friend since first grade at Hayes Elementary, Betty Wilson said Kirk was intensely competitive but everyone loved her anyway. She added, with a smile, 'There was never a dull moment around Evelyn.'

Holton Cramer recalled, 'She was a fierce friend.'

The library thoughtfully provided scratch paper and pencils by each terminal. I wrote down the names of Bess Hampton and Betty Wilson. After a moment's thought, I added Holton Cramer, ex-husband, 'A fierce friend.'

> Kirk was a first-rate tennis player and a singles champion in the Missouri Valley. It was through tennis that she met her second husband, George Kirk, when he became the tennis pro at the Adelaide Country Club.
>
> Kirk is survived by her husband, George of the home, and her daughter, Madeleine Cramer Timmons (James) of Lisbon, Portugal, and a cousin Alice Harrison.
>
> Services are pending at St Mildred's Episcopal Church. The family suggests donations to a favorite charity in lieu of flowers.

Now I knew the identity of the donor in the Kirk family. Not George. Not Melissa. The money belonged to Evelyn Kirk, the kind of wealth that flowed from early oil gushers, wealth that could provide largesse to a college, to a town, to members of her family. Likely the Outreach Office automatically invited George Kirk to the banquet and he included his sister, the visiting artist, and Evelyn's cousin in the guest list.

I would find out who now controlled her fortune. Surely a good portion went to her daughter. But George was in the home, George and his sister, Melissa, and Camille Dubois and Evelyn's cousin/secretary Alice Harrison. All four attended the banquet. All four left the table during the critical time. Any one of them could have been the person Matt Lambert saw in the mirror. George likely could arrange a substantial gift to the college. The others? One of them could have suggested a memorial to Evelyn and George might have easily been persuaded to provide a gift in her honor.

Which of those four was in the house on the cool March day – I looked at the dateline, Tuesday 20 March – when Evelyn died?

I looked up addresses for Bess Hampton and Betty Wilson. The high school yearbook offered a lovely photo of Evelyn's daughter, Madeleine. Unlike her mother, she was dark-haired and petite. Her wedding last year at St Mildred's received almost a full page of coverage in the *Gazette*. Madeleine was also an SMU graduate in fine arts. Her husband received his master's degree in business. There was a cute picture of them standing in a mock cockpit door with a banner reading, Lisbon Bound.

A single chime indicated the library would close in fifteen minutes. I searched for mentions of George Kirk. There were five, the announcement four years before Evelyn's death that George Kirk had been named head tennis pro at the country club, expansive coverage on the society page of Evelyn's wedding to George in an outdoor ceremony in the amphitheater at White Deer Park. I added the name of the matron of honor, Virginia Barrett, to the scratch paper. George was mentioned in the story about his successor at the country club and George was listed as the surviving spouse in the news story and also in the formal obituary.

I tried Alice Harrison, found nothing.

Camille Dubois:

FRENCH ARTIST ACCEPTS POST AT GODDARD

The library lights flickered, last alert before closing. I read fast. In January, the head of Goddard's fine arts department announced the arrival of Camille Dubois, artist in residence for the spring–fall semesters. 'This is an extraordinary opportunity for our students to learn from an accomplished French artist thanks to Goddard patron Evelyn Kirk.'

There was a list of Camille's academic accomplishments, awards won by her paintings, and a brief biography, a native of Nancy, a graduate of a prestigious art academy in Paris. The article was accompanied by photographs of several of her paintings. I recognized one quite similar to the hawk against a morning sky. There was a quote from Camille, 'I am very grateful to Mrs Kirk for making my visit to the United States possible and for providing a connection to this delightful college in such a lovely community. I look forward to working with students and sharing our joy in creating art.'

Evelyn Kirk not only sponsored a young artist at the college, she provided her with a place to live. I remembered George's hot gaze from ankle to hemline. Camille arrived in January. Evelyn died in March.

Melissa found her brother's pursuit of his guest amusing. Did George become enamored of Camille soon after her arrival? What was his attitude in March? What was Camille's response? There was an undercurrent between George and Camille that puzzled me. She still lived in Evelyn Kirk's house. No, now the house belonged to George Kirk. Of course the understanding when Camille arrived in Adelaide was that housing was provided. Camille was the guest of Evelyn Kirk. But Camille remained in the house after Evelyn's death.

Evelyn's bedroom was absolutely still. The hall door was closed. Someone brought a tray to Evelyn with a full glass which she drank without adding anything. I understood Matt Lambert's notation now. Matt Lambert looked in a mirror and saw Murder. There could be no other explanation for the note he wrote and secreted in his billfold.

Matt watched a reflection in the mirror in Evelyn's bedroom in March. This was July. The folded square of paper I found in his billfold was fresh. A square of paper tucked in with the bills for several months would be creased, perhaps smudged. Matt made the notation recently and Wednesday he walked near the trellis on the terrace and spoke to someone, demanding a gift to the college.

I was confident he called on a burner phone since there was no record of a call at that time on his cell phone. He was well aware that he was committing extortion, even if for a worthy cause, and wanted no link to his own phone. He called on a burner phone and insisted the listener come to the banquet with the promise of a big donation.

How did he make a connection between the glass he glimpsed in the mirror and Evelyn's death?

I promised Sam I would not disturb the residents of the Kirk house, but I had no compunction about Appearing on Joyce Lambert's front porch as Officer Loy. I rang the bell.

A kindly faced woman in her fifties with a fluff of white hair opened the door.

'Ma'am, Mrs Lambert has been very helpful to the investigation into her husband's death. We are hopeful she can give us some information about his activities in the week before his death. I promise not to keep her very long.'

My obvious deference was effective and in a moment I was in the small office to one side of the foyer. Joyce Lambert looked smaller in her clothes and her shoulders slumped. She settled on a sofa, gestured toward an easy chair for me. There was a flicker of fear in her eyes.

I saw no reason not to reassure her. I was brisk. 'We very much appreciate your helpfulness. Before I ask a few questions, as a matter of form, I want to inform you that you and your son are both accounted for during the time the crime was committed and have been eliminated from the investigation.'

She managed to keep her face quiescent, but her eyes closed briefly. When they opened, she exhaled a tightly held breath. 'I appreciate everything the police are doing. I wish I could help, but I told the other officers, I don't know anyone who was angry with Matt.'

'This is a matter of information, ma'am. Did your husband discuss with you the name of the donor he intended to honor at the banquet?'

She shook her head. 'He wanted the presentation to be a surprise. He was excited Thursday night.' Her voice was shaky as she remembered a man full of vigor, full of success, full of life. 'He told me if everything worked out, there would be a tremendous gift to the college and, of course, that was a triumph for him. He loved bringing in big donations.' She frowned. 'He said he was going down to check on some things. I thought it was about the gift, but I suppose not.'

'One day this past week, did your husband appear to have an air,' I tried to pick the right words, 'of a man who has discovered something amazing, something unexpected?'

Her pale blue eyes widened. 'How did you know?'

'We have reason to believe he obtained information that put him in danger.' Seeing Murder in a mirror put him on a path to doom. 'What day did you become aware of this?'

'Wednesday.' She spoke as if the word were strange, the gulf between that ordinary day and a Saturday consumed with funeral plans.

'Do you know what Mr Lambert did on Wednesday?'

Where did he find a link between a glass on a tray and Evelyn's death?

'He went to the office that morning as usual. I don't think anything happened there because he came home for lunch and he was his usual self. He told me he really enjoyed the slice of upside-down cake.' Her voice quivered.

'That afternoon?'

Joyce Lambert's cheeks had a faint flush, the first color I'd seen. She leaned forward, drawn into the search for answers, sensing perhaps that she might hold a key to her husband's death. 'Matt played golf on Wednesdays. It was the usual Wednesday when he left, but when he came home he was excited, looking like his thoughts were racing at a mile a minute.' She stared at me with rounded eyes.

'Who did he play golf with?'

'Ken Thomas.'

I made the connection. 'Dr Thomas?' Evelyn Kirk's physician. The man who pronounced her dead.

Sam's office was dim. It was about half past seven. Midsummer sunlight still spilled through his windows, affording enough light for me to see. I'd never before felt like an interloper. Was Officer Loy permanently retired from the Adelaide police? I couldn't leave a chalk message on the blackboard. Sam would dismiss any offering as another attempt to protect Iris Gallagher.

I looked at Sam's neat desktop and felt another sweep of despair. He was old-fashioned. He worked on legal pads, used pen and paper to make notes on cases. Later he created electronic files, but he started with a legal pad. There were no legal pads stacked to one side of the desktop. I sighed. He'd likely put them in a drawer, confident his work was done on the Lambert case.

I opened the top right drawer. Three legal pads lay on top of some folders. I picked up the first pad, found an hour-by-hour account of the investigation since receiving a nine-one-one call at twelve minutes after seven Thursday evening. I flipped pages. Surely somewhere in here – ah, a notation that Lambert

Folder 2 contained the register of guests at the banquet, their location during the critical time period, photos and addresses.

I was working as fast as I could, aware that minutes slipped into hours and hours into days. Monday morning at ten a.m. the mayor would greet the press on the steps of City Hall and revel in announcing the arrest of Iris Gallagher either as a material witness or on charges of first-degree murder in the homicides of Matthew Lambert and Nicole Potter.

Megan Wynn would defend Iris, stand with her, try to arrange bail, but Megan was not a detective.

Well, you aren't a detective either.

Exhaustion and pressure made me vulnerable. I tried to push away the terrible feeling that I couldn't manage the task ahead. Always before I'd been part of a team. I could count on Chief Cobb and Detective Sergeant Price to investigate when I pointed the way.

Not now.

Who wanted Evelyn Kirk dead?

Who was in the house the day she died?

What was Evelyn's relationship with her husband, her sister-in-law, her cousin, and the French artist?

How could a demand for an autopsy receive attention?

Most pressing of all, immediate action was necessary if there were to be any hope of casting doubt on the official conclusion that Iris Gallagher met Nicole, spoke with her, killed her.

I'd swung aboard the Rescue Express, certain I was one Heavenly answer to any challenge. Now I was alone in Sam Cobb's office, alone and close to panic at the task ahead of me. There was so much to find out, so little time.

Coal smoke swirled. Iron wheels clacked on steel rails. Whooo. Whooo. I tried to stand straight, head up, shoulders back. I'm not quite certain if Wiggins sees me even though I'm not visible, or if he is simply so closely attuned to his emissaries that he finds us wherever we are. Just in case, I was determined to go out in style. I chose a floral paisley georgette blouse with bodice pleats that flared below the waist and bell-bottom white linen trousers and tall, very tall, red heels that matched the background of the top.

I felt the warmth of his hand on my shoulder. 'Now, now.'

I heard the helpless tone of a man dealing with an emotionally distraught woman.

Tears spilled down my cheeks. 'She's awfully nice really. Iris, I mean. And she's going to be charged with murder Monday; and even if someday things are worked out, it's awful to be in jail and she's all alone in that cell and I thought I was up to anything, that I was a super emissary, the best ever, and here I am and I'm a mess. That's what happens when you think you're important. Mama always told us kids, "A nose stuck in the air makes it hard to see ahead and that's when you stub your toe and fall flat on your face." And that's what's happened to me. I thought I was special. I'm not.'

A handkerchief was thrust into my hand. I swiped at my cheeks.

'Of course you thought you were special.' Wiggins's deep voice was reassuring. 'Everyone is special. You are special and you will find a way.'

I thought of all the tasks that needed to be done. 'I need help.'

'That's the crux.' He sounded positive.

For a moment, I was impatient. Of course not having help was the crux. 'I can't save Iris by myself.'

A waiting silence. Waiting, but not cold, a silence of warmth, as though a soft afghan wrapped me in its folds.

I didn't understand what Wiggins expected of me. Didn't he understand the situation? On previous missions I could count on Sam Cobb to help me.

Help . . .

As Mama told us kids, 'If you don't ask, no one can say yes.'

Ask? Suddenly I was buoyed. It was like eating a Baby Ruth and bursting with energy. It was like finding a four-leaf clover and feeling the sun on my back. It was like turning a corner and seeing an old friend whose smile touched my heart.

'Oh, Wiggins, thank you.' Of course I could find help. All I had to do was ask. But getting help was only a beginning. There was another daunting task ahead. First and foremost Sam Cobb must be informed that Evelyn Kirk was murdered. Sam must be forced to act. He would dismiss a chalkboard message from Officer Loy. A telephone call? Sam knew my voice. Not even a whisper would likely fool him. How could Sam be persuaded that Evelyn was murdered?

'Good to see you thinking, Bailey Ruth. You will find a way to do what needs to be done.' Wiggins's deep voice was warm, encouraging.

Phone call . . . whisper . . . not a whisper . . . voice . . . It was as if a marquee blossomed with a thousand lights. Oh, yes, there might be a way, oh yes indeed.

It took me a moment to realize there was no more coal smoke and the sounds of wheels rolling on steel was fading, fading, gone.

I was as exhilarated as if fireworks exploded in my mind, but the brightness was from ideas: what I could do and what I could accomplish with confederates. I did have some qualms. If things went wrong . . .

Well, I'd simply have to make sure nothing went wrong.

I strode to Sam's desk. I reached for his Rolodex. I know the very term is meaningless in the digital world, but Sam, bless his heart, continues to keep information as he always has. I found the number I needed.

I was ready to execute my plan.

The corridor lights in the cellblock were dimmed, the bright glare of day diminished for sleep. Iris was not asleep. She lay on the bed, eyes wide, staring at the ceiling. I didn't know what she saw. Perhaps I didn't want to know.

'Will Megan request bail?'

She sat up, swung her legs over the side of the bed. Her gaze flicked toward me. 'I suppose she will.' She sounded weary. 'I doubt I can afford it.'

There are bail bonds.'

'I know. My young lawyer,' her face moved in a slight smile, 'treated me with great respect. I rather think because of you. She will do her best. There was the interrogation, that big man looking grim, the handsome detective sergeant acting like the good cop. None of it mattered. At Megan's instruction,

I declined to answer. Many times. Somehow she arranged for
Gage to see me.' A flicker of those violet eyes. Blinking back
tears because she foresaw separation from her daughter for
years and years? 'Gage brought an afghan. In case the cell
was cold.' Iris gestured at a beige-and-blue afghan at the foot
of the bed. 'They let me keep it.'

I admired her coolness. I'm afraid if I were in her situation I would immediately demand to know what was being
done, if there were progress, when I might be released. Instead
she gazed at me with those intelligent, grave violet eyes and
waited for me to speak.

'Did you know Evelyn Kirk?'

To Iris the question must have seemed utterly unrelated to
her, but she answered politely. 'To speak to. Not beyond that.
She seemed like a very fine person. Why?'

I told her everything. '. . . and so I have to have help. I'm
going to ask Gage and Robert to—'

'No.' Now she was alive in every way, a mother sensing
danger to her child. 'Absolutely not. I don't want her involved.
Someone is very dangerous. You're fine. You can disappear.
Gage can't.'

'Let me finish. I need their help tomorrow, but they'll have
no contact with anyone in Evelyn Kirk's house or anyone who
was at the Kirk table at the banquet.'

She regarded me steadily. 'What do you want them to do?'

I explained. In detail.

Iris gave a little sigh of relief, of acquiescence. 'That seems
reasonable. Safe. They'll be together?'

'Yes.'

'At all times?' Her stare was intense.

'Yes.'

'All right.' A pause. 'I see no harm. Or danger.' Another
slight smile. 'It's a very long shot.'

'A shot worth taking. I'll go see them now, make the arrangements. But Gage strikes me as nobody's fool. She might be
suspicious of a stranger. Can you give me something to tell
her that will assure her I've spoken with you?'

'Tell her you know Aunt Winnie's secret for a successful
Kool-Aid stand.'

I listened, smiled. Now I had everything I needed. And, of course, I didn't discuss with Iris what I planned for Gage to do tonight.

Gage's face, a young version of her mother's elegant features, looked haunted, hunted, and desperate. She sat stiffly on the decrepit green sofa in Robert's apartment. 'We have to do something.'

Robert would gladly have stormed a barricade for her, carried her away from raging flood waters, flung himself in the way of an attacking bear.

'Yeah. I wish we could do something.' He hunched his shoulders, cracked the knuckles of his tightly clasped hands, made miserable by his inability to ease her despair. 'But Megan Wynn's a good lawyer. She'll take care of your mom. Maybe we can talk to the police chief tomorrow.'

'Talk won't do any good. We have to do something.' Gage's voice quivered.

I said a silent yee-hah. Gage wanted to do something. I was glad to help. Back in the hallway, I took an instant before I Appeared. It was important to present myself as appealing and reassuring. I chose a dark blue silk blouse with a boat neck, mist gray linen trousers, and navy flats. As I lifted my hand to knock, I added a double strand pearl necklace and pearl buckles to the shoes. Real pearls have a presence. They indicate wealth, good taste, and respectability.

I knocked. The door swung in. Robert's expression was not welcoming. I would go so far as to say he looked downright hostile. He looked, in fact, as if he beheld something that was a cross between a tarantula and an evil sprite.

Before the door could close, I slipped past him, talking as I moved. 'Oh Gage, I'm sure you're Gage, so sorry we've not met before. But your mother was sure you would be here. Not a good night to be alone in a dorm. And Robert,' I turned to favor him with an approving smile despite his glower, 'is a fine young man. Glad to do everything he can to help you and Iris at this difficult time.' I was across the room and sitting beside Gage. 'I just left your mother—'

Gage's face lit up. 'Is Mom home? Why didn't she call?

Didn't they give her back her cell phone?' She started to
get up.

I put a restraining hand on her arm, a young, thin arm. 'Oh,
I wish that were so. I received special dispensation to speak
with her at the jail. It helps to have friends in high places.'

Robert looked befuddled. 'Special dispensation? Isn't that
like something religious?'

If all worked out and Gage eventually became Mrs Robert
Blair, Iris would surely have to be patient with Robert's literal
mindset.

'Not quite that high. In any event, I'm here to ask you and
Robert to do some investigating to help your mom. She
told me that she arrived at the park this afternoon and hurried
straight to the carousel and immediately found Nicole Potter's
body. At that instant, she called nine-one-one. If we can
find a witness who saw her park and walk to the carousel and
immediately use her cell phone, it will be some proof that
Nicole was dead when she arrived and that your mother's
actions didn't afford enough time for her to climb aboard the
carousel, speak with Nicole, strike her down, and hurry to
the lake to toss away the weapon.'

Robert stood a little to one side of the sofa, hands jammed
in the pockets of ratty jeans. 'Possible witness tampering.' He
sounded gloomy.

Gage glanced from him to me. Her eyes narrowed. 'I don't
want to do anything to mess things up for Mom. I don't know
you.'

I gave her a brilliant smile. 'I'm Bailey Ruth Raeburn and
of course your mom has many friends from Fort Sill.' Two
true statements. 'I happen to be in town and I heard she was
in trouble.' I talked fast before Robert, who was still frowning,
demanded to know how I found out about her arrest. The
literal of the world have a passion for connecting dots. I can
be creative, but even I have my limits. ESP? A text? Why
me? As Robert's mouth opened, I moved to forestall him.
'Your mom absolutely approves of my plan. And to confirm
I spoke with her, she told me Aunt Winnie's secret to success
at a Kool-Aid stand.'

Gage waited.

'Two black licorice strips with each glass of Kool-Aid.'

Gage's face lit up. 'You did talk to Mom. Is she OK? How does she look? What did she say?'

'You know your mom. Unflappable. She said you aren't to worry, she's fine.' Actually, Iris said, 'Make sure she's with Robert. She'll have him to hold to if I'm charged.'

'What's your plan?' Robert still stood, head lowered, as if he watched the approach of an anaconda.

'I have two tasks for you. One tomorrow. One tonight. Tomorrow I want you and Gage to arrive at White Deer Park by, oh, six a.m. Because it's Saturday.'

I saw Robert trying to figure out why Saturday required arrival at an obscenely early hour.

'On Fridays people work. Some of those who were in the park late in the afternoon can go much earlier on Saturday to jog or walk or take the dogs. I want you to spend the day there. Talk to every person who comes to the park. Say you're seeking Adelaide's Most Observant Citizen. If you were in the park yesterday between four and five, who did you see, where, when, for how long, what did they do? Make up a contest. Say it's a fun competition for the leadership class at Goddard. Hand out prizes. Fill a cooler with popsicles. Take a picture of each person with their popsicle and record the interview on your phone.'

Robert looked glum. 'False representation.'

Gage was tart. 'We aren't defrauding anybody. Actually we'll hand out free popsicles. I can see,' her eyes were shining, 'how this may make everything OK for Mom. This is great.'

Robert still looked glum. His mop of tawny hair, big brown eyes, and air of frustrated willingness to do whatever he could for Gage held great appeal, but I hoped his mouth didn't get a permanent downward slant.

Gage clapped her hands together. 'OK, that's tomorrow. What are we doing tonight?'

The less Robert knew about tonight the better. I stood up. 'I have a few things to check before we set out. Try to get a little rest, maybe a good snack. I'll be back at two a.m.'

Robert didn't look glum. He looked horrified. 'Two a.m.?' His mother must have told him ghoulies and ghosts were abroad at that hour. I can't speak for ghoulies and I surely prefer not to encounter them, but one ghost assuredly would be very busy then.

I gave him an encouraging smile as I hurried toward the door. 'Just a few preparations to make. Be out in front in Robert's car at two a.m. Wear dark clothes.'

THIRTEEN

José Altuve, all five feet six inches of him, whipped his bat and the ball sailed over the Crawford boxes, clearing the bases. As Astros players loped around the base pads, George Kirk upended a heavy tumbler, watched the huge screen, his face set in grim, hard lines. Baseball was not big on his mind this night.

Upstairs, I stood inside Melissa Kirk's dark bedroom, listened. Utter silence. I flicked the light. The bed was unoccupied. The disarray, scattered clothes, overflowing wastebasket, made the room cheerless, uninviting. Dinner out had stretched into a late hour.

Camille sat in an easy chair in her room, a sketchpad in her lap. The drawing captured the energy and movement in the partial figure of a cat crouched to spring. Instead of a nightgown, she wore shorty pjs, a candy-stripe top, pink shorts. I liked her house shoes, cerise with a feathery border. Her heart-shaped face was tinged by sadness, uncertainty, the pencil slack in her hand.

The coast was clear to reconnoiter the kitchen. I flicked on the light and turned to the wall above the kitchen counter. I had remembered correctly. An old-fashioned yellow landline telephone was attached to the wall. The kitchen was updated with granite countertops, new cabinetry with brass pulls, and laminated wood flooring. Just to be sure, l lifted the receiver, heard a dial tone. Reassured that the phone was in working order, I hung up.

I tried several drawers, found a catch-all drawer. I selected a thin flashlight. The narrow beam would be adequate and the light would not – I glanced toward a window – be visible outside. I unlocked the back door, placed the flashlight on the ground next to the bottom back step. I closed the back door, left it unlocked.

* * *

At Rose Bower, I once again settled in The Gusher room. In addition to the huge kitchen for banquet preparations, Rose Bower had a small kitchen which was always prepared for requests from honored guests in second-floor rooms. The kitchen was manned by part-time help. Possibly the operation was sophisticated enough that a room service call might be answered with a smooth, 'How may I help you, Mr, Mrs, Ms . . .?' But if a call came from a room without a guest registered, I doubted it would occur to room service that the caller was an interloper. The waiter would simply assume the guest would be included in an updated list.

I picked up the receiver, punched room service, ordered a cheeseburger, lettuce, tomato, and avocado with Thousand Island dressing, French fries, coffee, two dips of vanilla, extra chocolate syrup.

I was famished. And weary. I needed all the energy a good meal could provide. I settled at the desk, opened the center drawer. Rose Bower stationery was quite handsome, thick creamy paper. I shook my head. Roses spilled over the side of a basket in a lovely design at the top of the page. I wanted no identifying information on the sheet. Not that I intended for this missive to be left in the Kirk kitchen, but mistakes happen. I opened a side drawer and there, pristine and perfect, was a fresh legal pad. If ever I had the opportunity I would commend the staff at Rose Bower for its thoughtfulness in providing amenities for guests.

I sat at the desk deep in thought for several minutes. I wanted drama but I should be concise. I would be at Gage's side, but I intended to leave nothing to chance. I printed in large letters all cap:

SHE WAS MURDERED

A knock at the door.

I popped up, pleased at the quick service, and rushed to the door. I grabbed the knob and opened the door.

A cute girl with brown pigtails and a sweet smile held a tray. She looked puzzled as she gazed into the well-lighted but clearly unoccupied room.

Uh-oh. I wasn't visible. I backed up, called out, 'Come right in. In the bathroom. Put the tray on the desk.'

The girl blinked. She walked slowly toward the desk, her gaze moving from the bathroom door to the open hall door. She was pondering. The door opened, but no guest stood over the threshold. How did the guest move that quickly from the hall door into the bathroom?

She was almost at the desk.

Uh-oh. The legal pad lay there, a pen beside it. In a flash I was at the desk. 'Please close the door.'

'Yes, ma'am.' But she was already reaching out to move the legal pad. I imagine she intended to close the door as soon as she deposited the tray. The tray stopped a few inches from the surface.

Her eyes grew huge as she read my printing.

SHE WAS MURDERED

I moved to stand between her and the open door. I Appeared in a pink striped seersucker robe and matching pink flip flops. 'Just push that aside. Working on a mystery, you know.'

She glanced at the legal pad, at me standing between her and the hall, turned her head toward the open bathroom door. 'You came out of the bathroom?' She spoke through stiff lips. Anyone leaving the bathroom would be in her full field of vision.

I gave a little wave of my hand. As Mama always told us kids, 'If it couldn't happen, it didn't happen.' I asked brightly, 'Do you read mysteries?'

She balanced the tray on one hand, gingerly moved the legal pad with the other. She put the tray down. 'No.' Her voice was a little ragged. She backed up, her eyes darting from me to the bathroom door to the legal pad. She edged past me. At the door, she whirled and plunged into the hall. Running steps sounded.

I closed the door. I bolted it, although I doubted the room server would share her experience. By the time she reached the kitchen, she'd have figured out an explanation. She'd been looking down when I exited the bathroom. Maybe the printed words were HE WAS MERLIN.

I returned to the desk, lifted the cover. Mmmm. I sat down, grabbed the bun with my left hand, took a bite, picked up my pen. The statement had to be perfect.

* * *

No light glimmered in the Kirk house, dark windows, dark rooms. I made a final quick check of the ground floor and the second-floor bedrooms. George was sprawled on his stomach, his pillow toppled to the floor. Melissa curled in a ball. The Lab lifted his head and looked at me. Camille lay on her right side, cheek pressed against the pillow. Deep slumber should keep the residents in their rooms.

Downstairs, I eased out the back door. Still unlocked. I left the door ajar. An owl hooted. The water in the pool glimmered in the moonlight. I walked on an asphalt path down the hillside toward White Deer Park, making sure there were no obstacles. I carried with me a folded sheet from the legal pad. The sheet moved through the air, held aloft by my unseen hand. I'd brought the sheet with me from The Gusher room to the Kirk house. Unlike the evening at the banquet, there was no danger anyone would see the sheet. Not at this hour of the morning. At the edge of the woods, I judged that the pier parking lot was only twenty feet away. A perfect location.

I avoided the streetlight at the corner near Robert's apartment. I waited in the darker shadows below an elm. I Appeared dressed in black, blouse, linen slacks, sneakers. After I tucked my hair beneath a black cap, I tucked the folded sheet from the legal pad in a pocket. At precisely two a.m., headlights eased around the corner. Robert's black Toyota sedan drew up to the curb in front of the apartment house. I hurried, opened the rear door, slid inside.

Two faces turned toward me. In the light from the opening door, I took a quick look. Robert appeared wary. His gloomy expression indicated he didn't like the hour, the circumstances, or me. Gage was alight with anticipation and readiness for action.

'Where are we going?' Gage's voice was energetic and eager.

'Everything's closed at two a.m.' Robert sounded grim.

'Go to the parking lot by the pier in White Deer Park.'

'Why?' He sounded grimmer.

'That's where you'll wait for Gage and me.'

'You can't go to the carousel.' He bristled with resistance.

I was patient. 'We have no intention of going to the carousel. In fact, we are headed in the opposite direction. Gage and I will take a short stroll up the hillside. She is going to deliver a message that will help her mother. Let's get started. We don't want to be late.'

The car eased away from the curb. 'You're going to talk to somebody at this time of night?' His tone suggested disbelief that assistance for Iris could possibly occur in the woods long past midnight.

I was tempted to tell Robert in a cheery tone that it was actually early morning. But we needed a chauffeur. 'Don't worry. Everything is arranged.' If he understood this to mean Gage and I were expected by someone, that was his privilege.

'I'll come with you.' A flat, determined declaration.

'That's so sweet of you.'

Mama would have said, 'Missy, you can't fool me with that sugar voice.' I never doubted I could fool Robert. 'We would love to have you with us but the instructions were strict. Only Gage and me. But we won't take long and Gage can tell you everything when we come back to the car.' Robert would be horrified when he knew, assuming all went well and we returned as I planned, but the mission would be a fait accompli.

'Just a few minutes?' He sounded more positive. The car turned into the park, began to curl around the lake toward the lot by the pier.

'Possibly ten minutes, Not much longer.' I spoke as if I planned an outing to a Sunday school picnic.

The Toyota slid to a stop. Robert chose a parking spot in the dark shadows of some pines at the far end near an exit. Obviously, he feared he was part of a nefarious excursion.

Gage and I walked swiftly to the edge of the woods and the path that curved up the hillside.

'Who are we meeting?' she whispered.

'We aren't meeting anyone. We are going to use the phone in a kitchen and make a call. I have the number. I'll hold a flashlight and you are to read exactly what is on the sheet of paper. You are not to reveal your identity.'

She stood still. 'This doesn't sound right.'

'It is right. You'll understand when we're done.'

She didn't move,

I said, 'Black licorice.'

We started up the hillside. Moonlight slanting through the trees made it easy to keep to the path. When we reached the Kirk terrace, I put a hand on her arm. 'Wait here while I make sure everything is ready.'

I hurried to the back steps, bent, picked up the flashlight. I crept up the steps, opened the screen, pushed the unlatched door. The door swung in. Ahead lay darkness. I risked a quick flash. The door to the hall was closed.

I returned to the edge of the terrace. I spoke softly but urgently. 'We are going into the kitchen of that house.' I nodded toward the dark structure looming across the flagstones. 'There are people asleep upstairs. We aren't going to cause any disturbance or take anything. What matters is that this phone call originates in this house. Let's go.'

I put a hand on her slender arm. She hesitated for an instant before she drew in a quick breath and took a step. We moved together across the terrace. I led the way up the back steps. I entered the kitchen first and held the door open for her as I turned on the flashlight. I pointed the beam of light at the yellow phone mounted on the wall. I whispered, 'There's the phone.'

I led the way to the counter. I pulled the folded sheet from my pocket. Training the light on the phone, I punched in the Crime Stoppers number. I handed Gage the receiver and the flashlight. She held the receiver in her right hand, the flashlight in her left hand. I unfolded the sheet and placed it on the counter below the phone. She aimed the light down on the sheet.

Holding the receiver to her ear, she stepped closer to the counter so she could read the printed words. Her eyes widened and I knew she was hearing the Crime Stoppers recorded answer, which encouraged informants to provide information about criminal activity and promised confidentiality. In big cities Crime Stoppers is monitored 24/7 but Adelaide is a small town. Everyone knows to call 911 in an emergency.

'Speak clearly.' My tone was firm.

She stared at the sheet, read aloud, 'I have to tell someone.' Full stop, a sharp look at me.

I gave an emphatic nod, pointed at the receiver. 'Read.'

'Evelyn was murdered' – Gage's voice rose – 'on 20 March. The stuff in the glass of lemonade killed her. Matt Lambert . . .' Eyes huge, Gage looked at me, at the sheet. She struggled to breathe.

'Keep going.'

Gage had no inkling until this moment what the statement contained. Her uneven voice and halting delivery reflected her shock. No wonder her voice wobbled and rose higher as she understood why Matt Lambert was killed.

'Matt Lambert saw the person who brought the glass. He watched Evelyn drink the contents. Evelyn didn't add anything to the glass.'

I was attuned to everything around us, to our shadows on the wall, to the narrow shaft of light illuminating the sheet from the legal pad, to Gage's uneven breathing.

Abruptly, I was uneasy. Something was awry. Perhaps a primeval instinct was triggered. My eyes swept the area. The dark expanse of the kitchen. The partially open back door. The bowl of fruit on a kitchen table.

I looked toward the door to the hall. I drew a quick breath. There was a faint line of light between the edge of the door and its frame. The door was ajar, a scant quarter-inch, but that door was closed when we entered the kitchen.

Gage hunched near the phone, her voice shaky. 'You have to dig her up—'

I eased back a foot or so and disappeared.

In the hallway outside the kitchen, Camille Dubois gripped the knob to the kitchen door. She had taken time to dress before she came downstairs, a blue T, black yoga pants, moccasins. Likely she wakened, wanted something to drink, perhaps a snack, dressed because shorty pjs would be much too revealing if she met anyone else abroad in the night. Anyone such as George Kirk. The globe in the hall ceiling glowed. Behind her a door was open to the area with the stairwell. Light gleamed there, too. She had turned on lights as she came downstairs, and now she stood fully visible, leaning close to the narrow aperture, listening.

Gage's young, clear voice grew louder and shakier as she grasped what she was saying. '. . . and do those kinds of tests, find out what caused her heart attack. The doctor . . .'

I left Camille, stood behind Gage. I Appeared long enough to grip her arm. 'Leave. Now. Get to the car. Don't wait for me.'

Startled, she whirled around. 'What's wrong?'

I took the receiver from her hand, gave her a push. I hung up the receiver. 'Go.' My voice was low and urgent.

Gage dashed across the kitchen, opened the door, plunged outside, leaving the door ajar.

I disappeared as Camille eased open the hall door. She looked at the phone, the receiver firmly in its cradle. The kitchen was empty. She stiffened when she saw the door open to the terrace. She cautiously crossed the kitchen, grabbed the knob, slammed the door shut, locked it.

Camille stood with her back against the door, staring now at the counter below the wall phone and the sheet from the legal pad lying there. Camille took three quick steps. She snatched up the sheet, read the printed message. She stared helplessly around the empty kitchen. She gave one last searching glance as she moved toward the hall. She turned off the hall light and started up the stairs. She slowed as she climbed, looking behind her.

At the top, she gazed up and down the hallway. Her head was slightly bent as she listened, seeking any sound of movement. The quiet remained unbroken. Slowly, she turned toward her room, the crumpled sheet held tightly in her right hand. In her bedroom, the hall door firmly shut and locked, she walked to the chintz-covered chair, sank down. Her eyes were wide, fearful, despairing.

Was she afraid for herself? Or for someone else?

Camille opened her right hand. She spread out the crumpled sheet, smoothed it. Pushing up from the chair, she walked to a wall, removed a frame, a bright painting of a plains sunset. Turning the frame over, she unclipped the backing, slid the sheet inside, replaced the backing. She hung the painting on the wall and returned to the chair, sank down, buried her face in her hands.

Gage poked her head out the open window of the moving car as Robert drove slowly along Comanche, passing the Kirk house. 'There's somebody over there.'

'Looks like a big guy with a big dog. A *real* big dog.' Robert clearly had no interest in speaking to a man walking a dog at half past two in the morning.

'Slow down.' Gage was insistent. 'I'll ask him.'

'He'll think we're nuts. What are you going to say? We're missing a redhead, have you seen her? Look, Gage, she can take care of herself. And what were you and the redhead doing in somebody's kitchen? Did you two break and enter one of those houses?' He swept a worried glance at the expensive homes on Comanche.

My mouth opened. Robert needed elucidation. The door was unlocked, a trespass perhaps, but not breaking and entering. Just in time I recalled I was an unseen passenger in the back seat.

Robert jammed the accelerator. 'If we keep going up and down this street, you hanging out the window and wagging that flashlight, the cops are going to come for us. I don't want to talk to another cop. Ever.'

Gage thumped back in the seat. 'I guess she's all right. None of the houses have lights turned on and there would be lights blazing if anyone caught her in that kitchen.'

Robert gripped the wheel with both hands. 'Nobody caught her.' His voice had an odd tone.

Gage turned toward him. 'You know something I don't know. Who is she?'

'A friend of your mom's.' There was a distinct lack of cheer in his tone. At the end of the block, he veered on to the winding road that led down the hill. The car picked up speed. Robert wanted to get as far away from Comanche as he could as quickly as possible.

'She must be somebody special. Robert, she knows things you can't imagine.' Gage described the call to Crime Stoppers, words tumbling over each other. 'When I heard Matt talking to somebody and wanting money to keep quiet, he meant Evelyn Kirk. Evelyn Kirk was murdered.' Gage's tone was hushed. 'Matt should have gone to the police, but he didn't. Instead of going to the police, he planned to get big bucks for Goddard so he'd be an even bigger shot than he was. I don't know how she knew but she did and now the police know.'

Robert's literal mind was working its way forward. 'I get it. This can be your mom's ticket out of jail. But unless the redhead just likes to sneak around in the middle of the night, what's the point of you getting into somebody's kitchen and calling Crime Stoppers?' He pulled into the parking lot by his apartment house.

Gage turned her hands palms up. 'I don't know.'

I did. The call wasn't made in any old kitchen. The call was made on a landline in the kitchen of the Kirk house. The number would show up on Crime Stoppers. What mattered hugely was that the tip, the claim of murder, the call for exhumation came from the Kirk house and the speaker was an unidentified woman.

Sam knew my voice. He heard Gage speak when she described the call she overheard on the Union terrace, but her voice tonight was jerky, shocked, higher than usual. Sam would not associate tonight's call with Gage. He would not associate the call with me. He would accept the reality of a tip from someone who lived in Evelyn Kirk's house. Evelyn Kirk had been a prominent, respected, admired citizen of Adelaide. Even though Sam believed he knew the reason for Matt Lambert's murder, he would investigate this call. Sam would consider again the folded square of paper in Matt Lambert's billfold.

I gave myself a thumbs up for tonight's work. If only I could do as well tomorrow.

FOURTEEN

I luxuriated in the shower, absorbing the hot splash, taking deep steamy breaths. This morning I was combating the effects of too little sleep, a lethargic brain, grainy eyes, flaccid muscles. I steeled myself, switched the handle. Cold needles of water spat against me. I shuddered, but I was awake. This was my Mount Everest Day. It was up to me to scale the heights, rescue Iris. I didn't have a Sherpa guide at my side. Sam would investigate the Crime Stoppers tip, but the machinery of the law was still grinding against Iris. I was on my own. As Mama told us kids, 'When nobody backs you up, you have to stand tall.'

It was still early, just past seven, when I Appeared in a recessed entryway a few doors down from Lulu's. I was casual in a dolman sleeve pale blue pullover and ankle-length denim pants and sandals. I patted one pocket, felt a change purse.

Inside Lulu's I took a counter seat at one end, my back to the door. I ordered and nodded yes for coffee. Lulu's coffee is the perfect antidote for a late night, especially with two heaping teaspoons of sugar and a splash of thick fresh cream.

The stool next to me creaked. 'Thought you might be here.' The deep voice was polite, but lacked any sense of camaraderie.

Obviously the officer who listened to the Crime Stoppers recording this morning had contacted Sam. I was courteous though somewhat formal, given the stiffness when we last parted. 'Good morning.' Pleasant but distant.

He looked up at the waitress, ordered a double short stack with sausage and coffee. Side of whipped cream. As she turned away, he swung toward me. 'Late night for you.' A statement, not a question.

I preferred to think in terms of retiring as the birds were stirring. Thanks to my cold shower and my choice always to appear as I was at twenty-seven – I glanced in the mirror opposite the counter – I looked quite rested. Almost indecently so. I gave him an innocent wide-eyed stare. 'Actually rather early.' As I say, early or late depends upon interpretation. 'The beds are wonderfully comfortable at Rose Bower. I slept like a baby.' Since most babies don't slumber longer than three hours max, I was being quite truthful.

The waitress brought our plates, syrup, and fresh pats of butter.

I put two pats of butter on my French toast.

Sam poured syrup over the short stacks, cut into one, forked a big piece, poked it in the mound of whipped cream. 'You were in the Kirk house yesterday.'

'I visited there late in the afternoon. Quite a lovely home.'

'How about two o'clock this morning?' The fork didn't move and he watched me like a cougar stalking a fawn.

I sang a verse of 'Two O'Clock in the Morning'. 'That's a good time to sleep. If anything exciting occurred there at two a.m., it wasn't my doing.' It was Gage who spoke to Crime Stoppers. 'What happened?' My voice was eager.

'A phone call.' He still watched me with intensity.

I gave a disappointed poof. 'That's not exciting.' I leaned toward him. 'You wouldn't mention the call if it didn't matter. Who called whom? And why at two a.m.? Sam, do you have a break in the case?'

He asked quickly, 'What case?'

'Matt Lambert. He tried to force someone in that house to make a big gift. Do you know now who it was?'

Sam demolished the remainder of the first stack, ignored my question. 'Who did you talk to in the Kirk house?'

My gaze was steady and open. 'I have not spoken to anyone who lives or works in that house. Not yet. That's on my agenda today.'

He put down his fork, stared. 'You haven't talked to anyone there?'

I was firm. 'I have not talked to anyone in that house.'

He continued to frown, ate absentmindedly, likely not even tasting the sweet syrup.

I suspected his thoughts raced as he concluded that I wasn't responsible for the call, I hadn't maneuvered someone who lived there to call, and I hadn't given a resident of the house information based on the note in Lambert's wallet.

He stared at the mirror, eyes narrowed. He wasn't seeing his gray-flecked dark hair or remote expression. He was facing the reality that the informant was unknown to him and that Evelyn Kirk might be a murder victim.

'OK.' His tone was abstracted. He pulled out his billfold, slapped down a twenty and a five, plenty for two breakfasts, and a big tip. He turned on the stool, gave me a considering look. 'I thought I'd tag you with a clever ploy last night. Looks like I got that wrong. So I'll be checking out some information that I can't share. But I'll toss you a bone. An interesting fact turned up. Lambert's office was a mess, soggy ashes, charred rug, floor, desk. Detective Smith went through everything. He said the only time he got dirtier was on a case where somebody hid a stolen Stradivarius in a compost heap. Violin was wrapped up real good. Smith wasn't when he started tossing compost. Anyway, in the rubble of Lambert's desk, he found a burner phone. The fire damaged the phone to the point we couldn't get any information from it, but your idea that Lambert used a burner phone to make the call overheard by Gage is certainly possible.' Sam slid off the stool. 'Right now Iris Gallagher will be charged Monday morning. But I got some loose ends to see to.'

He turned and lumbered toward the door, didn't look back.

A burner phone wouldn't free Iris. But Sam was thinking and Sam would investigate the information left on Crime Stoppers. Would he force the exhumation of Evelyn Kirk's body?

Doctors don't hold office hours on Saturdays. Matt Lambert played golf with Ken Thomas on Wednesday, came home excited, likely picturing a pot of gold at the end of a rainbow. What did Dr Thomas say to Matt Lambert? Possibly they were close friends and Lambert was a man he trusted. The information the doctor shared indicated that the doctor was certain the lemonade caused Evelyn Kirk's death.

Lambert knew Evelyn added nothing to the lemonade, so when the drink arrived it contained a deadly dose. A deadly dose of what? Why did Evelyn's doctor conceal the reason for her death? He would not hide murder. No one accidentally adds poison to drink. There was only one possible reason. Dr Thomas decided Evelyn took her own life. He concluded that Evelyn put a substance in her lemonade. Matt Lambert knew that wasn't true.

I thought: *Dr Kenneth Thomas's home.* The rambling old wooden house had the charm of the last century, a verandah with a wooden swing, several cane chairs. A tall plastic pink flamingo graced the top step. Likely there was a cheerful family story behind the flamingo's presence. A half-dozen bikes were parked near the front walk. Shouts and calls came from beyond the house and splashes. A teenage pool-party.

I'd given a good deal of thought to my appearance, to my persona. A sleeveless lime-green maxi dress, notched neckline, tucked in slim waist, flaring skirt with a scalloped lace hem. I Appeared, confident the dress made a lovely contrast to red curls. Persona? Eager. Well meaning. But at this particular moment, sad and solemn. Committed to carrying out a quest for a friend but perhaps reluctant to bring up a difficult memory. Was I up to the task?

As Mama often told me, 'Missy, when you think you can't take another step, remember the pioneers. If the wagon gets stuck in the mud, push it out. If a rattler rears its head, chop it off. If there's a fire, pick up a bucket. Do what you have to do.'

I pushed the doorbell. Instead of chimes, a crow cawed, loud and raucous. I was startled then I smiled. Someone had a sense of humor at the Thomas house. And possibly respect for a highly intelligent bird capable of making and using tools

The door opened. A fortyish woman with an impatient air stood there, then called over her shoulder. 'Ice cream at this hour is decadent. But hey, it's July.' She turned back to me. Bright dark eyes scanned me, possibly making sure I wasn't a demanding patient. 'Yes?' Pleasant but coolly impersonal.

'I'm sorry to bother you at this early hour.' An apologetic smile. 'I'm Ellie Fitzgerald, a friend of Madeleine Timmons. Madeleine asked me to gather up memories of her mother's last day. I talked to Mr Lambert . . .'

Her expressive face was abruptly still and watchful.

'. . . and he was very honest. He told me everything. It's all dreadfully sad, but Madeleine wants me to tell Dr Thomas personally how much she appreciates his thoughtfulness to her mother.'

Her stillness revealed the woman at the door knew what I meant by *everything*. She was well aware of the circumstances of Evelyn's death.

'He just left. He plays golf on Saturday.'

'Oh, that will work out beautifully. I'll catch him before he starts his round. It's so important to Madeleine to understand what happened that day. Thank you.' I turned and walked toward the steps. When the front door shut, I disappeared and stood in the hallway beside her as she held a cell phone.

Her voice was low, the words rushed. 'A girl came to the house just now looking for you. A friend of Evelyn Kirk's daughter . . . She wants to know about Evelyn's last day. She's on her way to the country club. She said she talked to Matt Lambert. I've always been afraid someone would find out, but this girl seems all right. She says Madeleine appreciates what you did.'

Context determines outcomes. I didn't want the doctor to see me or my questions as a threat to his reputation or professional standing. I wanted him to respond to a plea from Evelyn Kirk's daughter. Now he would meet me as Madeleine's friend, coming to thank him.

I thought, *Dr Thomas's car.*

The silver BMW convertible, top down, occupied a shady slot beneath an oak tree in the country club parking lot. A dark-haired middle-aged man in a pale blue polo and navy Bermuda shorts that ended just above knobby knees slowly slid a cell phone into a back pocket. A leather golf bag leaned against the bumper. The bag held perhaps a half-dozen expensive-looking clubs. I remembered Bobby Mac's old canvas golf bag, chock full of assorted clubs collected over the years, most of them bought second-hand. Thomas lifted his head and gazed around the parking lot. Was he looking for Madeleine's friend?

Flaming red crape myrtles bordered the driving range.

Perhaps a half-dozen golfers worked on particular shots. A stocky blond teenager hit balls two hundred yards seemingly without effort. A tall lean woman practiced chip shots.

An evergreen screened a parking area for golf carts. No one was near. I Appeared and walked around the evergreen toward the dark-haired doctor.

His face was thin and sensitive. A serious man. When he entered an examining room, he would bring with him a gravity, an intensity. A patient would receive his full focus. A man who would listen.

'Dr Thomas.' I approached with a diffident smile. 'I just visited with your wife. I'm Ellie Fitzgerald, a friend of Madeleine Timmons. As I told your wife, Madeleine wants me to thank you for your kindness to the family. I was in Dallas visiting another college friend and Madeleine called Thursday morning and asked me to come here.' I was young and guileless, definitely not threatening. I clasped my hands together and now my voice was low and sad. 'It broke Madeleine's heart that she was so far away when her mom died. When she came back for the funeral, everything was such a blur and she wasn't able to spend time talking to people to find out more. She asked me to find out about her mom's last day.' Now I was grave. 'Of course I was shocked by what I learned from Mr Lambert. It's odd,' I sounded shivery, 'that he was killed that night. I talked to him in late afternoon and he was very honest. He said she died because of something in the lemonade. How did you know?'

'Evelyn shouldn't have died.' He looked into the distance but he wasn't seeing the first tee. 'Absolutely she shouldn't have died. Yes, unexpected heart attacks happen, but I think I knew right at that moment what she'd done. I went into the bathroom. The bottle of digitalis was empty and it should have been missing only a few tablets.' His face folded in sadness and a flicker of anger. 'I'm sorry Matt told you and that Madeleine knows. Suicide is a huge burden for a family.'

My tone was approving, not combative. 'Is that why you didn't tell anyone?'

He gave a defeated shrug. 'Evelyn was gone. What good would it do to tell the world she committed suicide? It would have been a big story in the paper. How do you think the family would feel? Suicide.' His voice was heavy. 'My aunt committed suicide. My mom never got over her death. She blamed herself. She thought somehow she should have known, should have done something. I wish,' his voice was low, almost inaudible, 'I'd been smarter for Evelyn. I thought she understood the arrhythmia was something we could handle. No problem. She was young, strong. She asked me if she was going to end up like her mother. Gail had a stroke, was incapacitated for years. The best of care but lying in a bed only able to move her eyes and one hand, never spoke again. Evelyn said she'd rather be dead. I told her she didn't need to worry, she was going to be fine. I thought she believed me.'

'How can you be sure she put the digitalis in the lemonade?' The question was offered in a wondering tone, with no hint of confrontation.

'She loved lemonade, drank a tall glass every afternoon. The glass in the bathroom was fresh, unused. The only glass in the room was the one with the dregs of the lemonade. I took a mouthwash bottle in the bathroom, emptied it, washed it. I poured what was left of the drink into the bottle, sent it to a lab. The report was clear. Digitalis. The report is in my safe.' He shook his head in regret. 'I'm sorry Madeleine will have this added sorrow. But,' and he was emphatic, 'she wasn't here. She won't feel there was anything she could have done, should have done. And maybe,' he was somber, 'I didn't want to face my own failure, have everyone know my patient cut her life short because I didn't see the depths of her fear.'

'You meant well.' I spoke in my own voice, a voice that held understanding and kindness, acceptance.

He was somber. 'Tell Madeleine whatever you wish. I meant well for Evelyn. And the family.' He hefted the golf bag, turned away, walking head down toward the driving range.

I didn't know who would ultimately speak with Madeleine. But now I knew the fact I needed. Evelyn Kirk was murdered with digitalis. Only Evelyn's doctor and the murderer and I possessed that knowledge.

*   *   *

An early fisherman lounged in a canvas chair on the pier in White Deer Park, rod wedged between two boards. Dog walkers moved fast with big dogs, slowed their pace for little ones. Size ranged from a St Bernard, mercifully with a shaved coat, and a Chihuahua no bigger than my hand.

I hovered above a beach umbrella that shaded a card table and two unoccupied folding chairs. A white Styrofoam cooler sat on the table. Gage wore a floppy straw hat, tank top, brief shorts, and tennis shoes. She held a tube in one hand, squirted sunscreen in the other. She spread thick white cream on an already pink arm. 'Some people aren't very nice.'

Robert, face flushed from exertion, flopped in a chair. 'Honey, I love you when you say things like that and sound surprised.'

'Can you believe that woman told me contests are un-American? I almost informed her George Washington was a whiz at horseshoes.'

'At least she didn't waste your time. That grumpy guy who looked like his dachshund asked me at least eight questions about the contest then said he wasn't in the park yesterday but told me everything he observed when he walked Fritzi Thursday morning.'

Robert fished a chilled bottle of water from the cooler, twisted off the cap, offered it to Gage. She smiled, took several deep gulps, handed the bottle to Robert who glugged the remainder.

A petite blonde in a white top, blue shorts, and sandals came around a tree.

It was as if Gage and Robert were on point. They moved toward the path, Gage smiling. 'Good morning. We're Gage and Robert and we're out here to share popsicles on a hot day and find out who in White Deer Park qualifies as Super Observer.'

The woman, possibly in her mid-forties, stopped to listen. Her face was kind and her eyes soft. Perhaps she was remembering herself with a tall thin young man on a sunny day in a park.

I smiled, blew them a kiss. All three of them.

*   *   *

Bess Hampton's buff brick duplex in a modest area of Adelaide was well kept. A porch swing creaked in a gentle breeze. Mandevilla twined over the wooden railing, the trumpet-shaped blooms a bright rich red. The flower bed, thick with pansies, was a riot of color.

I wasn't surprised when Bess opened her front door neatly dressed for the day though it was only a quarter to eight. People who work hard for a living don't lie abed just because it's Saturday.

The Kirk housekeeper loomed over me, tall, sturdy. Her broad face was wary. An early morning visit by a stranger would be unusual. She said nothing, waited for me to speak.

For Bess Hampton, I intended to pose as Madeleine's ditzy friend, young and eager, trying to help out a friend. '. . . A favor to dear Madeleine . . . sorry to be so early . . . heading back to Dallas soon . . . would be such a kindness to Madeleine to help her deal with her mom's death . . . please just a few questions about That Day.'

'And your name, Miss?' Bess's voice was surprisingly soft.

'Ellie Fitzgerald. Just call me Ellie. Madeleine says Ellies are supposed to be cute and pixyish and I don't qualify but we are who we are.' I beamed at her. 'I know you'll help me help Madeleine.'

Bess's face softened. 'Poor Miss Madeleine. So young to lose her mother; even though they were as different as night and day, they were close. Miss Evelyn, well, she grew up in a house where no one paid her much attention so she tried hard to not let that happen to Madeleine. Miss Evelyn deserves a lot of credit there. She and Miss Madeleine were so different, Miss Evelyn always elegant and cool and controlled and Miss Madeleine bouncy and loud and never-met-a-stranger. Like her papa. If you'll take a seat in the swing, Miss Ellie, I'll get us some coffee. I'd invite you in but my husband works nights and he's having himself breakfast right now.'

I waited on the porch. She returned carrying a tray with two pottery mugs, steam wreathing above them, a cream pitcher, and bowl of brown sugar. In a moment, I took a sip of delicious sweet creamy strong coffee. She sat opposite me in a porch chair, sat straight, her strong face composed. 'What do you want to know, Miss Ellie?'

I leaned forward. 'I want to tell Madeleine everything that happened. How did the day start?'

Bess placed her mug on a small side table, folded her hands in her lap. 'It was awfully cold. In the forties. I forgot my coat that morning and froze all the way to the house. My heater was broken. I got there at six as usual. I put out breakfast on the buffet in the dining room at seven. That was for Miss Camille and Mr George.' A pause. 'Miss Melissa came down at eight and took food up to her room.'

Camille, George, Melissa. Three of the four attendees at the banquet were in the house that day.

'I always took a tray up to Miss Evelyn. Coffee, a brioche with strawberry jam and butter, a small bowl of fruit. Papaya that morning.' She pressed her lips tight together. 'I'm so glad I had the papaya. She loved that fruit and it isn't easy to get. I was in Norman that weekend and I went by Whole Foods and bought six of them. Since it was her last breakfast, I don't know, do you think' – she looked at me earnestly – 'that somehow she knew her time was done?'

I stiffened. Was this an affirmation of the doctor's insistence on suicide? But the digitalis was in the lemonade and Matt Lambert insisted Evelyn added nothing to the glass after it was delivered to her room. And that last entry in the journal, *Tahiti definite*, was surely an indication of anticipation of a journey. 'What do you mean?'

'I served her on the little table in a nook that overlooks the terrace. Just as I reached the door, she lifted the cover on the fruit. She said, "Papaya! Bess, you spoil me. Thank you, Sweet Bess." I was so pleased because she didn't often give a compliment. I'll always remember standing there and seeing her smile. Somehow she didn't smile often. I'm so glad the papaya made her happy.' Bess lifted a hand to wipe away a tear from her cheek. 'I don't know. It just seems like maybe she knew she wouldn't see me at breakfast again.'

'I'll tell Madeleine her mom was happy that day.' I felt a huge sweep of relief. There was no hint of depression or worry or fear in Evelyn's speech, only a woman who appreciated the effort Bess made to bring her favorite breakfast fruit. 'I'll tell Madeleine how much she appreciated you and the papaya was a reminder of all you did for her through the years. Madeleine will be glad to know her mom's day started with smiles. Did Alice arrive for work at her usual time?'

Another nod.

Suspect number four accounted for.

I led her through the day. Evelyn met Betty Wilson for lunch at a new little teashop near the campus. 'When she got back, Miss Evelyn poked her head in the kitchen, told me the quiche at lunch wasn't nearly as light as mine.' Bess gave a sigh.

'Did you see her after that?'

'I didn't see her, but she had company. A little after two, that man from the college came to see Miss Evelyn. He gave me a big smile and said she'd told him to come right up. He knew the way. He came here a lot, always had a big smile.' Her tone was neutral.

I expect Bess would have agreed with Mama when she said, 'Crocodiles show a lot of teeth but that doesn't mean they love you.'

'What time did he leave?'

'I don't know. I didn't see him again.'

'Madeleine said her mom loved lemonade. Did she have one that afternoon?'

'Oh yes.' Bess spoke with pride. 'Always. Every afternoon. Lemonade with four maraschino cherries on top. Lots of sugar. Oh, I wish I'd taken the tray up. I would have seen her again. Maybe I would have known if she wasn't feeling good. I could always tell when she was getting sick when she was a little girl. Her eyes had little purple crescents under them.'

Her pain and regret throbbed in the room. I didn't hesitate. 'I talked to the doctor this morning. There was nothing you could have done. If you'd seen her again, she would have looked fine, been cheerful, herself.'

'You think so?' A plea. Large dark eyes wanted to believe, prayed to believe there was no way she could have helped Evelyn.

'I know so.' I spoke with the authority achieved through

ruling a classroom filled with football players. This voice was
never ignored, always obeyed.

It was as if she shed a burden, grew younger as I watched.

'But it was nice that someone saved you a trip up the stairs.
Who took the tray to her?'

She turned her hands, work-worn hands, palms up. 'I don't
know. I put the tray on the side table near the hall door and
Reggie, that's the black Lab, asked to go out. I opened the
door and he hung back. Like I said, it was such a cold day.
He's old but I knew he needed to go. I shooed him outside
and stood on the porch and waited. Reggie saw a squirrel
and forgot he was old. The squirrel went up a tree.' Almost
a laugh. 'Reggie used that tree. Anyway, we came inside and
I dried him off because he'd gone into the long grass. I turned
to get the tray and it was gone. Everybody knew lemonade
was for Miss Evelyn. I thought maybe she came down to
see Mr Lambert out and took the tray up herself. I suppose,'
she sounded doubtful, 'it could have been someone else.
Maybe Miss Camille. Or Mr George.'

In other words, Alice and Melissa were unlikely to save steps
for Bess.

Murder made easy. I wondered if a clever killer urged the
dog into the kitchen. If Bess had taken the tray up as usual,
perhaps the killer planned to arrive soon after and ask Evelyn
for an aspirin, got a bump that aches, any excuse to send
her into her bathroom while a plastic baggie was opened
and the ground-up digitalis tablets dumped into the lemonade
and stirred.

Bess was mournful. 'She died alone. Mr George found her
in bed a little after four. He called Dr Thomas and nine-one-one
but they weren't able to help her.'

'I'd like a cherry popsicle.'

Gage grabbed Robert's arm. 'Did you hear that? It sounded
like somebody wants a popsicle, but there's no one here.'

Robert's face reminded me of his expression Thursday
evening as he listened to Iris exchange not quite pleasantries
with an unseen woman.

I'd disappeared outside Bess's house, decided to check on

the survey, but neglected to Appear before speaking. I stepped close to Robert, gripped his jaw – very gently – with my right and turned it toward the pier.

Actually Robert bore up gallantly, though his voice was a little jerky. 'Gage, look over there by the pier.'

In an instant I was behind Gage.

Robert watched colors swirl with the same enthusiasm he might have afforded an IRS summons.

I smiled anyway. 'Hello.'

Gage jerked around. 'Where'd you come from?'

I gave a casual wave of my hand. 'Here and there.'

Robert made wavy gestures with his hands.

Smirks aren't attractive, though his response likely was the equivalent of whistling past a graveyard to manifest nonchalance. I gave him a warning look, then smiled at Gage.

My white T with charming ruched sleeves and very short batik print skirt were summery, but the heat was intense. 'A popsicle would be great.'

Gage was still puzzled at my presence where absolutely no one had stood a moment before. She blinked twice, gave me an intense look, almost spoke, stopped. Was she remembering the woman who gripped her arm in the fiery office? Another look, then she shook her head, perhaps deciding guardian angels, if that's who I was, must be permitted to come and go without question. 'Well, you're here now, and,' a huge smile, 'we found someone. The police will have to listen. He's a math professor. Precise. Definitive. And memory? He could probably tell us the color of the teething ring he had at six months.'

Robert handed me a popsicle, avoided touching my fingers.

'Thank you.' I stripped the paper, bit a cool sweet chunk.

Gage burbled, 'His name is Waldo Whiffle. But I doubt anyone ever kids him. He's about seven feet tall—'

'Six seven,' Robert interrupted.

'—and he was walking his Pomeranian. We got a picture. Him and Fifi. They got to the park yesterday at ten to four, started over by the llama pens. He said Fifi is old and can't go fast, that they came even with the carousel at about ten minutes after four. He saw a red Malibu pull into the parking lot. A tall, dark-haired woman got out. He thought she looked worried. She walked really fast to the carousel. Fifi had to stop so he found a shady spot near the willow. The woman – it was Mom – hurried to the carousel and this is what matters' – Gage's voice rose with excitement – 'she got on the carousel and he saw her stop, hold her hand to her throat. She started to reach out, shook her head, backed away. By this time he was interested. He said she got off the carousel and came toward the willow. She was talking on her cell phone. Fifi darted after a prairie dog and he hurried to catch her. He said the last time she cornered a prairie dog she had to get five stitches. He wanted to show us her scar and we got pictures of that too. But we have every word he said recorded. This proves Mom is innocent.'

I was excited, too. 'One statement is great. More will be even better. Keep after it. There's a chance someone else may remember too.'

'We'll be here all day. We'll talk to everyone.' She was shining with success and hope and relief.

Coal smoke swirled around me. Wheels clacked on steel.

I gave Robert a hard stare.

He looked confused.

I cut my eyes toward the willow, gave a tiny nod, mouthed *prairie dog*.

Perhaps I underestimated Robert. Literal, yes. Eager to see me gone, for sure.

'Hey Gage, look over there. Maybe that's Fifi's prairie dog. Let's go see.'

Gage turned toward the willow.

'Hey, that prairie dog moves fast. Daytona next stop.'

I disappeared. Let Robert explain where the nice redhead went. Or perhaps Gage wouldn't be surprised.

FIFTEEN

Cottonwood leaves rustled in the breeze. Coal smoke swirled around me. The Rescue Express was quite near, quivering to be underway. I stood my ground in the shade of the big tree. 'Not yet, Wiggins.' I felt his presence beside me. His disapproving presence. Earlier I fled the Express. Now I was stubbornly rooted to the ground. What next? Wiggins must be thinking.

I rushed to divert him. 'I'm thrilled you are here for this celebratory moment.' Not to hijack me from my work. 'It's a huge step forward to provide a statement proving Iris had no opportunity to deliver the blow in the carousel. Wiggins, you were my inspiration. You value teamwork. But,' pause for emphasis, 'you always have your eye on the goal. It's obvious we must unmask the evildoer to effect Iris's release.' If the language was a bit early twentieth century, remember my listener. I continued rapidly because Wiggins would never be rude enough to interrupt a lady. In Wiggins's view, all women are ladies. Rather dear of him, really. 'Though we have taken a huge step forward, we must not rest on our laurels. Never flag, never fail. I know you understand I will require today and possibly most of tomorrow to determine the murderer's identity. One of four people killed Evelyn Kirk, Matt Lambert and Nicole Potter.'

'Your mission is to protect Iris.' Indeed Wiggins kept his eye on the goal.

Determined to neither flag nor fail, I persisted. 'The testimony of those in the park yesterday afternoon will be useful for the defense in a trial. Wiggins, I know you don't want Iris charged and tried.'

A silence as he thought. 'It seems definitive that she is innocent of the student's murder.'

'She is being held for the homicide of Matt Lambert. Iris

won't be safe unless I succeed in showing that he was murdered
to hide the truth about Evelyn Kirk's death.'

Another silence. 'Very complicated. I'm afraid you are
correct.' His tone indicated surrender.

'Oh, Wiggins, you are the best.'

As Mama always told us kids, 'Always give praise when
praise is due.'

There's a reason we talk about comfort food. Chicken fried
steak. Mashed potatoes. Cream gravy. Green beans with ham
hock. Ice cream. Chocolate. When we need a pick-me-up, we
turn to the food we remember from childhood when we sat
at a table buoyed by succulent tastes and love.

Once again I sat at the counter in Lulu's. Saturday morning
at eleven wasn't packed. The work week saw every seat taken,
the booths jammed, a line near the register. I spread creamy
butter on a biscuit, added a drizzle of honey. Brave words
when I spoke to Wiggins. I asked for time, and implicit was
the premise that time was all I needed, that I had a plan and
would execute.

I had a plan, all right. I intended to zoom like a Hoover
through the lives of the Four – George, Melissa, Camille, Alice
– and suck out who was crossways with Evelyn and why. I'd
worked hard all morning trying to dig up information that
would lead to a murderer. At this point the tally read: Murderer,
ace of Spades, Bailey Ruth, deuce of Diamonds.

I started out with confidence. I had names. I had addresses. I
had my spiel. What could go wrong? I ticked names off my
checklist. Matron of Honor Virginia Barrett moved to Toronto
before Melissa and Camille arrived in Adelaide. She Facebooked
with Evelyn but had only spoken to her twice since moving.
'She put up the cutest video of Doobie, that's the Siamese,
watching a cardinal through a window, and you should have
seen that cat's tail flick.'

When I called Holton Cramer's office, it's possible the
receptionist misunderstood and thought the call was from
Madeleine. In any event, I succeeded in getting the director
on the line.

'Oh, a friend of Madeleine's?'

'So many happy times.' If he took this to mean Madeleine and I were BFFs, that was fine. 'Madeleine loved what you said about her mom, that she was a fierce friend. I'm putting together a memory book for Madeleine. I thought it would be wonderful to include that quote from her daddy and the inspiration for it.'

Cramer spoke softly but there was underlying authority in his voice, a glimpse of a man who could draw forth depths of emotion from actors, a man who had insight and understanding of the human psyche. 'Tigers are beautiful. But dangerous. That was Evelyn. Beautiful, but fierce. She was one thousand percent for you. Or,' a wistful note, 'against you. She had a good friend, great actress, who had a roulette problem, had to watch that little ball and she always thought it would stop on the red for her. Got in debt big time. Stole some money. Went to jail. Husband dumped her. Kids turned away. Evelyn visited her, was there the day she got out, drove her to an apartment Evelyn had rented in Santa Monica, told her everything's better if you look at the water. Monica got her life back together, always said Evelyn made it happen. You can take it to the bank. If Evelyn was your friend, she would stand by you all the way.'

I took a last bite of chicken fried steak smothered in the best cream gravy this side of my mama's table. Betty Wilson, the old elementary school friend, apparently never met a committee meeting she could ignore. I glanced at my watch. She was due out of the Friends of the Library meeting in fifteen minutes. She was my last hope of finding chinks in the armor of the Four.

Betty Wilson beamed at me. Short brown curls framed a sweet face. Kind eyes. Few wrinkles suggested a nature impervious to worry. Her rosebud mouth slipped up in a kind smile. 'It's so good to meet you, sugar. Dear little Madeleine. Sometimes I think Evelyn was amazed that she had such a carefree daughter. Evelyn was always serious.' Betty spoke as if this were a failing but one that must be excused for a good friend. 'Evelyn was always a little stiff. Gorgeous, of course,' Betty added hurriedly. 'She was already gorgeous with that golden hair and blue eyes when we were in elementary school. She was sophisticated even then, so no wonder she grew up to go to Paris to buy her clothes. Not just Dallas, Paris. I told her Pappy, that's my husband Joe, thinks Target is plenty good enough for clothes and I agree, it's all in how you look at things—'

I began to feel slightly dazed.

'—and Joe pronounces it TarJay and says what's the difference between a label from France and one from China and of course I could tell him—'

I broke in. 'Madeleine was a little concerned. She thought perhaps her mom and George were disagreeing and she wants to know what happened so she can tell George he really mustn't feel bad.' It was graceless but I didn't think anything less than a body slam would get Betty's attention.

Blue eyes widened. 'That's just not at all the thing that dear child should be thinking about. George was always sweet to Evelyn. Pappy stopped opening doors for me the year we got married.' Light laugh. 'He said he was all for this women's lib thing' – she rolled her eyes – 'and women should be free to handle everything, and I could get my own door. Not that Pappy isn't sweet, he's just a big blustery guy with a heart of gold and—'

I resisted the urge to slap my hand across her mouth. 'George.'

She batted her lashes. 'George?'

'George and Camille.'

There was a flicker in those sweet-as-pie eyes. Betty pretended all was fine and good in her world, but she was nobody's fool. She knew George was attracted to Camille. 'Camille is just the nicest girl.'

I suppose I was like a dowser on a sun-parched plot, determined the stick should wobble toward water, even if only a drop. 'Madeleine didn't think George was right for her mother.'

'Now you tell Madeleine that Evelyn and George were always on the best of terms. The best.'

I gave it one last shot. 'Madeleine was surprised at what her mom said about Alice.'

Another pretty laugh. 'I don't know anything about that.

I know Evelyn was so generous. You know, a big bonus at Christmas.'

'Madeleine said her mom talked to you almost every day.' I would have bet the ranch that Betty placed the daily call. Evelyn didn't strike me as the kind of woman to seek out spun sugar on a daily basis. 'What did she say the last time you spoke?'

Her smile was unwavering. 'We had the loveliest lunch at a sweet little teashop.' The smile slipped away and her voice was mournful. 'I can't believe that was the day she died. She looked wonderful and she was her usual self. The last thing she said was she was going on a big trip and she'd send me a card from Tahiti. She said, "How about Tahiti to kick off a new chapter in my life." I asked what she meant and she just laughed.'

There were a few more cheery comments as I thanked her. I promised to give her love to Madeleine. She shepherded me to the door, smiling sweetly.

At the door, I paused, crinkled my face in a worried frown. 'Oh yes. I promised Madeleine. There's that friend of her mom's – I can't remember her name – you know, the one who's wild and crazy and you never know what she's going to say.' Almost everyone has one friend like that.

It was refreshing to see a genuine spark from Betty. Her cheekbones jutted for an instant. 'Oh. Sybil.' Her voice was cold.

I clapped my hands together. 'That's the name. Where does she live?'

'Oh you young people. So proper. So correct. So boring.' The dark-haired woman with a pixie cut and wicked brown eyes pointed at my glass of iced tea. Evelyn's wild-woman friend Sybil flung herself into a cushioned wicker chair opposite me. Shaded by a thatched roof pergola, we were cooled by mist from water tumbling over boulders into the pool.

Sybil's mobile mouth stretched in a grimace. 'Perhaps I should create a primer for Millennials. First rule: Never turn down a drink. Second rule: Especially not a gin and tonic from

Sybil. Third rule: A midmorning gin and tonic will give your day a kick.' She picked up a big tumbler, drank. 'My gin and tonics are famous.' A dark eyebrow quirked. She gave a husky laugh. 'Infamous?'

A gin and tonic sounded appealing, but I needed every wit I ever possessed to see me through this day. 'I'm heading for the highway as soon as I leave here or I'd follow the house rules.'

That evoked a pleased laugh. 'House Rules. I like that. So you're the right sort. I'll send you off with a thermos guaranteed to keep drinks cold for four hours. That will see you to Dallas and then you can hoist a glass to me.'

'With pleasure.' I grinned at her. I could imagine sardonic Sybil and elegant Evelyn tossing acerbic observations back and forth with ease. And perhaps a malicious delight.

Sybil drank a bit more. Quite a bit more. Looking like a cat with a feather in her whiskers, she leaned forward. 'So Madeleine sent you to see me. I love Madeleine.' Those dark eyes were intelligent, thoughtful. 'Why?'

I doubted Sybil Warwick was discreet. At this point I didn't care. 'Madeleine says her mom wanted to live.'

Sybil's face quivered for an instant. 'Evelyn called me the day before she died. She wanted to go to Tahiti with a side trip to Portugal. No matter the directions didn't gibe. She said airplanes flew in all directions. That was Evelyn. She did what she wanted when she wanted and she decided Tahiti and Portugal were her next stops and she wanted me along. She said, "You make me laugh. I want to do a road trip like we did right before college." We went to SMU together. I got kicked out second semester but had fun until then. I'd already looked up bookings. Then I got the call Tuesday evening.'

I no longer needed the persona of a flighty, charming friend of Madeleine's. I held her gaze, spoke crisply. 'I know who was in Evelyn's house that day.'

There was no fuzziness, despite the gin, in those dark bright eyes. 'Why does it matter?'

'I want you to help me find out which one killed her.'

She took a moment before she spoke, those dark eyes studying me. 'Killed?' The single word bristled with anger and heartbreak.

'Poison in the lemonade she drank that afternoon.'

Her drink forgotten, fingers laced tightly together, Sybil never moved until I finished. 'Oh yes, I'll help you.' Her voice was cold and hard, unforgiving, determined. 'When Evelyn felt that sharp ugly twist, when her heart began to fail, she would know it was something in the drink. She was fine when I talked to her. She knew the heart problem was easily solved. I want one of them to pay for her last few terrible minutes.' She twisted a cocktail napkin in a tanned hand with bright red fingernails then grabbed the tumbler, took a deep swallow.

'One of four.' Her tone was appraising. 'Was it George, the stud who strayed? Or maybe Melissa, his pissy sister. Then we come to Camille, the much too pretty artist. And there's Alice, the cousin who's always a downer.' Sybil rolled the crumpled napkin into a tight ball. 'George landed in clover. George probably never had an extra thou in his bank account until he put his arm around Evelyn to help with her forehand. Evelyn and I didn't mince words. I told her he was good for an affair, not a husband. She wasn't dewy eyed. She decided to marry him because Madeleine wasn't programmed to have her mother sleeping around. There was a pre-nup, of course. At her death he inherited the house and a couple of million. But if she divorced him for any reason, it was Bye Bye Boy with a hundred thousand in his pocket.' Sybil took another drink. Those dark eyes locked with mine. 'Anybody in the same room with George and Camille got the picture. The Saturday before she died, Evelyn gave him a week to move out. Ditto Camille. When she called me on Monday, she said Tahiti and Portugal would be her freedom fling.'

Sam Cobb once told me crimes happen when they do for a reason. Evelyn ordered the lovers to leave on Saturday, died on Tuesday. Matt Lambert learned about digitalis in the lemonade on Wednesday, died on Thursday. Nicole Potter made a threat on Friday and died that day.

Sybil replaced her tumbler on the glass surface with a bang. 'George doesn't fit my bill for murder. He smiles too much and loves to stretch out on a couch like a house cat. But maybe he was willing to do what he had to do to keep his soft life. I don't know about Camille. Beautiful manners. Hard to read.' Her gamine face, intelligent, malicious, perhaps a trifle cruel, was intent, remorseless. 'Alice is a different matter. I wouldn't put anything past Alice. Alice is a pain. Always has been. Always will be. A pain and a craven crook. Not a good combo. Alice cooked the books at a local church, came to Evelyn, begged for money to make the accounts good. She had some fancy story about why she took the money. Evelyn gave her the money to repay the church. Evelyn said she wanted to keep the family name unsullied. It was about the time Evelyn's longtime secretary moved away so she hired Alice. But Evelyn was keen about money. Maybe Alice was a good girl for a time. Maybe she can't resist dipping her fingers into pools of money. Whatever, Evelyn figured out Alice was skimming some accounts. Evelyn said Alice had played her last trick.'

'It's interesting that Alice still works there.'

'George probably didn't know. He and Evelyn weren't sharing pillow talk at that point. But he knew about Evelyn's ultimatum to his obnoxious sister Melissa.'

I leaned forward to hear.

It was a moment of déjà vu as I watched Bess Hampton prepare a tray. Today she added chunks of pineapple to two tea glasses, removed the cap from a frosty bottle of Heineken's. A small bowl brimmed with cashews. Party toothpicks poked from a silver container. Assorted crackers shared a serving plate with chunks of Brie, Cheddar, and Muenster.

The same trio was beneath the umbrella by the pool. Melissa glanced at her watch, had a tethered look, as if straining to be up and gone. Camille looked oddly formal in a crisp white blouse and navy skirt and flats. George, his hair damp from a plunge, once again lounged in swim trunks.

They were silent as Bess approached. Only Camille spoke as Bess deposited the tray. '*Merci.*'

Melissa ignored the housekeeper, her restless gaze skating from Camille to George to sunlit water splashing over boulders at one end of the pool.

George grabbed the bottle, upended it. He looked at his sister. 'If you have an appointment, don't let us keep you.'

Her mouth curled in a satisfied smile. 'Thanks, bro. I'm counting the minutes. Who knew I'd have such fun in Adelaide.' She stood, gave him a derisive glance. 'You could try meditation. Helps some people. Not everybody,' a flicker toward Camille, 'knows how to have fun.'

Camille took a swift breath, then her lashes fell as she stared down at the mint atop the tea glass.

George glared at Melissa's retreating back.

A screech of metal on the cement. Camille was on her feet. She didn't look toward him, murmured in a hurried voice, 'I need to sort some prints in the studio.'

George stood, too. 'Don't go. I want to talk to you.' He was a travel poster model for a mid-thirties male, broad face, muscular chest, stalwart legs, a very attractive man wearing only swim trunks. His voice was low, urgent. His eyes held hot desire.

Camille's slender hand touched the crimson scarf at her throat. Her young face was vulnerable, forlorn. Despairing. 'Not now. I must think. Not now,' and she whirled away. Her steps clattered across the terrace to the path to the studio with its bank of tall windows.

He lifted a hand, took a single step. Then, face twisting in misery, he turned and walked heavily across the terrace.

I was a little surprised to find Alice Harrison in her office at the house on Saturday afternoon. She wasn't at the desk. Her blonde hair was pulled back in a ponytail, not flattering at her age. She was comfortably stretched on a sofa, two pillows behind her back. She held a travel magazine.

I looked over her shoulder, admired the rugged cliffs near Dubrovnik, dark blue waves crashing into boulders. A hiker with a bright kerchief toiled up a narrow path. Alice plucked a piece of toffee from a candy dish, popped it in her mouth.

The computer monitor glowed. The screen held an airline reservation page. I checked out the white notepad on her lap. Sums were scribbled. I glanced at a sidebar. All-inclusive travel packages ranged in price from four to nine thousand dollars.

I stood unseen on the front porch of the Kirk house. The street was quiet, the house screened from visibility by sycamores and elms. I would have one shot at the Four. The time for charm was past. I intended to be the equivalent of an avalanche pounding down without warning, engulfing everyone in my path.

Demeanor is destiny. That wasn't one of Mama's dictums, it was my own, learned by living, daughter, wife, mother, friend, employee. A warm glance, warmth in return. Sneer, dislike forever. Everything depends upon demeanor. Madeleine's good friend Ellie Fitzgerald was a redhead with curls and lightheartedness and the ever-dancing movements of a hummingbird. I will always be a redhead, but there are redheads and redheads. Contrast Lucille Ball and Agnes Moorehead.

I jabbed the bell.

When the door opened, I looked sternly at Bess Hampton, spoke in a brusque tone slightly deeper than my own. 'Michaela Shayne here to see Mr Kirk.' Not a curl was apparent, my hair drawn back into a sleek bun. No makeup. Black two button jacket with a Chinese collar. White blouse. Short black skirt. Tall black heels. Small embroidered purse. Sleek gray leather attaché case. Michaela Shayne was not Ellie Fitzgerald.

Bess accepted me as presented. 'Yes, ma'am. Is he expecting you?'

'Tell him Mrs Timmons sent me.'

'Oh yes, ma'am. Please come in.' She led me to the living room and offered a sofa. 'I'll tell him you're here.'

I nodded, unsmiling. I remained standing.

George walked into the living room, hair freshly combed, neatly dressed in a Madras shirt and chino pants and loafers.

No socks. Maybe bare feet in shoes made him feel young, a guy about town.

I didn't give him a chance to speak. 'Michaela Shayne, Shayne and Gillespie Private Investigations, Kansas City. Mrs Timmons has authorized me to speak for her.'

'Private Investigations?' His broad face was puzzled.

'Yes, sir. Perhaps we might step into the library. Mrs Timmons indicated the room is suitable for confidential conversation.' I walked forward, nodding to the hallway. I led the way, opened the library door, held the panel for him. 'If you will sit there.' I pointed at a straight chair near the desk. I closed the door and moved behind the desk, sat in the swivel chair. 'Turn the chair to face me.'

He remained standing. 'Who did you say you are?' He gave me a hard stare.

'I am a private investigator authorized to speak to you on behalf of Madeleine Timmons. There is an urgent matter to discuss.'

He was wary and somewhat resentful. 'Why does Madeleine need a private detective?'

My stare was level, 'If you will be seated, I will explain.'

George turned the chair to face me. When seated, he made the chair look small, less than adequate. He was bigger than I'd realized. We looked at each other across the expanse of the desk. The Kirk library wasn't the Adelaide police interrogation room, but the positioning was similar, the subject alone on a hard, straight chair facing authoritative questions.

I pulled a legal pad from the attaché case, picked up a pen. 'I have some particulars here I want to confirm.' I'd done my homework. 'George Randall Kirk. Thirty-seven. Native . . .' I sped through his bio, ended with his marriage to Evelyn.

He looked both irritated and bewildered. 'Why do you have stuff about me? What's going on here? What do you want?'

'Information, Mr Kirk. Mrs Timmons has been apprised of some ugly rumors.'

Abruptly he was utterly still. 'Rumors?'

I continued at a rapid clip. 'Mrs Timmons received an anonymous letter with this message.' I carefully enunciated

each word. 'Evelyn was poisoned. People know who was in
the house that day. The letter was signed *A Friend*.'

'Evelyn poisoned?' George barely managed to push out
the words. He stared at me as if I'd sprouted two heads or
suddenly brandished a sword. 'Poisoned? She had a heart
attack.'

'I'm sorry, sir. Dreadful news, I know. But you can understand why I was hired. Mrs Timmons gave me several names
and I have secured information about them. Mrs Timmons told
me to speak with you first. She wants your help before she
contacts the police.'

'Police.' Was there a hint of fear included in his stricken
stare?

'This will ultimately be a police investigation. But for the
moment, where were you the afternoon Mrs Kirk died?'

'You're asking me where I was when Evelyn died?' There
was outrage in his voice.

I held the pen poised over the pad. 'Sir, everyone in the
house that day must answer. I know you want to help.'

'Help . . .' He suddenly looked up at the painting over the
mantel. For an instant it was as if we could feel salty spray
as a very alive woman exulted in speed and life. His eyes
dropped. He took a breath. 'I think Madeleine's making a
mistake. She should toss that kind of letter. Someone doesn't
like her, wants to cause trouble. But yeah, I guess she had to
do something. That day.' He blew out a spurt of air. 'I'd been
out for lunch. A fellow I got to know at the country club.
We were thinking of a chicken place. Fried chicken but like
home, not that tasteless stuff you get at chains. I got back here
around one.' His gaze slid toward the windows. 'I took a walk
down to the park.'

As he spoke, I made notes. 'Did you see anyone you
knew?'

'Actually,' he spoke slowly, 'I walked down with a guest.
An artist. My wife arranged for her to teach at Goddard. We
happened to go down that way at the same time.'

'What time did you return from your walk?'

'Around two. I wasn't paying attention to the time.'

'Did you and the guest return to the house together?'

'Yes.'

'Where did your guest go?'

'I seem to recall she went to the studio behind the house. I came inside. Ready for a cup of coffee.' He was casual. 'I watched some golf in the den.'

'Did you see Mrs Kirk that afternoon?'

'No.'

The word hung between us.

'Had you started packing?'

He stared.

'Mrs Kirk planned to divorce you. But she died. You inherited a nice amount of money. Not her fortune. That went to her daughter. But this house and money enough for you and the artist to continue to enjoy each other's company.'

George came to his feet, his face empty of expression, but his eyes were hot and watchful.

I slid the legal pad into the attaché case, stood also. 'The police will be informed.' I started for the door.

'Look,' His voice was loud, forceful, 'somebody's been lying to Madeleine. Evelyn and I were fine. We'd worked everything out.'

How easy for George to claim all was well with him and his wife, but Evelyn was dead and couldn't contradict him.

George talked fast. 'I told Evelyn there wasn't anything going on with Camille, that I'd been stupid. Yeah, Camille's attractive, but Evelyn misunderstood.'

'She didn't misunderstand, Mr Kirk.' I was at the door. I gripped the knob, turned, said one word sharply, loudly. I watched his face.

I opened the studio door.

Camille Dubois looked up from the drawing table. Light spilled through the tall windows, illuminating her heart-shaped face and the half-finished sketch of an Irish setter bounding after a multicolored ball, golden coat shimmering in the sun.

I closed the door behind me, walked toward her. 'Michaela Shayne, Shayne and Gillespie Private Investigations, Kansas City.'

As she rose, she said slowly, her face creasing in concern, 'I do not know what that means, investigations? Something about my papers? They are all in order.'

'Not your papers, miss.' I spoke firmly. 'I am here to speak to you on behalf of Evelyn Kirk's daughter, Madeleine Timmons.'

'Oh, I see.' Clearly she didn't, but she was indebted to her late hostess and sponsor, so she said politely, 'How may I help you?'

'Evelyn Kirk was murdered.'

She reached out, held to the back of the chair for support. 'Oh no. No. No.' It was as if she cried for deliverance, for relief. There was no surprise in her face. My pronouncement was her worst fear confirmed. Camille spoke rapidly in English with French phrases, rapidly, desperately. 'You must be the one. Last night. On the telephone. Please, how do you know these things?'

I understood the connection she made. Last night she stood in the hallway outside the kitchen and heard Gage's shocking call insisting on murder.

Again, she cried, 'How do you know these things?'

'A wife is murdered after she discovers her husband in an affair with a young woman she has befriended—'

'Not an affair.' Her voice choked in a sob. 'There is no truth. I couldn't help that he wanted me. And my heart breaks. I would love him if I could, but now I'm afraid. I pushed him away after she died. She was strong. Do you know? She played tennis. She was such a tennis player. She shouldn't have died. Oh, they said there was something with her heart but my *maman* has the heart that beats this way and that and she still skis and laughs and lives. I didn't think Evelyn should be dead. I kept thinking I must move but I have so little money and I was offered the place to stay and the young lady, Madeleine, urged me to continue. Still I have been thinking. But I didn't want to leave George. Now there is this talk of murder. I don't know what to think. I am so afraid.'

My stare was unyielding. 'Mrs Kirk ordered you and her husband to leave.'

'I spoke with her.' Camille's speech was rushed, insistent. 'I told her I would look for a place to go, but she must believe me, I never responded to George. Never. She even smiled, said, "Poor baby," when I told her there was no truth, that I would not love a man who belonged to another. She said, "Poor baby. Even though you love him." And I cried and she told me to go back to my room, we would speak of it later. But the next day, she died.'

'She was murdered.'

'Murder.' Her voice shook.

'Murder. The police will be informed. About you.' I walked to the door. Again, I put my hand on the knob, turned, said one word sharply, loudly. I watched her face.

I returned to the house. I entered by the kitchen door, nodded pleasantly to Bess Hampton. I didn't ask permission. I walked briskly to the stairs, climbed. In the upstairs hallway, I opened the door to Alice Harrison's office, stepped inside, closed the door behind me.

Alice turned her chair toward the door, looked inquiring, polite enough but with no interest. The harsh light from the ceiling globe emphasized the dark roots to her blonde hair, the fan of wrinkles by her eyes, the permanent lines that bracketed her lips. She looked like a woman in her fifties who had not enjoyed the journey.

Clothes tell us much about their wearer. A retiring person chooses simple apparel in restrained colors. Outgoing lively people see no reason not to flare bright feathers like a macaw. New wealth can be ostentatious. Old wealth may be incredibly expensive but understated.

Alice's clothing was casual, it was Saturday, a beige cotton shirt, blue cotton pants, espadrilles. There was an ink stain on one sleeve. If she embezzled, apparently fashion wasn't the impetus.

'Michaela Shayne. Shayne and Gillespie Private Investigators. Kansas City.'

She didn't say a word. Her tight face signaled a woman immediately on the defensive, marshaling arguments, readying a defense. Not the reaction of innocence.

I walked across the uncarpeted floor, heels clicking. 'The audit is scheduled Monday.'

'Audit?' Her hands clenched into tight claws.

'Evelyn Kirk's papers indicate you were responsible for irregularities.' The charge was made in an impersonal level voice, as if a bewigged judge were gaveling a courtroom to attention.

'What are you doing in Evelyn's files?' Her voice was uneven, choked. 'I swear everything's absolutely all right. Who said you could look in her papers?'

I repeated my name and title. 'I am authorized to interview you by Madeleine Timmons.'

'Madeleine?' Alice straightened her hands, the fingers stiff in front of her. 'Why is Madeleine doing this to me?'

'Irregularities.' I spoke with finality.

'This is absurd, insulting. I won't be hounded about a mistake. That's all that happened. I made a mistake.' Bluster. 'Evelyn understood there was a mistake. I didn't try to take Evelyn's money.'

I was matter of fact, almost conversational. 'You took the church's money.'

'That's all in the past. Evelyn helped me. I was saving a friend. I thought he was my friend. And he was terrified. He said they would hurt him, break his legs. Because of the gambling. He owed so much money. I helped him.' Tears welled. 'And he took the money and never came back and he'd told me . . .' Told her he loved her? I imagined so.

'What did Evelyn say when you told her?'

'She said I was a fool to believe him.' Alice's voice was tired.

'How much did you take from Evelyn?'

'That was an accident.'

I was not an accountant. In fact, Bobby Mac always urged me simply to record checks and Not To Subtract. I can't understand why everyone is so picky about balances. As long as you know where you are, well, that should be good enough. I had no idea if one could accidentally siphon off a sizable sum. I rather doubted it.

'Evelyn didn't believe you.'

Something shifted in her eyes. She lifted her chin. 'Oh yes she did. Everything was all right. And,' was there a taunting gleam in her cool blue eyes, 'I'm so glad we worked everything out. Since she died.'

I nodded. 'Of course you understand the audit is scheduled.'

She didn't look worried. She was good with figures. Perhaps she'd had plenty of time to make irregularities regular. 'I'll be glad to help. I'll be here all day Monday.'

Once again I paused at a door, looked back, said one word sharply, loudly. I watched her face.

Melissa's untidy room was empty except for the Siamese cat curled in a nest of silk hose. Bright blue eyes gave me a glance, then he turned over, batted a stocking, rolled to his feet. Stockings flew in all directions. He raced across the floor, a flash of gray fur, rose effortlessly to land on a valence. He turned his back to me, suddenly bored.

I disappeared; thought, *Melissa's car.*

The black Jeep was parked in front of Room 19 at the Sweet Slumber Motel. The car was empty.

Inside the motel room, Melissa lounged in a red short silk nightie. She held a margarita glass frosted with salt. She relaxed on the divan, two cushions behind her back, legs stretched out, reading a fashion magazine, awaiting her lover.

I was struck by the emptiness in her face. I saw no anticipation. Instead she looked restless, irritable, as if poised to flee. I cautiously turned the knob, eased the door open a fraction, just enough for an easy entrance.

I returned to the sidewalk outside, made sure no one was about, and Appeared, once again in the black suit and heels. I turned the knob, stepped inside the room.

At the sound, she put down the magazine and looked around. She jerked to sit up, swinging her legs to the floor. 'You have the wrong room.'

'No mistake.' I shut the door behind me. 'Hello, Melissa

Kirk.' I introduced myself. I doubt she heard anything but Private Investigations. She scrambled for her cell phone.

'You don't need to warn him. I'm not here from his wife.'

She held the phone, glared, spoke rapidly, 'Private investigator here,' clicked off.

'So sorry he won't join us. The red nightie wasted.'

'Get out. I'll call Security.'

'That scares me.' Did I get a whiff of coal smoke? Precept Five. Do not succumb to the temptation to confound those who appear to oppose you. To my surprise and consternation, I was swept by sadness at the impersonal, clean enough but tawdry motel room in late afternoon and a young woman with hot, haunted eyes.

'I'm sorry.' And I was. Sorry for the forces that led her here, for a life that appeared to have no direction. 'You shouldn't waste your time with a married man.' In her last conversation with Sybil, Evelyn described a stormy meeting with Melissa over her affair with a good friend's husband, told Sybil she'd ordered Melissa to pack up and go. 'If he cared about you, why doesn't he leave his wife?'

Those tormented eyes stared, shining with tears. Of rage? Of despair? Of defeat?

I made a guess. 'He's staying because of the kids. You should have your own life and kids—'

'Shut up.' The words were hard as rocks flung against a barricade. Tears flooded down her thin face, a thin young face. 'She would have been three years old the next week. Three years old. He slammed out of the house after we had a fight. He was mad, almost mad enough not to see anything. He didn't see her. He screeched in reverse and she was in the drive on her tricycle. A neighborhood girl was watching her and he almost hit her, too.' Melissa came to her feet, stood, wounded, wretched, wasted.

'I'm sorry.' Her pain flooded the room, was a weight I felt.

'Sorry doesn't help. Sorry isn't worth anything. She's dead. She'll always be dead. So take your sorry and your camera somewhere else. I don't give a damn about him or his wife or you or anything. Get out.' She reached for a blouse, pulled it over her head, grabbed slacks, stepped into them, stuffing the nightie inside the waistband.

I stood at the door. I waited until her gaze swung toward me, said one word sharply, loudly. I watched her face.

SIXTEEN

Robert answered the knock on his door. I did think he could be a bit cheerier when he saw me. To say I have him spooked puts it mildly. His eyes get a wide stare and he lurches backward. And I'd thoughtfully changed into the white blouse and batik skirt I'd worn in the park. Michaela Shayne might truly discombobulate Robert.

For an instant, Gage looked at me with a considering expression and then it was as if she gave a mental shrug, decided – whoever I was – clearly I was helping her mom. Her voice was warm. 'Bailey Ruth, I'm so glad you've come. We have great news.' She talked a mile a minute as I sat on a chair opposite her. Her face was awfully pink from the day in the park.

'Calamine lotion will take out the sting.' Even good sunscreen has its limits for a full day in the sun.

She waved her hand as if brushing away a caterpillar. 'I'm OK. And listen, we transcribed the recordings. We have names and addresses and cell-phone numbers. They loved us. Proud as peacocks to be The Winners. I sent Robert to Walmart and he bought a half-dozen twenty-dollar gift certificates . . .'

Robert looked glum. I expected the hundred and twenty he spent was way over his budget. I must remember to ask Iris to reimburse him.

'. . . and we found three more people who saw Mom get out of her car and go to the carousel and immediately walk away talking on her cell. And we went to the police station and that big man—'

Robert was meticulous. 'The police chief.'

'Actually, he was pretty nice and he took everything from us and set up a file. I asked him how soon Mom would be released.' The glow diminished. 'He said she was being held as a material witness and at this point he was concerned for her safety since she had been in contact with the last victim and he thought the murderer acted fast and might start to wonder if Nicole had told Mom anything. He said she was safer in custody until Monday.'

A cell on Saturday night isn't a happy place to be. Iris was no longer the sole occupant of the jail. Two more cells were occupied. In one a disheveled woman sat on the bed, arms wrapped tightly across her front, staring disconsolately into the corridor. From the other cell came a deep lugubrious voice indistinctly singing 'The Sloop *John B*'.

Iris gestured toward the singer. 'He has a point.' There was the barest wobble in her voice.

I was glad I'd come. I didn't want to raise her hopes too high, but I could give her a boost. 'Gage and Robert spent the day at the park. They found three witnesses who will testify you arrived at the carousel and immediately departed. The police chief has been informed.'

Her face was alight. 'Oh that's wonderful. Maybe I'll get out of here tomorrow.'

I gave her a thumbs up. I didn't want to tell her she was only on first base and it would take a double to get her home. Let her think freedom was almost hers. It was much more comforting than another verse of 'The Sloop *John B*'.

'It's cold enough to hang meat in here.'

The hamburger gripped in Sam's right hand stopped midway to his mouth. 'I turned the thermostat down to sixty-five in honor of Her Honor. You can punch it up.'

I was at the wall in an instant and nudged the control. A cashmere cardigan offered instant warmth. I settled in the chair opposite Sam's desk, my eyes riveted on the hamburger. It was almost seven o'clock, way past my suppertime. 'I don't suppose you have an extra?'

'It unsettles me to talk to an empty chair.'

The room had warmed a bit. I discarded the cardigan and Appeared in a brightly tropical shift but I decided on three-quarter length sleeves and ballet flats. Very comfortable.

His big heavy face managed a tired smile. 'Thanks. So fill me in on the Kirk house.'

I was relieved that his tone was weary but companionable.
'Will do. But,' my voice was longing, 'do you have an extra?'

'Extra what?'

'Hamburger.'

A sigh. 'Claire's in Tishomingo visiting her sister. Yeah, I
got two cheeseburgers, cheddar, lettuce, tomato, onions,
mustard, mayo. They came with onion rings on top. Tonight's
special. So I didn't order fries. Anyway, when I talk to Claire
tonight I'll admit to the cheeseburger, but stress no fries. She'd
be happier if I ordered grilled chicken but a man has his limits.
I've had a long day and I have this funny feeling it's going
to get longer.' As he spoke, he spread out the morning newspaper on the desk near me.

I picked up the fried onion ring and munched, a big onion
ring with crispy cornmeal crust. 'Lulu's?'

'Yeah. They know I'm on a diet. Libby slipped in some
celery sticks. Wait 'til I tell Claire I had celery sticks instead
of fries. Maybe I'll get strawberry shortcake for my treat next
week. Dessert every Thursday. Don't know why she picked
Thursdays. Yeah, I guess I do. The mayor has all the department heads in on Thursday mornings, trying to chisel another
thou off everyone's budget.' He finished his cheeseburger,
looked morose. 'Speaking of money, the overtime is piling
up. I called Judy Weitz in to deal with the info Gallagher's
daughter and boyfriend brought in. They did some smart work.
I asked them how they came up with the idea. She couldn't
say enough nice things about Bailey Ruth Raeburn, an old
friend of her mom's at Fort Sill.'

I smiled.

Sam was dry. 'The guy not so much. I said I always liked
redheads. He looked like he wanted to burrow under a blanket.
So you and the girl are chums. About halfway through their
spiel – and she did most of the talking – I kept thinking I'd
heard her voice before in addition to the other time I talked
to her. After they left, I ran the Crime Stoppers tape again. So
do you want to tell me how you got Gage Gallagher into the
Kirk house at two in the morning to make that call?'

'These things happen,' I said airily.

'When you're around.' He tried but didn't quite manage to

suppress a grin. 'I fell for it. But it turns out you steered me right. I talked to the doc. Huffed. Puffed. Then crumpled like a crushed beer can. Yes, he knew she died from medicine ground up and dropped in her afternoon lemonade. I got the papers ready to file for an exhumation. The autopsy will prove how she died. The text of the note in Lambert's wallet definitely indicates she didn't take the stuff herself. No way it could be accidental. Not with the amount in the glass. So it's murder. I started looking because of that call to Crime Stoppers, even though I had a feeling it was somehow rigged.' A head shake. 'My instinct was right. Nobody living there called with a first-person view of that glass of lemonade. You based the call on Lambert's note. But the doctor's actions prove what Lambert wrote. As for the doctor, he meant well. It's funny how people do things with the best of intentions and the results bleed through a lot of lives. If only one fact or another changed, Matt Lambert and Nicole Potter might still be alive. Instead a murderer succeeded, never had a worry until Lambert called on a burner phone, demanding a big donation. I gather you've talked to them all now, the ones who were at the banquet Thursday night.'

'I have talked to them.'

'How easily could the killer make that donation happen?'

I was thoughtful. 'George Kirk inherited enough to make a donation. His sister? No money, but if she suggested a gift in Evelyn's memory, George likely would have agreed. The artist? George is nuts about her. If he thought a donation would please Camille, he would provide whatever she asked. The cousin? She handled money. She has a history of taking money if she needed it. The person Lambert called could have paid off. But it didn't cost a penny to kill him.'

'When you announced you intended to find out everything about the banquet guests at the Kirk table, I told you they were off limits to Officer Loy.'

'Right.'

He was intrigued. 'How did you manage to question them?'

I was touched that he took it for granted I'd not Appeared as Officer Loy. 'I found out as much as I could about each of them before I contacted them. I pretended to be a college chum of Madeleine's and talked to several people who knew a lot about Evelyn and those around her. When I thought I had a handle on them, I showed up at the front door as a private investigator sent by Madeleine Timmons.'

He raised a dark eyebrow. 'That could be dicey. What if one of them called or texted Madeleine?'

'No one was that close to her. I was authoritative. Michaela Shayne of Shayne and Gillespie Private Investigations, Kansas City.'

He gave a low rumble of laughter. 'My grandad had a used bookstore. Lots of paperbacks. I grew up reading tattered old copies of the Brett Halliday books, Michael Shayne, redheaded PI. OK, Mike, what did you find out?'

I tried to give him a sense of each person.

He listened intently. When I was silent, he was brisk. 'George married an older woman for her money, was the handsome lover, but one day a bewitching young woman arrives. He was probably used to money by then, liked living well. But he wanted the artist. The sister is bitter, mad at the world, aching to make other people miserable. Maybe she's attracted to that husband of Evelyn's friend. Maybe she just hated seeing someone else be happy. But she probably liked the money there, too. The artist?' Sam looked cynical. 'Lots of innocence on parade but she's still in the house. The bookkeeper? If Evelyn tossed her out, she probably would never get another job that paid as well. If she called the police, she could face time in prison.' He looked discouraged. 'Good work, Mike. But we aren't a step closer to knowing which one of them killed Evelyn, slipped down the stairs at Rose Bower to break Lambert's neck, and walked to the carousel to kill the student.'

My voice was grave. 'I know.'

Sam stared at me. 'What have I missed?'

'After PI Shayne interviewed each one, she walked to the door. With no hint of what was to come, PI Shayne stared into the watching eyes, a long, hard stare. PI Shayne spoke a single word. Loudly. Sharply.'

I pushed back my chair, rose, walked to the blackboard. I printed in block letters:

DIGITALIS.

Sam crumpled the greasy paper wrapper from the cheese-burger. 'Oh come on, Bailey Ruth. A three-time murderer gasps and clutches his/her bosom and all is revealed.' His voice was heavy with irony.

I continued unabashed. 'One looked at me with no change in expression. One took a step back, convinced I was unhinged. One was puzzled, trying to make sense of an unfamiliar word. But Sam, one knew exactly what I meant. And why. My concluding comment to the killer? I spoke quite pleasantly, "It's a pleasure doing business with you. I'll be in touch."'

Sam was dour. 'Judges want facts. A judge won't be impressed by a description of this face or that face. Furthermore, there's a small but important matter of appearing in the witness stand. The defense gets a list of witnesses. So are we supposed to create an identity for you? You can't testify even if it ever got that far. This face and that face isn't proof. We need proof. And we need a witness who can testify.'

Poor Sam. He was probably still hungry since I'd taken half his planned meal. And the mayor was driving him crazy. And I would admit a spectral detective lacks authority. I was sanguine. 'Of course we'll get proof. The murderer expects PI Shayne to get in touch. How about a red wig for Judy Weitz? We'll set up a meeting at night so the difference between us' – probably a good forty pounds – 'won't be evident. We can use a phone with an unknown number—'

'You *think* the murderer expects a call.'

'The murderer expects a call.' I remembered the eyes looking at me, the eyes that said I would be dead if we were in another place, if there were any way to safely be done with me, but there could not be murder in a house filled with people who saw Michaela Shayne arrive, could describe her.

Sam gave me a level look. 'We'll find out. Call. Set up a meeting. Detective Weitz. Red wig and all.' A slight smile. 'Better set it at night.' A sigh. 'More overtime. I'll have to deploy officers an hour or two in advance, cameras ready. Have to get some people close enough to the meeting to keep the murderer from whacking Weitz. Say we set the time at midnight. It will have to be tomorrow night.' Another weary sigh. 'Sunday night. Yeah. Everybody likes to work on Sunday nights. It will really lift morale—'

'Sam.' My tone was chiding.

He managed a grin. 'All right. Actually they're like race-horses. Sound the bugle and off they go, doesn't matter, rain or shine, night or day. Wish we could set something up on Monday morning. That would avoid overtime. Do you have any idea how much overtime will be involved? I'll have to call people in tomorrow, spend most of the day making the arrangements for tomorrow night. All overtime.' He swiveled to the computer, tapped his mouse.

I relaxed. Sam might grouse about overtime to keep the mayor from tearing holes in his budget, but Sam didn't like killers. I remained quiet, let him work on a plan of attack.

I thought about the call I would soon make. I might suggest hiring Shayne and Gillespie on a retainer. A monthly retainer. Maybe ten thousand—

Sam's office door burst open, banged against the wall. Heavy steps sounded.

I disappeared, jerked around to look.

Mayor Neva Lumpkin strode across the floor, hand outstretched, index finger pointing at Sam. 'Do you know how much it costs to dig up a body, do an autopsy?'

Sam was on his feet. There was a curl of mustard on his chin.

I grabbed a napkin, eased around the desk with my hand out of sight, put the napkin in his hand, and lifted his hand to his chin.

He got the idea, scrubbed.

In her fury, the mayor stumbled into the straight chair I'd just vacated, knocking it sideways. She was too angry to notice. She plumped broad hands on his desk. Her fingers glittered with rings, three on her right hand, a ruby, a sapphire, and carnelian, engagement and wedding bands on the left with diamonds fat as early morning dewdrops. 'Did you ask how much an autopsy was going to cost?'

Sam's face hardened. 'As the duly appointed chief of police, it is my duty to investigate suspected homicides.'

'Eight thousand dollars.' Her voice quivered. 'My budget.

My campaign. You are trying to sabotage me. Well, it won't work. I have ordered the application to the court be withdrawn.'

His voice was clipped. 'Who carried out that order?'

She pushed up from the desk, drew herself to her full height. 'It is fortunate that I keep a close eye on the activities of this department.' Her voice grew stronger. 'I keep a close eye on the activities of every department.' Perhaps she realized this was not a dais. Her voice dropped. 'Detective Harris will assume temporary command of the department as of this moment. You will officially go on administrative leave immediately.'

She turned, stomped across the room. The door slammed behind her.

Sam still stood. 'Howie strikes again. I heard some foot-steps when I picked up the printout for the exhumation request. He must have lurked. Howie's good at lurking. Too bad he doesn't show the same curiosity when he's on a case. There's some button or other you can push to print a copy of the most recent print job.'

Detective Howie Harris was small, plump, and tried to spread thinning locks over a balding pate.

'Can't you go ahead and figure out a plan and arrange everything?'

'Tempting,' Sam said. 'But Howie would find out and I'd get fired for insubordination. I could handle that. But I can't order detectives and officers to work when I don't have the authority. Would they turn out for me sub rosa? Sure. But that would get them fired, too. Neva would make a clean sweep. She'd fire Hal and quite a few others. She'd be like Midas running gold through her fingers with the money she'd save on salaries. Plus you can bet Chief Harris would toe the line on overtime. If somebody's life was at stake, I'd do it in a heartbeat. But right now PI Michaela Shayne is the only person in danger and we both know she's safe.'

I felt stricken, remembering the wobble in Iris's voice. 'Howie Harris will charge Iris Gallagher with murder Monday.'

Sam said nothing, but his silence meant he well understood.

As Mama always told us kids, 'If you get boxed in, be an Oklahoma buffalo. Lower your head and charge.'

Sam and I together might not be a herd of buffalo, but we could raise some dust. 'The mayor nixed Chief Cobb. We can't call on anyone in the department. But long ago in the Old West, sometimes you had to handle your own problems. You and I together, Sam, we can do it.'

'We? I don't see you.'

I Appeared.

'Thanks. I don't feel quite so nuts when I can see you. As for your idea . . . The Old West.' Sam's dark eyes gleamed. 'A sheriff could deputize civilians, create a posse if he had to.' A frown. 'But there's no one we can call on to help us.'

My voice was loud, firm, emphatic. 'Of course there is. The SIVF.'

Sam peered at me. There was a curious uncertainty in his gaze. Was he wondering if I'd come untethered from reality?

I talked fast, and the faster I talked, the more excited I became. 'We can. I swear we can.'

Sam sank down in his chair. Perhaps he looked a bit dazed. 'The Save Iris Volunteer Force. Only you could come up with an idea like that. But you know, just maybe . . .' He turned to the monitor. 'It's certainly reasonable for a man going on administrative leave to deal with any outstanding matters that require disposition. Such as . . .' He typed rapidly, waited a moment, nodded at a reply, gave me a thumbs up.

He looked ten years younger than when I first arrived this evening. Cats love catnip. A policeman revels in outwitting criminals. And I supposed Sam was taking some delight in outwitting a woman obsessed by overtime.

We waited in silence, I suppose both of us considering how a posse of five could corner a killer. I had some ideas.

Sam had a faraway look in his eyes. He pulled the bag of M&Ms from the left lower drawer, politely offered me a handful, poured a mound into his palm. We munched in companionable silence.

Matters move quickly when the head man issues an order. In less than five minutes, there was a knock at his door. The door opened. A uniformed attendant with faded blonde hair and thin hands held the panel. Her nails were a mournful purple. 'In here, please, ma'am. And here's your stuff.' She held out a plastic bag. 'Please confirm you have received all of your valuables.' The blonde pulled a sheet of paper from a pocket. 'Sign here.' She tapped the bottom of the page.

Iris Gallagher, her thin face drawn and uncertain, looked from the plastic bag to Sam Cobb to me. Despite her wrinkled lacy white top and turquoise slacks, she was still lovely and there was the beginning of hope in her face. 'They said I'm free to go?' Her voice wasn't quite level.

'Come in.' I hurried across the room, put a hand on her arm.

The attendant still held the sheet. 'Ma'am.'

Iris fumbled in the plastic bag, pulled out a watch with a silver band, a golden wedding band, a cell phone, a purse. She took the pen from the attendant, signed the sheet, slipped on the watch, tucked the purse under her elbow, held tight to the cell phone.

'Ma'am, please confirm there is thirty-six dollars in bills and four dollars and twelve cents in change.'

Iris nodded agreement, made no effort to open the purse. 'Confirmed.'

The attendant checked a box. 'If you'll initial here.'

In an instant Iris handed her the initialed sheet and the attendant turned away. Iris listened to the clip of receding footsteps, turned to look at Sam. 'Am I free?'

Sam nodded. 'Charge dropped. You are released.'

Tears welled in her eyes. 'I can go home.'

'Sam will drive us there.' I was across the room, holding to her arm. 'Sam and I need help from you and Gage and Robert. You can call Gage and Robert on the way.'

Sam jerked a thumb toward the hallway. 'I don't blame her for taking a shower. I feel that way about cells, too, but we keep a clean jail. No mice. No roaches.' Sam appeared relaxed in a large easy chair, but it was the relaxation before effort, a man poised to sprint from the starting block at the sound of the gun.

The front door opened. Gage and Robert spilled into the small living room, still in their casual dress from the day in the park, both decidedly pink from the sun. Gage ran past us.

'Mom, Mom?' Robert stood somewhat uncomfortably in the center of the rose-and-silver Persian rug. His wary glance slid from me to the chief.

Sam was genial. 'Sit down, Robert. When the ladies join us, we'll talk.'

His face glum, Robert walked to a table in one corner, pulled out a straight chair, turned it to face us. When seated, he was as stiff as Wiggins's starched white shirt.

I tried to put Robert at ease. 'Such a lovely day to spend in the park.'

'Hot.' His posture was on a par with a fence post.

'July,' Sam observed.

I turned to Sam. 'I noticed Judy Weitz is a bit more fashionable.'

Sam looked utterly blank.

I looked from Sam to Robert and decided neither was open to casual conversation. Happily, footsteps sounded in the hall. Gage clung to her mother's hand as they entered the room. Fresh from a shower, Iris was crisp in a navy striped cotton T and white slacks and sandals.

Robert stood up, remained standing until Iris and Gage settled on the couch. He sat again, still glum. Clearly he sensed impending activities were unlikely to enhance the professional standing of a fledgling lawyer. His eyes moved to Gage. He took a quick breath. Professional standing went overboard.

I rose and walked to the fireplace, faced an attentive audience. 'Chief Cobb and I are here to ask the three of you to join us in gathering facts that will exonerate Iris. We intend to trap Evelyn Kirk's murderer, who is also responsible for the deaths of Matt Lambert and Nicole Potter.' I described digitalis in lemonade, Matt seeing a reflection in the mirror, Matt's talk with Evelyn's doctor, Matt's decision to trade a donation to Goddard for his silence.

Gage shot Sam a hot look. 'I knew he was leaning on someone.'

Sam was equable. 'You were right.'

Nicole's glimpse of a murderer and her attempt at blackmail, the meeting in the carousel, the arrival of Michaela Shayne of Shayne and Gillespie Private Investigations in Kansas City, PI Shayne's taunting *digitalis.*

Evelyn leaned forward, her gaze intent. Gage's mouth formed a perfect O. Robert appeared to be sorting topic headings in his mind.

I looked at Sam.

He nodded approval.

I was bolstered by his presence, a big man, a good man, a man who would always try to do the right thing. I hoped he saw the admiration in my gaze.

A slight flush tinged his cheeks. 'Throw it out.'

'When I said *digitalis*, Melissa Kirk looked at me with no change in expression. Alice Harrison took a step back, convinced I was unhinged. Camille Dubois was puzzled, trying to make sense of an unfamiliar word. George Kirk looked at me with a murderer's eyes.'

Sam immediately frowned, shook his head. 'Evelyn Kirk intended to divorce him. Remember Tahiti? Why wouldn't she slam the door in his face? She wasn't having anything to do with him.'

I was quick to reply. 'Remember that Matt Lambert was in the room though George was unaware of his presence. She was a proud woman. She may have been surprised to see George, but she wouldn't have given any indication of anger. Perhaps she merely nodded, took the tray, closed the door. She probably thought George brought the tray to try and gain a moment to speak to her. Perhaps she said something like, "I'll talk to you later." However it happened, it was George that Matt saw in the mirror because George understood immediately when I said, "Digitalis." Only the doctor and the murderer and I knew that Evelyn died from an overdose of digitalis.'

Sam slowly nodded.

Robert cleared his throat. 'Inadmissible.'

I sent him a sweet smile. Robert was Robert, literal, factual, legalistic.

I spoke firmly, 'George ground digitalis pills into a powder. George let the dog out to distract the housekeeper. George spilled powder into the lemonade, carried the tray upstairs.

George opened the door, handed the tray to his wife. George eased down the stairs at Rose Bower, met Matt Lambert, pulled a weighted sock, likely tucked inside his jacket, and swung with the strength of a superb tennis player. When Nicole called him, George Kirk used a charming and reassuring tone to persuade her to come to the carousel.' I looked at Sam. 'When Michaela Shayne calls George, you will know he is guilty.'

Iris turned to Sam. 'Why haven't you arrested him?'

Robert repeated, 'Inadmissible.'

It was Sam's turn to clear his throat. 'If I had the power, detectives would be swarming everywhere to find proof. Look for his fingerprints downstairs at Rose Bower, anywhere, a wall, a door panel, somewhere in the room, out on the terrace. Detectives would canvass White Deer Park with his mugshot. Somebody will have seen him in the park just like,' he nodded at Gage and Robert, 'you found people who saw your mother walk to the carousel and immediately leave. But the mayor's running for re-election, she's doubling down on the budget, and she's put me on administrative leave because I ordered the exhumation of Evelyn Kirk's body. A big expense. I can't order officers to investigate. At this moment George Kirk is probably hustling the French artist and enjoying a bourbon and soda.'

'But George,' my tone was silky, 'has a worried mind. He's expecting a call from Private Investigator Michaela Shayne. He knows my voice. He knows that I know. He's figuring out how to dispose of another blackmailer. If he meets Shayne, she can be wired to record their conversation. If Sam was in charge, he would put a red wig on a police officer and George would be trapped.'

Robert was skeptical. 'Kirk knows she doesn't have hard evidence. Why not blow off her demand? If she persists, he could call the cops, say he's being harassed by a woman making up false claims about his wife's death.' Robert spoke in the reasoned tone of a lawyer listing facts.

I looked at him with a new respect. He might be literal, but he was smart. Maybe literal wasn't a bad approach. 'He can't afford to have Shayne go to the police. He thinks Madeleine Timmons hired Shayne. She could insist on exhumation.

George wants Shayne to inform her client that there is no truth
to the ugly rumors.' I glanced at Sam. 'George won't ignore
my call. If there is an autopsy and death is determined to be
the result of an overdose of digitalis, a police investigation
will follow. He won't ignore the phone call from Michaela
Shayne. But here's the problem. Sam can make a citizen's
arrest, but we need a woman in a red wig to meet Kirk and
record the conversation.' I looked at Iris.

Gage immediately stretched out an arm in front of Iris, the
cub protecting her mother. 'I'll do it. You're a lot younger than
Mom and I have a red wig in the closet from the Follies we
put on at school for a charity skit. I can look like you and I'll
drop my voice—'

Robert was on his feet. 'Absolutely not. I forbid it. Not you.
Not your mom.' He swung toward me, shoulders hunched.
'So why don't you finish what you started? You're Michaela
Shayne, you talk to him, record what he says.'

There was the challenge. Sam needed a witness who could
later testify in court about recording a conversation with a
murderer. I could hear the question from the defense attorney,
'Let's see now, Bailey Ruth Raeburn under the alias Michaela
Shayne. Let's establish your identity for the record. Where do
you live?' Heaven was heavenly but not an address likely to
be acceptable to the court.

'That won't do.' Iris's glance at me indicated she understood
my plight. 'Of course you can't meet with George. Because
of your disability.'

I suppose we all looked surprised.

Gage's face was instantly sympathetic.

Robert looked glum again, remembering the voices at the
murder scene in Rose Bower and my sometimes-here some-
times-not assistance with the seed pod and our meetings in
the park. 'Oh, yeah. I guess not.'

'Thanks for your understanding.' I managed a sweet, sad
smile. 'Of course, you know I never like to discuss my situation.'

'Of course not,' Iris agreed instantly. 'There's no more to
be said.'

'Yeah.' Robert eyed me like a pile of fish entrails somebody
left on the dock.

Gage was much too well-mannered to inquire for particulars about my disability.

'Definitely I will meet him. This is for my benefit. It's my responsibility.' Iris was emphatic. 'What do we need to do?'

'Not.' Robert took a deep breath. He strode the few feet across the room to look down at Sam. 'Kirk's not stupid. He had to deal with Lambert and the student. They saw him. All Shayne has is a reaction to a word. Shayne can make all the claims she wants about looking in the eyes of a murderer, but that's not evidence.'

I spoke out. 'He doesn't want an autopsy. He can't afford to have an investigation into her death. It would be sure to include the possibility of murder, and who do they look at first? The husband. Especially a husband who's been ordered to leave the house.'

Robert was judicious. 'The autopsy results won't convict him. We need evidence. I will get evidence.'

SEVENTEEN

S am said mildly, 'What do you have in mind?'

Robert spoke in short, direct sentences. He no longer looked glum. Nothing he suggested would get him disbarred.

Sam gave an approving nod. 'That works. Good idea, man. I have some stuff out in my car. Be right back.' He strode to the front door, banged the screen behind him.

Iris looked worried. 'Robert, I can't let you take this kind of risk.'

Robert reminded me of an RAF fighter pilot climbing into a Spitfire, moving with speed but no panic. Robert had the same aura of quiet confidence. I almost mentioned the Save Iris Volunteer Force to tell him he was in charge of the mission, but I decided the moment wasn't right. Sam came back from his car with a blue canvas sports bag. He carried the bag to Iris's small dining-room table, pulled the zipper. He lifted up an index card. 'Here's Kirk's cell-phone number.' He reached in, retrieved a nondescript cell phone. 'The number won't mean anything to Kirk but he'll answer because the caller might be the private eye. Good phone for this purpose. Records. Has a speaker phone. An upscale burner. The mayor would fuss at the expense.' Next came a slim rectangular black plastic box. 'Recorder. Picks up a sneeze at fifty yards.' He looked at Robert. 'Wear a loose shirt over your undershirt. Recorder comes with Velcro.'

Robert looked blank.

Iris understood modern mores, intervened. 'Most young men don't wear undershirts. Robert can wear a T under his shirt.'

Gage came to her feet, hurried to the table. She looked at Sam, not Robert. 'Robert can't go by himself. That man's dangerous. I'll go with him.'

Iris walked to the table. 'Robert, you're wonderful,' and she meant every word, 'but it's too dangerous.'

'No danger.' Robert spoke loudly, a courtroom voice. Bobby Mac's cousin Cimarron, yes, Cimarron after the river and they called him Ron, was a trial lawyer. Ron could be heard to the farthest rafter. 'I've worked everything out.' There was total confidence in his tone. He picked up the cell phone and index card. As he tapped numbers, he said firmly, 'Absolute quiet. I've put it on speaker so you can hear.' The cell rang, once, twice.

'Hello.' George Kirk sounded gruff, wary.

'Vince Gillespie here. I'm calling for Michaela Shayne. Shayne and Gillespie Private Investigations, Kansas City. I'm fully informed about her dealings with you. We have some business to discuss, Mr Kirk.' Robert spoke pleasantly, a businessman setting up a meeting, one hopefully that would prove satisfactory to all concerned.

George's silence was absolute. He expected a call from the woman who threatened him. Now he confronted the totally unexpected – not one threat, but two.

Robert was brisk. 'You understand we need to work out a business plan. I'll bring a prepared contract for you to sign. A monthly retainer to Shayne and Gillespie. Twenty thousand a month for services rendered. You will receive bills that list all charges. All perfectly aboveboard. A business arrangement. Very beneficial to you. There will be a separate document, you understand we need some protection, for your signature. That document contains details about the digitalis in your wife's lemonade, the weighted socks you used to kill Matt Lambert at Rose Bower and the student seated in the carousel in White Deer Park. We can discuss this at some length in the morning in City Park. I'll be waiting on the pier in the pond at nine a.m.' Robert clicked off the speaker, ended the call.

'I don't want you on that pier with him.' Gage clapped her hands together in a tight grip.

Robert slipped an arm around her shoulders. 'We have him cornered. He has to come. He has to agree to a payoff. Maybe he'll claim he can't do twenty K a month. I'll demand financial records.'

Gage's lips trembled. 'He'll bring one of those awful socks.'

Robert gave her a squeeze. 'He won't try anything with me.

Remember, it's Shayne and Gillespie. If Michaela Shayne'
– he shot me a look of active dislike – 'met him, of course
he'd plan to kill her. But he can't swing at me because Michaela
knows everything. He has to face the fact that he's trapped.
Since Michaela knows I'm meeting him, I'm perfectly safe.'

Iris brushed back a strand of dark hair, her gaze intense.
'We have to be certain you're safe. We'll all come to the park.
There are always people near the pond and on the pier. If there
are people around – and we will be – that's a protection.'

Robert folded his arms, looked mulish. 'No way. You and
Gage stay here.' He jerked his head at Sam. 'He can be there.
We'll come here as soon as we get him in jail.'

Iris reached out, patted his cheek. 'I love manly men. But
we are womanly women. We'll be there.'

I recalled the good and the bad I'd observed at City Park over
the years. Happy couples hand in hand. Sad solitary walkers.
Dogs and their devoted owners. An occasional homeless
person with empty eyes and a trash bag to carry stuff. Children
running barefoot in summer, pulling sleds in winter. This
morning the pond shimmered beneath the early sun. A
graveled path circled the small pond. Occasional benches
offered a good view of the water and the fishing pier.

It was only eight thirty but Sam and Iris and Gage were
already in their designated places.

Evergreens crowded close to the path, but there was space
enough for Iris to sit on a campstool in front of an easel and
daub at a watercolor. A large floppy sun hat shaded her face.
Ties on either side obscured her profile. Not that George Kirk
likely knew her. She was an anonymous woman painting early
on Sunday morning.

Gage merged into a shadow of an evergreen, almost
invisible in a gray T-shirt and yoga pants. She stood stiff and
straight, watching the pier, alert to every movement. A car
passing the park backfired and the sharp crack brought her
hand to her mouth. Gage's face was suddenly still and I had
a sense of what she would look like when she was old.

A small maintenance shed was situated about twenty feet
from the pier. The corrugated metal roof and sides gleamed

in the sunlight. If anyone looked closely, the padlock on the metal hasp hung loose. The shed door was slightly open, a very narrow crack. I hoped Sam Cobb had brought a folding chair. He would be rather cramped in that shed but he had a good view of the pier.

I dropped down beside the easel.

Iris spoke through gritted teeth. 'Watching you move through air disorients me. I've had about as much stress as I can manage. Please walk on the ground when you go away.' She moved her head, scanning in all directions. 'Is anyone coming?'

'A woman and a Great Dane.'

'You know what I mean.' It was the first time I'd heard Iris sound querulous.

'I don't see . . . oh.'

'What?' she demanded.

City Park boasts a wide sidewalk that runs from the pond through a grove of trees to the gazebo in the center of the park and picks up on the other side of the gazebo.

I pointed.

A large man ambled from behind a row of willows. Muscular, athletic, he moved easily. He stopped to survey the pond. And, of course, the pier. The pier was unoccupied. An oversized straw hat rode low on his head, hiding any glimpse of hair. Aviator sunglasses, also oversized, masked his eyes. A blue work shirt not tucked in, cargo pants with many pockets, running shoes.

Likely he wore the cargo pants with the capacious pockets when he went to the carousel to meet Nicole and he carried a weighted sock in one of those large pockets.

Iris's fingers gripped my arm. 'That's him, isn't it? Look how he's dressed. A description wouldn't sound anything like George Kirk except for his size. I'm going to the pier. He won't dare hurt Robert if someone's there.'

I twisted free, grabbed her arm. 'You say you admire manly men. Let Robert be a man. He's constructed a brilliant trap for a very dangerous person. Don't mess everything up.'

Her violet eyes were enormous, beseeching. 'It's hideous to stand here and wait for Robert to confront a killer.' She was breathing quickly. 'Look, I know Robert's sure of himself. Who isn't sure at his age? But he doesn't have a weapon.' She pulled free, reached down for a large canvas tote, scrabbled within it. Her hand came out clutching a blue metal canister on a key ring. 'We should have insisted that he have a gun, something to protect himself. Take this to him. It's pepper spray. Insist he have it ready in his pocket.'

I took the canister. 'All right.' I didn't blame Iris for being afraid. George Kirk wouldn't hesitate to kill. Not now.

I eased the canister to the ground, pushed it with my toe until I was deep in the shadows of a stand of bamboo. I Appeared Sunday morning cheerful in an embroidered sheath dress, tiny violets stitched near the notched neckline of the white top. Daffodils cavorted on the pale blue skirt. Yellow slippers. I picked up the small canister, cupped it in my palm.

I walked toward the evergreens. When I stepped into the shadows, Gage gestured at a bench near the pier. 'Is that him?'

I nodded.

'He's big.' Her voice trembled. 'He's so big.'

George Kirk was big and obviously strong.

'He's bigger than Robert.' She tried to suppress a sob.

'Robert will be fine.' I showed her the canister of pepper spray. 'From your mom. For Robert.'

She almost managed a laugh. 'Mom and pepper spray. I was never out at night without it. At least it's not night.'

'That's another reason Robert will be fine.' I moved away, stepped beyond the evergreens. Out of sight, I disappeared. The canister in my hand, I barely skimmed above the ground, an odd sensation, quite close to ladybugs and discarded plastic cups and patches of clover. I reached the steps to the pier. I tucked the canister in the shadows beneath the first step.

I stood by the steps. George Kirk sat on a bench, those dark lenses turned toward the pond. Then his head moved and the opaque lens were turned toward the pier. There was no sign yet of Robert.

Inside the shed, a Maglite illuminated bags of fertilizer, two mowers, and assorted tools. A folding chair sat near the door, but Sam was on his feet, peering through the crack.

He hummed softly, a sound that wouldn't reach beyond the shed, a rousing version of 'When the Saints Go Marching In'.

'I hope St Jude is listening.'

He was startled for an instant, then relaxed. 'I thought you'd be on the pier.'

'I will in a moment. Robert's not there yet.' Perhaps the fear that quivered within Iris and Gage was contagious. I thought suddenly of how much we should have told Robert: stay several feet away from George, watch what he does with his hands, be ready to duck.

'Five to nine.' A pause. 'St Jude?'

'The saint for desperate causes.' I spoke soberly and realized indeed that I was tight and tense, worried, uncertain. I liked Robert, every literal inch of him. Gage loved him. Iris loved him because he loved Gage Oh, Robert, be careful.

Sam looked energetic, positive, and not the least concerned. 'Kirk's the one who needs intervention, not Robert. The last I heard, saints don't rescue bad guys.'

My tight muscles relaxed. I smiled at Sam and noticed he wore his usual office suit, brown, baggy and wrinkled. I was puzzled. 'Did you go to the early service?'

He turned and looked toward the sound of my voice. He patted the right-hand pocket which appeared to sag. 'Concealed carry. I have a blue suit for church.' He turned back to the slight opening and was suddenly a dog on the hunt, every sense alert. 'Here comes Robert.'

I was on the pier as Robert walked confidently toward the steps.

The pier stretched empty – I don't count when I'm not visible – out into the water. The wooden boards were painted gray. The railings were natural wood with a middle and top rails. A pair of white swans moved majestically in the middle of the pond.

Robert wore a blue polo loose over jeans. His Tony Llama boots looked well worn, boots that were at home in a corral. The breeze stirred his sandy hair. He held a green file folder in his left hand.

I presumed the Velcro equipped recorder was safely attached to the equivalent of an undershirt.

The city clock tolled the hour. Church bells caroled not far away.

Robert looked down at his watch, frowned, moved up the steps on to the pier, once again checked his watch.

George Kirk watched Robert. He rose unhurriedly, walked the fifteen feet to the steps, gravel crunching under his steps.

Robert waited, his angular face composed, his dark eyes intent.

Kirk climbed the steps, stopped a foot or so away from Robert. 'Gillespie?'

Robert nodded, took a step back. 'Stay where you are.' He moved again, increasing the space between them. 'I prefer not to be in arm's reach. You have a nasty habit of cracking people's necks.'

Once again I'd underestimated Robert. In his meticulous way, he'd considered how George attacked and he intended to maintain a good distance between himself and danger.

'You don't have any proof.' The voice was cold, harsh.

'I don't need proof. That's what police do. They'll find proof if they start looking. They'll get a witness who spotted you downstairs at Rose Bower. They'll pick up some finger-prints. Are you sure you didn't touch something in the room? Maybe on the way out to the terrace. A good solid print of your hand on the side of the door. You sat down on the swan bench on the carousel. That will have prints. Trust me, the police will find evidence if they look. Whether they look is your call.' Robert held up the folder. 'I have a statement ready for your signature. Then we can discuss your payments to Shayne and Gillespie.'

The tendons in Kirk's neck bulged. 'You think you've got me. You and that redhead. Partners, right? She sics you on me, but she's the kind that has to run things. She's here in the park, isn't she?' His right hand unsnapped the top pocket in his cargo pants. His hand slid down and the pocket bulged outward.

There was no doubt that a gun barrel poked against the fabric.

Kirk's smile was ugly. 'See the bulge? That's the barrel aimed at you. I can't miss at five feet. The bullet will rip your guts out. If you don't want to die, get on your cell, call

Shayne, tell her you need for her to come, you're at the pier, then click off. She'll come if she wants her sidekick to live a while longer. She knows I'll kill you, just like I killed them.' His rage was mounting. 'Everything worked. The digitalis knocked Evelyn out easy as you please. It was rotten luck Lambert saw me bring the lemonade, but he learned blackmail doesn't pay off. It didn't pay off for that kid who called me, asked for five thousand. It isn't going to pay off for you. Give me that folder.'

I was at the steps, easing out the canister of pepper spray, holding it carefully so the key ring didn't jangle against metal.

The door to the shed opened. The recorder Velcroed to Robert's T-shirt transmitted to Sam in the shed. Sam ran across the grass, intent on reaching the pier, a gun in hand, holding his fire to protect Robert. He knew Robert still had a moment of safety. Kirk wanted Robert to summon Michaela Shayne.

Robert held out the folder. Robert looked poised to jump forward, balancing on the balls of his feet. He wasn't nearly as big and solid as Kirk. Robert was tall and thin with long arms. No match for the tennis player.

Kirk grabbed the folder with his free hand. His right hand was deep into the top pocket of the cargo pants, holding the gun. If he pulled the trigger, a bullet would slam into Robert's chest. 'Make that call, Gillespie. Or you're a dead man.'

Where did Kirk intend for this to end? Did he want Michaela Shayne here at the pier? Did he plan to take them hostage, maneuver them into the woods, leave them dead, hope to escape before police responded to shots? He was angry, desperate, determined.

I stood behind Kirk, held the pepper spray in my hand. I lifted the spray, my finger poised to flip up the cap. If I pushed the tab, spray would envelop Kirk's head, but in the instant before he choked, Kirk would start shooting.

Start shooting . . .

I flipped the lid up, shifted the canister, and pressed the nozzle hard against the top of his spine. 'Move and you're a dead man.'

For an instant, Kirk tensed. Then he yanked his right hand from the pocket, pulling out a black gun.

Robert took two steps, kicked with his right leg. Robert kicked hard, hard enough to crack bone. The blunt toe of the cowboy boot struck Kirk's wrist.

Kirk doubled in pain, cradling a shattered wrist, and the revolver spun out of his grip to clatter on to the wooden pier. Another crack, this one as the gun struck the plank, and a bullet splintered a portion of the railing not far from Robert.

Robert's gaze jerked from the railing back toward Kirk and then his eyes widened. The pepper spray canister was clearly visible, hanging in the air some feet above the ground.

Slowly, easily, like a feather drifting down, I lowered the canister to the planked pier.

Robert's eyes followed the canister, down, down, down.

Sam thudded up the steps, gun leveled at Kirk. Sam's broad face was stern, implacable. 'George Kirk, you are under arrest for the murders of Evelyn Kirk, Matthew Lambert, and Nicole Potter.'

EIGHTEEN

The gun in Sam's hand never wavered. Big, stocky, and muscular, Sam looked immovable as a mountain. Face twisting in pain, Kirk clutched at his forearm. The big straw hat tilted back as he jerked his head, seeking a way out.

Sirens shrilling, two police cars, followed by a fire truck and an ambulance, drove across grass, slammed to a stop only feet away. Perhaps the crack of a bullet in the park brought them. More likely, Sam used a mouthpiece radio the instant Kirk's gun went off. More uniformed officers came from across the street, swarming the area, joining the officers, several with drawn weapons, encircling the chief and Kirk.

Kirk's head swung back and forth. The straw hat slid from his head, fell on the pier. The aviator sunglasses glittered in the sunlight. His mouth twisted in fury.

'Don't move.' Sam walked nearer, held the gun in two hands leveled at Kirk's chest. 'Do not move.'

'Chief, we have him covered.' Detective Weitz stood at the foot of the steps. She looked formidable with a gun rock steady in her hands, an odd contrast to a very stylish knee-length white dress with rows of pineapples, the green stems a lovely contrast to the golden fruit. And high white strap heels. Likely she'd stopped by the department on her way to church.

Sam nodded. 'Handcuff him. Get him to the emergency room. Full security.'

A uniformed officer took Weitz's gun, supplied handcuffs. Weitz was wary as she snapped handcuffs on Kirk, clicking the right handcuff above the limp wrist. A few feet away an officer stood guard over the gun kicked from Kirk's. Crime techs would film the pier, the gun in situ, make sketches, measure, then finally slip the gun into an evidence bag.

Sam pushed the safety catch, returned his gun to the saggy

pocket of his suit. 'After he's fixed up at the emergency room, book him. Assault with intent to kill. More charges to follow. One phone call.'

A tall, rangy officer gripped Kirk's left arm. A petite blonde officer gripped the other. They turned him, headed to the path that led across the park to the street and City Hall.

George Kirk's cheekbones jutted. He looked what he was, a feral creature who would attack if he could.

The line of officers parted for the captors with their prisoner, but a ring of blue uniforms still protected the pier and the arrest scene.

'I have to get through. Oh Robert, Robert.' Gage's voice shook.

Sam nodded at an officer. 'Let her through and the woman in the floppy hat.'

Gage flew up the steps and across the short space and into Robert's embrace. 'The gun . . . when it went off . . .' She trembled.

'Hey, it's OK. I kicked him good, honey.'

Iris reached them, clutched at both her daughter and Robert. Iris's low voice was breathless. 'I knew there was danger.' She turned a bit, her gaze seeking, and then she saw me. She whispered, 'Thank you.'

I reached her, gave her a big hug. Had anyone been looking they might have been puzzled at her posture for a moment, arms encircling, head bent for an instant to press against mine.

'Robert and Gage. Think of the good years to come,' I murmured.

'Thanks to you.' She spoke softly.

Yet I think both Iris and I were aware as we looked at George Kirk that a good ending for her and Robert and Gage brought sorrow and pain to those who loved Evelyn Kirk. And George.

Sam turned and moved toward Robert. He stopped in front of Robert and Gage and Iris. 'You play a little football, Robert?'

Robert nodded. 'Cougars.'

'Kicked the winning point at the high school state championship, as I recall. Knew you were a kicker when you kicked that gun out of Kirk's hand. Good work.'

Robert got an odd look on his face. 'Yeah. I kicked. But behind him . . .' He broke off.

After Kirk doubled over to clutch at his hurt arm, Robert saw the pepper-spray canister hovering in the air without visible means of support. He wanted to speak up, but he knew he couldn't tell anyone about an airborne pepper-spray canister.

'Right. Something behind him startled him.' Sam wasn't going to talk about a pepper-spray canister either. 'Who knows what it might have been. But you thought fast, kicked hard. You know how things happen.' His gaze at Robert was commanding. 'Probably a hummingbird darted down, maybe clipped the back of his neck. Something like that.'

I hoped no one noticed the slow but steady progress of the small metal canister across the gray boards. I got to the edge of the pier, pushed, heard a tiny splash.

'Something like that.' Robert determinedly didn't look toward the spot where he'd seen the canister.

Sam nodded agreement. 'That's probably what happened. Anyway, you got a chance, took advantage of it, saved your life. Now you folks,' his nod included Gage and Iris, 'go over to the station. Probably you can use some coffee. Detective Weitz will take charge of that recorder. There will be lots of paperwork to see to. And I'll start work on an official commendation for the three of you for assisting the police in a murder investigation.'

He waved them away, took out his cell. He walked a few feet from the pier to a quieter area, tapped a number. 'Mayor, good morning. A very good morning to you. And for you. I want to give you a heads up. I'll be in your office in about twenty minutes. I know you'll have on that big purple hat you wear to church. That will make a great shot for the *Gazette*, look good on TV tonight, probably give a big boost to the campaign. And you know we all want the campaign to succeed. We'll have lots of good details for the reporters. Like you at work in your office even on a Sunday morning when duty calls. Reporters? Oh they'll be on their way to City Hall right now. I'll have Detective Weitz send them up to your office. Reporters pick up everything on the police radio frequency. You remember how you chopped the budget item to arrange to block access? Oh well, probably a good thing. This will be a great opportunity for you to explain how you always have the public interest at the forefront of your mind, you spend many hours scouring expenditures to save money for citizens, but how you never hesitate to provide what is needed to protect Adelaide from criminals and you approved every penny necessary to make it possible for the police department to arrest the murderer of Evelyn Kirk, one of Adelaide's leading citizens.'

Coal smoke swirled. Wheels clacked on silver rails. I swung aboard the caboose of the Rescue Express, grateful for the strength of Wiggins's firm grip. We stood at the railing as the Express soared away from Adelaide.

Wiggins peered at me with a hint of awe. 'My, oh my.' His stiff blue cap with rounded black bill rode high on curly auburn hair. Appropriate to the moment, he wore a navy coat over his stiff white shirt. The breeze tugged at his baggy gray flannel trousers. His large spaniel eyes were wide. He appeared overcome.

I was anxious. 'Are you all right?'

'To be truthful,' he sounded dazed, 'I've not been this over-whelmed since the Fourth of July – I believe it was in 1910 – that a youth with a strong arm threw a large firecracker that landed atop my station and set the shingles ablaze. Everything turned out well in the end, the youth was eager to help the volunteer fire department and you called on volunteers as well, but, Bailey Ruth, my, oh my is exactly my state of mind as you progressed through Adelaide on this mission. My, oh my. However, I almost intervened when you flouted Precepts Three, Four and Six.' His tone was morose.

'Wiggins, I always honor the Precepts in my heart.' I spoke rapidly, 'Precept Three: Work behind the scenes without making your presence known. You will certainly agree that I had no choice. What if Madeleine's friend hadn't spoken with the doctor or Michaela Shayne used that knowledge to unmask a killer? As for Precept Four: Become visible only when absolutely necessary. The doctor and others certainly wouldn't have responded to an unseen questioner. As for Precept Six:

Make every effort not to alarm earthly creatures. Oh Wiggins, these things happen.'

'Things did happen. I heartily agree. Things did happen. In fact, I have never seen so many things happen.'

'There were moments when I doubted our outcome, Wiggins.' It is well to speak in the plural and especially appropriate now. 'When Officer Loy was dismissed from the force, when Kirk house seemed such a haven of innocence, when Iris Gallagher was found at the scene of violence, I feared all was lost.' Talking to Wiggins elicits speech suitable for any 1910 parlor. 'When Chief Cobb was put on leave, the future was dark.' I looked up into his brown eyes, saw understanding.

'Future was dark,' Wiggins repeated.

'Yet we never flagged or failed.' This assessment would surely meet with Wiggins's approval. 'Working together, we triumphed.'

He clapped an approving hand on my shoulder. 'A triumph!'

I was modest. 'A ghost must do what a ghost must do.' But he was, in fact, too generous in his praise. 'I didn't manage alone, Wiggins. Saving Iris took all of us, Iris and Gage and Robert and Sam and me.'

Wiggins boomed, 'Huzzah to the Save Iris Volunteer Force.'

Huzzah. The exclamation might be an echo from Wiggins's 1910 train station, but I thought his shout had rather a nice ring, and the wind sweeping over us as the Rescue Express roared Heavenward was fresh and fine and good.

Huzzah!